LOST CITIES OF THE MAYA

Coba
Tulum

from NY

GULF OF HOND

HONDURAS

ASA BATTLES

JOURNEY TO THE SKY

Jamake Highwater

By the author of Anpao,
winner of the Newbery Honor Award

The jungle-covered Maya ceremonial centers have been a source of mystery and awe to all who have seen them, from the first European explorers to the tourists of today.

The remarkable Maya civilization rose and crumbled long before the Spanish invasion in the sixteenth century. Since that time the remains of the magnificent Maya world have been slowly discovered. The dramatic beginning of that adventure was when a young American attorney and his British sidekick, a gifted architect and artist, became intrigued by rumors of great cities lost in the deepest jungles. John Lloyd Stephens and Frederick Catherwood journeyed by steamboat and mule through the green hell of Central America, where almost by chance they stumbled upon a civilization so utterly forgotten by Indians and white men alike that it had no name.

(continued on back flap)

Journey to the Sky

Also by Jamake Highwater

Indian America

Song from the Earth:
American Indian Painting

Ritual of the Wind:
North American Indian Ceremonies, Music and Dances

Anpao: An American Indian Odyssey *(novel)*

Many Smokes, Many Moons:
A Chronology of American Indian History Through Indian Art

Dance: Rituals of Experience

"Journey to the Sky ;

*A novel about the true adventures
of two men in search of the lost
Maya kingdom."*

Jamake Highwater

Thomas Y. Crowell, Publishers
New York   Established 1834

FIRST EDITION

Designed by Suzanne Haldane

Library of Congress Cataloging in Publication Data

Highwater, Jamake.   Journey to the sky.
1. Mayas. 2. Catherwood, Frederick. 3. Stephens,
John Lloyd, 1805–1852. 4. Highwater, Jamake. 5. Mexico
—Antiquities. 6. Central America—Antiquities. I. Title.
F1435.H53   1978   972   78-3324
ISBN 0-690-01758-8

---

78 79 80 81 82 10 9 8 7 6 5 4 3 2 1

For Alfred Hart

Contents

If you do not expect it, you will not find the unexpected.

—HERACLITUS

Journey to the Sky

John Lloyd Stephens stepped into a waiting carriage at dawn on the third day of October 1839 in the company of a few acquaintances and his traveling companion, Frederick Catherwood. In a moment the horses lurched forward. With snorting nostrils and sweating flanks they clattered through the deserted chilly streets where the first frail light of day streaked across the cobblestones. White curls of smoke rose from chimneys as escaped slaves kindled cold stoves in the fine houses built in the Dutch style, their steep gables decorated with weathercocks twisting listlessly in a delicate breeze. The carriage jostled and rolled as it swept past Pearl Street and swung into Broadway, which was piled with so much debris from the houses being pulled down and remodeled that it was nearly impassable. Dogs and scavenger pigs scattered from the wheels of the hurtling

The Stephens residence at 13 Leroy Place, Greenwich Village
(From a drawing by Andrew J. Davis, engraved by Dick. Courtesy The New York Historical Society, New York City)

coach, and then scrambled back into the street to devour the heaps of refuse tossed there by New York's housewives. And as the sun came over the low rows of houses, the constables, huddled against the autumn morning chill, called out the hour and extinguished the gas lamps which had been used to light the streets of America's prime city for little more than a decade.

The Battery, at the tip of Manhattan Island, was deserted as the carriage made its way toward Pier Number One on the North River. A few whaling ships moved silently against the gray sky as they made their laborious way out to sea on the ebb tide, bound for the distant Pacific. The wharfs were desolate except for the steady flow of humble immigrants staggering from rude ships and pouring into the muddy streets, where many of them immediately sought relief from the almshouses of their new country.

At seven o'clock in the morning, Stephens and Catherwood found their ship, the British brig *Mary Ann*, with its anchor aweigh and its sails loose in the breeze, ready to sail for Central America. They were about to embark upon a search for a lost world, a world so obscured by jungle and time that it did not possess a name or a history, not even among the Indians whose tales of vast vine-ensnarled cities kept alive the legends of a forsaken ancient Indian civilization. The two young explorers were going in search of these cities. With a daring rare among the most adventurous of their contemporaries, the lawyer Stephens and the artist Catherwood stood at the ship's rail as the *Mary Ann* was slowly drawn into the current and slipped gradually into seas where few men had ventured. For a moment they stared uncertainly at the deserted New York landscape and the diminishing figures of their friends. Then they turned toward the vast open waters beyond which lay the southern trade winds and the tangled scrub jungles of Central America, where incredible rumors of temples and great stone causeways kept alive the apparition of a forgotten civilization as rich and mysterious as that of ancient Egypt.

* * *

The extraordinary story of the search for that lost world belongs to John Lloyd Stephens and Frederick Catherwood, two laymen who lived in an era when the potential for discovery was still accessible to ordinary people. Though Stephens was an attorney and his British friend Catherwood was an architect, it was not in the fields for which they were trained that they made their important contributions. There were few scholars of American archeology when these young men, still in their mid-thirties, set off for Central America. So they had to invent their own expertise. Nonetheless, they quickly became heroes of a breed of amateurs whose daring and imagination often resulted in discoveries beyond the reach of professionals who did most of their field work in libraries and universities.

Stephens was born to a well-to-do merchant in Shrewsbury, New Jersey, in 1805. His family soon moved to New York City, where he attended Joseph Nelson's School for three years, majoring in Latin and other classical studies.

At thirteen he was enrolled at Columbia College, and he was graduated in 1822 at the age of seventeen. In order to prepare for a profession in law he went to Litchfield, Connecticut, for fourteen months of study at the famous law school founded by Tapping Reeve.

Stephens had been allowed one adventure before he was expected to settle down for the rest of his life in a Manhattan law office. He traveled into the new West on a trip that eventually took him to New Orleans, where he embarked rather sadly on his homeward voyage. He dutifully hung out a shingle at 67 Wall Street and tried his best to be a respectable attorney, but his heart wasn't in it. During the nine years that he occupied that office, politics attracted his attention far more than legal briefs. Then Stephens was advised by his doctor to get away for a rest. He spent two eventful years wandering through Europe. After a respectable tour of England, France and Italy, he turned to the lands which attracted his real interest and imagination: Greece, Turkey, Russia and Poland. He traveled down the Nile and he explored the ruins. Donning the disguise of an Arab, a peculiar but prevalent sort of behavior in his day, Stephens trekked across the desert to ancient Petra in Palestine. Then he returned to New York and resumed his work in law; but he was restless, and he had been distinctly changed by his adventures.

On a hunch, he dashed off two volumes concerning his tour of Egypt and Arabia, and the published books received enthusiastic attention. The next year he wrote a sequel, this time relating his travels in Greece, Turkey, Russia and Poland. Clearly John Lloyd Stephens did not want to pursue the profession for which he had been meticulously trained.

Frederick Catherwood was six years older than Stephens, and though he had much the same sort of background as a world traveler, his upbringing in a London suburb was a good deal less comfortable than that of his

American friend. After completing the sort of vigorous classical education expected of a young English architect, Catherwood visited Egypt, Arabia and Palestine and made a great many architectural drawings. After returning home, he was invited to exhibit a huge canvas of Jerusalem at Burford's Panorama in London's Leicester Square. The advertisement out front read, "A painting of the largest class . . . 10,000 square feet from drawings by Mr. Catherwood brilliantly illuminated every evening by upward to 200 gaslights!" When Stephens was en route home from his European tour of 1836 he stopped at Burford's, and there he met the artist Catherwood. The two young men became friends at once.

At Stephens' urging, Catherwood moved with his wife and children to New York City, where recent catastrophic fires had created a good market for architects. By 1836 Catherwood had taken a house on Houston Street and leased a piece of ground from John Jacob Astor at the corner of Broadway and Prince Street, where in 1838 he opened his own exhibition: "The Splendid Panorama of Jerusalem."

About the time that Catherwood was opening his "Panorama," John Stephens came upon an old report by a Colonel Juan Galindo. In this report, which was essentially concerned with military levies among the natives, the Colonel mentioned seeing the remains of some strange and extremely old buildings located in the wilds of Yucatan and Central America. Stephens was so impressed by the document that he decided almost at once to leave New York and go in search of this lost world. When Catherwood heard about his friend's plans he happily accepted employment as the expedition's artist, and a casual agreement was signed.

Catherwood had hardly completed his signature on the contract when he looked up at Stephens and asked, "So much for the formalities. When are we leaving?"

The gulls made tireless circles about the masts of the brig *Mary Ann*, their forlorn calls mingling with the sharp snapping of the sails in a brisk wind. By dusk the October air was cold and the outline of the New Jersey coast was a pale smudge upon the misty horizon. Captain Hampton, master of the ship, turned to his only passengers, Stephens and Catherwood, and shook his head in amusement, for the two men were so intent upon the diminishing landmarks of America that they had hardly left the ship's railing since the morning's departure. "By dawning," the Captain called down to them with a smirk, "I guarantee we will be fairly at sea, gentlemen, and you will be seeing more ocean water than you bargained for."

Captain Hampton knew what to expect of the sea, but for his passengers the ocean was always an adventure in the unexpected.

Hurried on by a strong northeasterly wind which sang in the gray sails, the *Mary Ann* was swept into the region of the trade winds by the ninth day of the journey. Then the dull cast of fall began to leave the endless sky, and by the morning of the tenth day the sailing ship was within the tropics. The sailors shed their jackets and woolen caps. The sun set trails of silver across the green sea, and great flocks of strange garish birds umbrellaed the *Mary Ann*, sending up an exotic medley of cries and songs. By the eleventh day of the voyage, as the ship glided through the waterway that separates Cuba and Hispaniola, the thermometer climbed rapidly to seventy and then to eighty degrees. The sailors stretched in the scorching daylight as they tugged upon the lines, which opened more canvas to the power of the wind. Mr. Catherwood hid his pallid complexion from the tropical sun under an elegantly sporty wide-brimmed hat. Then he joined the ruddy-skinned Stephens, who was relaxing in the shadows of the loudly flapping sails. The ship swept through a sea turned to glowing white crystals by the sunshine.

The explorers gazed into the distance, eagerly anticipating their first joint venture. Though Central America was entirely new to them, and though neither spoke fluent Spanish, they possessed a command of circumstance which bordered on bravado. This nineteenth-century attitude was composed of equal parts of confidence and sheer showmanship, cultivated by Stephens and Catherwood during their remarkable prior adventures in the real world and through a fantasy which most people of their generation knew as Manifest Destiny. Though they were both men of exceptionally liberal attitudes for their day, they nonetheless carried with them a naïve sense of self-righteousness as representatives of the civilized world.

* * *

The America of John Lloyd Stephens was under the stress of several complicated issues. The Monroe Doctrine of 1823 prohibited European nations from establishing any new dependencies in the Western Hemisphere and declared that Europe must no longer interfere in the affairs of the Americas. From the patriotic viewpoint of John Stephens this was a necessary protection of nations which had only recently liberated themselves from Spain, but from the British point of view of Frederick Catherwood the Monroe Doctrine seemed like the basis of the American continentalism espoused by President Andrew Jackson and his successor Martin Van Buren, who hoped to control Latin America and to annex a vast Mexican territory.

Therefore, while John Lloyd Stephens was secretly in search of lost worlds, he was officially a legal observer sent by President Van Buren to deal with the government of Central America, whose white leaders were reportedly under the revolutionary fire of an army of savage Indians.

Stephens and Catherwood awakened on the eighteenth day of their voyage to great growls of thunder which broke and cascaded over their heads. When they staggered to the portholes they found the morning sky as dark as night. A constant succession of lightning bolts cracked open the black heavens, illuminating the surface of the water with a white glow for miles around them. The ocean, which had only yesterday glittered with sunshine, had turned into a turbulent giant on which the little vessel pitched and rolled helplessly.

It was nearly impossible to stand in the ship, but Stephens and Catherwood slowly made their way toward the deck, where they hoped to confer with Captain Hampton about the vessel's ability to withstand the storm. Just as the two men forced back a door in the bulkhead a torrent of rain threw them back, and a bolt of lightning explosively struck the sea a few feet from the ship's prow. Wind slammed the door closed with a resounding roar, and the two men fell back into the ship, glancing uncertainly at one another as they sat in the darkness and discussed, disjointedly, the practical danger of being struck by lightning on shipboard.

Somehow the day passed without disaster, and by the following morning Stephens and Catherwood were sufficiently accustomed to the turbulence to consider taking tea for breakfast. The storm, however, continued unabated. The gale was terrific; nothing could stand upright to windward, and it was only with the greatest difficulty that the travelers managed to find the Captain, who sat under the quarter rail watching the compass and turning anxiously to the misty horizon from which the winds tumbled down upon them. At breakfast large drops of sweat stood on his forehead, and though at first the Captain was unwilling to admit it even to himself, Stephens and Catherwood discovered that the ship was in real danger.

The *Mary Ann* was being driven as fast as the wind could push her into the barrier of sunken rocks known as Lighthouse Reef. Directly under the ship's lee was the worst part of the whole reef, marked on the chart "Dangerous rocky shore!" But on the twenty-ninth day of the voyage, by good fortune alone, the *Mary Ann* was driven narrowly past the rocks and slipped into the shelter behind the reef.

Gradually the thunder and lightning, the swells, wind and turbulence of the Gulf of Honduras, faded as the ship edged toward the British settlement of Belize. The clouds opened slowly, and the vast unbroken dome of the tropical night was filled with stars and moonlight. Finally at midnight they reached St. George's Cay, about twenty miles north of Belize. A large brig, cumbersomely loaded with mahogany, was lying at anchor. A pilot was already on board, patiently waiting favorable weather to put to sea. The pilot's booming voice came over the water, welcoming Captain Hampton and informing him that he and his son, a boy of about sixteen, were on board the mahogany brig. The Captain was overjoyed with the news and invited the lad on board.

There was full moonlight and a calm sea when the pilot's son eventually climbed to the deck of the *Mary Ann* and gave Captain Hampton the pilot's formal welcome. Stephens could not quite see the lad's face, but he could tell that he was not white. Without delay the young man took his place at the wheel, and, loading the *Mary Ann* with full canvas, he knowingly guided the ship toward Belize as he rambled on about the great gale on the coast, about the apprehension he and his father had had for the safety of the *Mary Ann*. He also spoke of recent disasters and shipwrecks in the Gulf of Honduras, and of another pilot who on that very night had driven his vessel into the terrible sunken reef which had very nearly claimed the *Mary Ann*.

John Stephens had heard enough. He quietly withdrew and sought the solitude of the highest level of the ship, where he could enjoy the fact that he was still alive.

He stood facing the sky as the ship silently slipped through the blackness, illuminated only by a distant twinkle of firelight on the shore and by the tiny halos of the ships' yellow lanterns. Over him was the unbroken vastness of a sky full of stars. The breeze was hot and damp. A new fragrance mixed with the salty stench of the sea; the perfume of vegetation and earth. John Stephens inhaled this scent and threw back his head as an exuberance filled him. Then they glided into the appalling darkness, surrounded by nothing but the enormity of the black water and the opulence of the sky whose luminousness increased fantastically as the world fell back into the night.

At seven in the morning the tropical sun gradually lifted Belize from the darkness with an orange light which spread across the world like wildfire. The landscape was perfectly horizontal and flat. The sea rose to the very brink of the single row of white dwellings, reminding Stephens and Catherwood, as they were rowed ashore in a mahogany dugout, of Venice or Alexandria.

The sea was calm in the little harbor where four ships, three barges, schooners, bungos, canoes and a hefty old steamboat were quietly riding at anchor. The fearful storm which had battered the *Mary Ann* had also passed over Belize, leaving the streets flooded and muddy. At closer view the town was a good deal less romantic than it had appeared to be from the sea. It was the gateway to Central America, though heavy naval traffic had done little to alter its rustic character since 1670, when the port was settled by the British. Just behind the frail settlement was a stand of cohune palms and pitch pines. And back of this succulent savanna was a solid wall of jungle permitting no contact with the interior. Belize hung on the sandy edge of a world of mahogany and vines, providing barely a foothold for those who came to it by the sea.

The boatman in the dugout was black, as were the faces which appeared on the ships and barges. And when the explorers finally landed and stepped knee-deep into the mud which filled the streets, they found themselves in a town which seemed in the possession of blacks. At once they were overcome by a curious and troubled feeling. For the first time in their lives they felt outnumbered, utterly alien and conspicuous. Though Catherwood and Stephens had traveled in Arabia and North Africa, they had never encountered an entire population which was so predominantly black. Of the settlement's six thousand population, at least four thousand were Negro. The bridge, the marketplace, the streets, and the stores were thronging with them. Catherwood looked a bit distressed, while John Stephens seemed delighted. "Astonishing," he whispered to his friend. "I almost fancy myself in the capital of a Negro Republic!"

Stephens was intrigued by the blacks. They were a fine-looking race, tall, straight and athletic in build, with deep ebony, glossy and marvelously smooth skin. The men dressed in handsome white cotton shirts and trousers, with straw hats typical of the region; and the women had immaculate white frocks with short sleeves revealing their long, sensuous arms. They stitched bright red borders on their dresses and adorned themselves with massive red earrings and elegant necklaces. Stephens could not keep his eyes off the women. Coming from a world in which ladies' ankles were the most intimate part of the anatomy exposed in public, he could not resist noticing that the frail, billowy frocks were the women's only coverings. It was the fashion of these sable ladies to wear one sleeve well off the right shoulder, and to carry their skirts in the left hand, raising them to whatever height necessary when crossing the numerous puddles in the streets.

The explorers stopped at the house of a merchant who was in the midst of what was locally called a second breakfast. At the table was a British officer as well as the merchant and his wife. The other guests were quite unexpected in the company of these white people: several blacks and mulattoes. By chance the place provided for Stephens at the table was between two blacks. He paused momentarily, wondering what his countrymen might think of him, and then cheerfully took his place. These ebony gentlemen proved to be extremely refined and hospitable, talking about their mahogany works, of England, hunting, horses, ladies and wine. And before Stephens and Catherwood had been in Belize an hour, they learned that the work of racial amalgamation which was at that time such a stormy subject in North America had been going on quietly in Central America for generations. Color was considered hardly more than a matter of taste. Most of the respected citizens of Belize had black wives and mulatto children. In matters of education and economic success there were no distinctions made in regard to race. And to Stephens and Catherwood's surprise, no one seemed in the slightest concerned about the wide variation among the townspeople.

*   *   *

Blacks had been a vital part of the life of Belize ever since the Spaniards introduced them to the region in the seventeenth century as forced labor for the mahogany works which were the major source of the land's great riches. The black population steadily outnumbered other races. Gradually the situation of the slaves improved, until in August of 1839, just prior to Stephens' arrival, the British overlords eliminated slavery by an act of general abolition.

The wealth which blacks drew from the land had made Belize an enviable, exclusively Spanish outpost for a century and a half despite the ambition of expansionist nations like England. But with the aggression of Britain's

Oliver Cromwell, the Spanish domination of Belize came to an end. Panama, Porto Bello, Cartagena, and Cuba evaded Cromwell's grasp, but he grabbed Jamaica and Belize, thus getting a significant foothold in Central America, which soon led to British political dominance.

At the time of the visit of Stephens and Catherwood, Belize was a curious blend of two centuries of Spanish culture with a subtle residue of the lifestyle of the Mopan tribes of the Maya that had been assimilated into the blacks' half-forgotten African culture. The administration of the English interests in the region was almost entirely in the hands of the colonies' superintendent, Colonel Archibald MacDonald, who, even as he invited the U.S. diplomat John Lloyd Stephens for a visit of the state, had elaborate plans to seize the Bay Islands in the Caribbean, a move which would greatly challenge the terms of the Monroe Doctrine and seriously unsettle the balance of power then existing in Central America.

John Lloyd Stephens, being relatively uninformed in the complexities and power plays of the world of diplomacy, was unaware of these political intrigues. As this was his first government appointment, and he was not certain of ever holding another, he decided to make the most of it, and accepted at once Superintendent MacDonald's invitation to Government House.

In Cairo, Stephens had arranged a theatrical entrance when given an audience with Mehemet Ali—arriving astride a gorgeously ornamented Arabian steed. He was determined to make his meeting with Colonel MacDonald equally impressive. So he arranged for the use of a pitpan—the kind of boat the Indians had been using in Central America for centuries before the Spaniards arrived. The boat was forty feet long, pointed on both ends and made of the six-foot-wide trunk of a mahogany tree. Part of the boat was covered by a light wooden shelter, supported by stanchions, with curtains for protection against the sun and large cushions for comfort. This elegant gondola was manned by eight huge black soldiers whose six-foot paddles sliced the water into a foaming wake. Just a few touches of these paddles and the pitpan dashed across the surface, running the length of the town in moments.

The blacks on the shore gazed at the two white strangers in the handsome boat. The excitement of the people grew, and throngs of them hurried to the bridge to cheer. This uncommon attention impressed the boatmen, who, with a wild chant reminiscent of the songs of the Nubian boatmen of the Nile, swept under the bridge and hurried the explorers into the still expanse of the wide Belize River. Even before the cheering of the people had died away they found themselves in a perfect solitude.

The Belize River, coming from sources then little known, was in its fullness. The flanks of the river were walled by a dense, unbroken forest, overflowing so that the black trees grew directly out of the silvery water, their wide branches spreading almost across the river and shutting out the light of the sun, which sent frail, shadowy beams onto the silent surface.

Colonel MacDonald met his guests on the steps of Government House. He was the most military-looking man Stephens had ever seen—a great six-foot fellow uniformed to the teeth; his tunic a mosaic of medals and ribbons, and his face flushed and ruddy. He was very much the professional soldier, one of a breed, Stephens thought, fast passing out of existence. His style was pure Empire and his conversation was full of hyperbole; listening to him was like reading a page of old-fashioned history. He was unyielding in his round of toasts. He toasted the Queen, the health of Mr. Van Buren, President of the United States, and the success of his guests' perilous adventures in Central America.

Stephens, although unused to taking the President and the people of the United States upon his shoulders, managed a splendid show of diplomacy. Friendliness so abounded that the Colonel was moved to toast "the strong and perpetual friendship of England and America."

Colonel MacDonald's words possessed more sentiment than his

actions, for he was fully advised of the archeological purpose of the visit of Stephens and Catherwood beyond their diplomatic business with him, and he was determined that the Stephens party should not achieve its scientific objectives. Unbeknownst to his guests, he had sent, without official Foreign Office approval, two men—Patrick Walker and Lieutenant John Caddy—into the jungle with instructions to discover and document all ruins in the district. Walker and Caddy were already en route to the ruins of Palenque.

For the moment Stephens and Catherwood were unaware of the Colonel's duplicity. They sat back and thoroughly enjoyed the company of their host and his dignified guests—the cream of Belize's white population. In the midst of these comforts, Stephens noticed through the large window of the dining room the steamboat on which his party intended to make its journey to Guatemala and up the Dulce River. The steamboat lay immediately in front of Government House, and the black smoke rising in steady columns from her stack announced that it was time to embark.

When the guests rose from the table, MacDonald took Stephens' arm and informed him that he was venturing into a country in turmoil. "Mr. Savage, your American Consul in Guatemala," he explained, "was once so good as to protect the lives and property of British subjects, for which we are most grateful to him." The Colonel wanted Stephens and Catherwood to know that should any danger threaten them, they must assemble all Europeans, run up the British flag, and send at once for Colonel MacDonald.

With this bit of bravado, Stephens and Catherwood stepped into the awaiting dory which was to transport them to the wood-burning steamboat *Vera Paz*. It was an unexpected and colorful moment: flags were flying everywhere—on the fort, the courthouse and on the government schooner. With a thunderous report a gun was fired in honor of the United States diplomat John Lloyd Stephens. Then, as the two visitors crossed the bay in their little boat, a thirteen-gun salute was fired, and the brightly uniformed soldiers at the fort presented arms as the dory passed. The government schooner lowered and raised her ensign, and when Stephens mounted the deck of the steamboat, the Captain, with hat in hand, told him that he had strict instructions to place his vessel under Stephens' orders, stopping absolutely *anywhere* he pleased.

Stephens grinned with unrepressed delight. He had visited many cities, but this was the first time that flags and cannons had announced to the world that he was going away. He was a novice in such matters of state, but he managed to behave as if he had been brought up to be king. "To tell you the truth," he mumbled to Catherwood as they stood on the deck, "I could live very nicely with this sort of thing."

The *Vera Paz* trembled and finally lurched into motion. Captain Hampton of the anchored *Mary Ann* was not to be outdone in the tributes paid to his friends Stephens and Catherwood. He had loaded his two four-pounders, and when the steamboat got under way he managed to fire one of them, but the other simply would not go off. He stamped and shouted to his crew, but still the second gun would not fire; so with a mortified grin he looked up as his friends sailed past and gave his best salute.

Then the harbor was behind them and silence fell upon the *Vera Paz* except for the constant churning of her wheel and the wheezing of her boilers.

Belize was surrounded by jungle. Between this coastal settlement and the other inhabited parts of Central America was a barrier of ferocious vegetation, unbroken even by an Indian footpath. Within Belize there were no wheeled vehicles, for there were no roads. The only causeway which had once penetrated the jungle was abandoned long ago and totally overgrown. There was no other communication with the interior except by way of the Dulce River in Guatemala or the Belize River. Therefore, to penetrate the jungle Stephens and Catherwood had to rely upon a raucous old steamboat which was the last remnant of an abandoned transportation network.

The *Vera Paz* was commanded by a small weather-worn Spaniard whose cavalier manner helped make up for his vessel's many deficiencies. The engineer was an Englishman; and the crew were

Spaniards, Indians and mulattoes who had no particular acquaintance with the management of a steamboat. And to complete this
ramshackle cast of characters was Augustin, a young cutthroat
with a machete scar on his cheek, whom the explorers had
engaged in Belize as a servant despite their doubts that he was
very smart and the fact that he looked very much like a common
criminal. Augustin had been born on the island of Santo Domingo and raised in Omoa after being abandoned by his French
father. What his mother had been no one could say for certain,
but he spoke a fluent if peculiar French, and this language soon
became the expedition's lingua franca.

The *Vera Paz* had hardly begun its journey and already life was
becoming difficult; the luggage was thoroughly mixed up, for one
thing, and it also turned out that the steamboat made no provi-
sion for feeding its passengers. They were expected to take care of
themselves. Fortunately the new servant, Augustin, had the good
sense to include among the cargo such strange luggage as a
coopful of chickens.

Despite such problems, it was a beautiful day. The steamboat's
course lay nearly south, along the coast of Honduras. The sun was
gloriously bright and the sea was calm. Only the mechanical
gasps of the *Vera Paz* spoiled the idyllic scene. The age of steam
was just beginning, but already John L. Stephens saw in such
"progress" the end of the romance of travel. The wood-burning
Vera Paz smudged the enormous sky with its great heaves of soot
and beat the shore with its aggressive wake. Steamboats had
destroyed some of the most romantic moments of Stephens' life.
And he was annoyed by the sacrifices his world was willing to
make in exchange for speed. He had been rushed through the
Hellespont, past Sestos and Abydos, and past the Plain of Troy
deafened by the clatter of a steam engine, and now, even in this
far sea still on the brink of paradise he found himself being
hurried past incomparable sights by a clamorous, steam-devour-
ing monster made of sticks and iron.

Nevertheless, the spirit of romance filled the day. The two
adventurers relaxed under an awning to escape the intense heat

of the sun. A delicate breeze swept through their shelter as they looked out on the coastline where nature was putting on a display of vegetable pyrotechnics. The dense forest came to the water's very edge. Beyond were mountains matted with perpetual green, running off into purple ranges, higher and higher, until they were lost in the clouds. Of all this natural beauty it was the sky which dominated the green world. Everything appeared to reach toward the sky and to be consumed by it. Even the thunderous steamboat was dwarfed by the immensity of the great porcelain dome of the tropics.

*   *   *

It was the hope for just such an impossible journey which had brought John Lloyd Stephens and Frederick Catherwood to Central America. Though their apparent mission was diplomatic, they hoped to undertake quite a different kind of adventure, one which would crown all their prior explorations. Ever since the day that a book dealer named John Bartlett had shown Stephens a folio of drawings of ruins supposedly located in Yucatan, he and Catherwood had confidentially planned their most fantastic journey. This bizarre folio had been published in Paris and was the work of a flamboyant French adventurer, Count Jean-Frédéric Waldeck, who was widely regarded as a hoaxer and eccentric. Yet Stephens could not resist hoping that Waldeck's unbelievable drawings possessed some elements of truth. He was amazed by the images which suggested that a civilization had once existed in the Western Hemisphere which was as advanced as that of Egypt. It was dubious, however, that a dreamer who claimed friendships with Alexander von Humboldt, Lord Byron, Beau Brummell, not to mention Marie Antoinette, could be trusted.

Also there were puzzling details in Waldeck's drawings, such as Egyptian pyramids decorated with Romanesque statues in the full round. So Stephens, unwilling to

discount the evidence, decided to do more research. A
certain Captain Don Antonio del Rio claimed the rediscovery of ruins called Palenque in southern Mexico. As
incoherent and romantic as the descriptions of these ruins
were, Stephens felt that there was sufficient proof to
suggest that some sort of elaborate masonry culture had
once existed in the tropics of Central America. It was an
entirely preposterous idea for his day, and was refuted by
respected historians and theologians. Yet Stephens found
another book which seemed to confirm his conviction: a
large folio of writings, including the report of Captain
Guillermo Dupaix, an officer in the Mexican Army, who
had explored the ruins of Palenque. Another ruin was
vividly described in a book called *Antiquites Mexicanines*,
and this ancient city was called Uxmal by the author,
Lorenzo de Zavala, who claimed that it was located quite
near his birthplace, in the state of Yucatan, where he had
seen the ruins with his own eyes.

Though such evidence of American civilizations was
still generally unavailable in the United States, a learned
American journal finally published the first information
about a ruin in Honduras called Copan. To Stephens'
dismay, even this impressive article did not electrify the
public and passed almost without notice. The research of
the great German pioneer of American archeology, Alexander von Humboldt, also met with considerable resistance. The public and specialists were simply not ready
for the fundamental alteration of viewpoint which the
discovery of ancient American civilizations required.

Humboldt had visited the Valley of Mexico at a time
when it was as closed to aliens as China was closed to
foreigners in Stephens' day. Humboldt made drawings of
Mitla and Xochicalco, and he surveyed the great pyramid
of the Temple of Cholula; but he knew very little about
the ruins to the south, in Central America. These earlier
sites, created by a shadowy people later called the Maya,

were buried deep in the forests. The temples and pyramids lay broken in jungles. Of these Humboldt had heard little or nothing. And his own discoveries to the north, in Mexico, were largely discounted. The distinguished *New Quarterly Review* was shocked: "If Humboldt claims that these ruins lie out of prehistory then he rejects the biblical origin of mankind."

For politicians of the America of 1839, the acknowledgment of such a thing as an "Indian civilization" was unthinkable. This was the era of the most ferocious Indian resistance to the invasion and expansion of the white man. Indians, like indigenous people all over the world at the time, were considered the enemies of civilization. They were almost universally considered a race of barbaric, naked and primitive beasts, barely on the margin of humanity. They were said to relish scalping and the wanton slaughter of women and children. They possessed no warmth or ties of family. They were cannibals who devoured their own infants without a thought. They were vermin who plagued a marvelous "new" land which God intended for Europeans. So how could such a race produce anything which remotely resembled civilization? And if, by some remarkable chance, America did possess wondrous masonry temples and pyramids, they would certainly not be found in the humid scrub jungles of Central America. The notion was preposterous to all thinking people. Except John Lloyd Stephens, and his colleague Frederick Catherwood.

Copan . . . Palenque . . . Uxmal . . . such names appeared on no existing maps. Aztec . . . Maya . . . Toltec . . . Inca . . . these names were not to be found in any dictionary, and were known to few historians of the day. These worlds and their peoples were beyond the grasp of history; they were so utterly lost in time and space that it seemed as if they had never existed. The Scottish historian and churchman William Robertson had decreed in his

History of the Discovery and Settlement of America that the ruins reported by the Spanish conquistadores were "more fit to be the habitation of men just emerging from barbarity than the residence of a polished people. If the buildings corresponding to such descriptions had ever existed in the Mexican cities, it is probable that some remains of them would still be visible. It seems altogether incredible that in a period so short every vestige of this boasted elegance and grandeur should have disappeared. The Spanish accounts appear highly embellished."

Even when undeniable evidence of some kind of curious ruins finally came to light, historians adamantly denied that Indians had anything to do with their construction. These mysterious ruins were apparently built, they claimed, by Egyptians, Norsemen and Mongols who briefly imported elephants to America and then apparently shipped them back home. If prehistoric American ruins existed, they were the masterful work of Romans, Phoenicians, Carthaginians or perhaps the Lost Tribes of Israel. For quite apart from the storm of controversy among historians, churchmen were even more enraged by the suggestion that Indians were outside the historical reportage of the Bible. If the Flood had in fact annihilated the world of men except for Noah and his family, who thereafter repopulated it, then what was the origin of American Indians? By the beginning of the eighteenth century the question was universally answered by the acceptance of American Indians as descendants of the Lost Tribes of Israel.

In 1839, John Lloyd Stephens—a man with a modest classical education, trained in law at the famous Tapping Reeve School in Litchfield, Connecticut, and more traveled than most of his countrymen—stood in the avantgarde of his era simply by wondering if there might be some truth in the rumors of lost cities in Central America. Being by nature a practical man, Stephens decided that there was only one way to find out. And so he and Catherwood planned their voyage. While making final arrangements, Stephens was unexpectedly appointed the U.S. diplomatic agent to the Central American Confederation. With this appointment, he became President Van Buren's confidential agent in Central America and was given a considerable subsidy for his travels. And so while Catherwood was putting his "Panorama" in the hands of a partner, and busying himself buying artist's supplies and a camera lucida, Stephens visited his tailors on Broadway, where he had a blue diplomat's coat made to order, with embroidered golden braid and as many bright brass buttons as they could possibly stitch on it.

"I figured," Stephens told Catherwood, "that I am not likely to get another appointment, so I decided to make the most of my grand position!"

Catherwood chuckled, and Augustin with unsteady hands and dirty fingernails took advantage of the pause in the conversation to pour tea for the diners.

At eleven o'clock the Vera Paz came in sight of Punta Gorda, a tiny settlement of Carib Indians, about a hundred and fifty miles down the coast from Belize, and the first place at which Stephens had directed the accommodating Captain to stop. As the steamboat approached, Stephens could see an opening in the jungle barrier, with a few low houses huddled together in the clearing. Punta Gorda was hardly a speck on the expansive coastline of vines and primeval trees. As the *Vera Paz* turned in toward the shore, where a steamboat had never anchored before, the entire village was in commotion. Women and children ran along the bank, and four sturdy men came from shore in a canoe to meet the strangers.

The only passenger beside Stephens and Catherwood was a priest who had become friendly with the Carib Indians during his appointment at Belize. He was determined to go ashore for the purpose of marrying and baptizing the inhabitants. So when it came time to disembark, the padre appeared on deck with a large washbasin in one hand and a packet of priestly vestments in the other. In his eagerness to do the work of God he very nearly fell overboard, but finally had the good sense to stand back while the *Vera Paz* anchored a short distance from the beach and a small boat was lowered over the side.

The visitors landed in a dense shade at the foot of a steep, barren embankment. Ascending to the top they suddenly came into the full burning sun and a green tide of lush vegetation. Bananas, coconuts, pineapples, oranges, lemons and plantains grew with such luxuriance that their fragrance was nearly overwhelming. The Indians, less formidable in build and attitude than the native people Stephens had seen in the Wild West, were excitedly gathered in the shade of the trees. The priest immediately gave notice that he intended to marry and baptize them. After a short conversation a house was picked for these Christian rituals, and the priest became solemnly ecstatic at the prospect of saving all of these people from the religion that they had practiced for centuries.

Meanwhile Stephens and Catherwood went off for a bit of sightseeing with an old Carib man who knew some English from his numerous canoe expeditions to Belize. About five hundred Indians lived in Punta Gorda, where they sought to retain their own customs and avoided intermarriage with their conquerors. Their hostility was either veiled or broken—Stephens could not tell which—for they were exceedingly ingratiating. And yet these were the descendants of the fiercest of all the tribes the Spaniards had conquered.

Their manner had changed drastically but their lifestyle had remained the same for thousands of years, far longer than anyone at the time realized. These handsome brown people with passions for beads and ornaments conducted their lives exactly like their ancestors, who—beyond the reach of memory—had carved and lifted the stones of the mysterious cities which Stephens and

Catherwood were seeking. Their huts were built as they had been built for countless generations: a construction of poles set upright in the ground, tied together with bark string, mortared with mud and thatched with leaves.

These attractive primal houses extended along the bank where the guide was coaxing the visitors, for he wanted them to see "the old woman," his grandmother. Despite the oppressive heat and humidity, Stephens and Catherwood followed their guide until they came across a crouched figure—a woman of very advanced age. No one knew how old she was, but it was considerably over a hundred. She came from the island of St. Vincent, the home of the most indomitable band of her tribe, and she was very proud that she had never been baptized.

The old woman suddenly giggled and raised her shrunken hand to point at the white men. Then her shriveled face became very grave and she turned her eyes away and did not look at Stephens or Catherwood again. "Old woman," their guide repeated again and again as he led them away. "Old woman . . . old woman . . ."

When they returned to the center of the village they found the priest dressed in his official costume and conducting religious business with zeal. At his side was the washbowl from the steamboat, filled with holy water. In his hand was a prayer book from which he was reading without pause. The servant Augustin stood patiently by, holding the stump of a tallow candle for lack of an appropriate candleholder. Stephens, though not a very religious man, was respectful if somewhat amused by the sight.

* * *

Catholics were not very popular back home in his America. They insisted, for one thing, on the absolute authority of the Pope at Rome, and this potential division of loyalty convinced American Protestants of their unassimilability and undesirability. The Catholics were also relatively late arrivals in America; and they were seen as an economic threat to the Protestant working class. As recently as 1834, a mob of Protestant workers had burned down an Ursuline convent in Boston and had rioted in the streets for three days as an expression of their hatred for immigrant Irish workers.

This same religious turmoil involved a number of the other sects which had sprung up during a wave of fire-and-brimstone revivalism in America. The Church of Jesus Christ of Latter-day Saints was created by the Mormons. Soon William Miller would produce the Seventh-Day Adventist Church. Both groups were disdained by other Protestants, who openly forced them into the wilderness in search of friendlier territories. Meanwhile Ralph Waldo Emerson and his group were founding the Transcendental Club. It was an era when Americans were far from passive about their religious beliefs, and John Lloyd Stephens was no exception.

Most of the Caribs had been Christianized by the priests of Spain with considerable help from Spanish soldiers. The Indian grasp of Catholicism was a blend of their own ancient customs and those of the priests. They were strict observers of their own conception of the prescribed rites of their new religion. A visit by a priest was normally considered a great occasion, but the Indians were suspicious of the expedition's priest because he did not speak Spanish. But when they saw him in his cassock and surplice, with the burning incense which they adored, all their distrust vanished.

Distressingly for the zealous priest, there was very little to be done in the way of marriages, since the settlement had a great scarcity of men at the moment—most of whom were away at work. A long line, however, was formed by women carrying babies for baptism. Of the first mother he asked a question which Stephens did not think could be found in the book, and which, in some places, would be considered impertinent to ask a mother offering her child for initiation into the Church: whether she were married.

The handsome brown woman hesitated, smiled, laughed and then answered, "No, Padre." There was a silence. The women on line crowded forward and innocently gazed into the face of the priest trying to understand his expression of disapproval.

"My child," he said, "this is very wrong and very unbecoming a good Christian woman. You must take advantage of my presence and immediately marry your child's father."

The woman hesitated, smiled uncertainly and then laughed again. "Well, Padre, that would be nice. Yes, I would do it, but he is away cutting mahogany." And then she continued, along with all the other women, to gaze into the padre's face, awaiting his response.

The priest hesitated and looked around. He became uncomfortably aware that he had touched upon a very delicate matter and so, without speaking, he quickly passed on to the next woman.

John Stephens looked on with considerable dismay, for he was rather conservative on the subject of unwed mothers. The subject was unmentioned in his own family, because his very respectable father, Benjamin Stephens, had been a bastard. The circumstances of father Stephens' birth were extremely awkward. It seems that his mother, Amelia Shepherd, had been exposed at an early age to something called "The Trouble." In 1771, when Benjamin Stephens had been born, "The Trouble" was caused by a rowdy lad named Shore Stevenson who had fathered Amelia's child without the slightest intention of marrying her. In the America of that day, contrary to history books, it was not entirely wrong for a couple to engage in sex now and again if they were truly anticipating matrimony, but it was socially unforgivable to sire a bastard. As the time of Benjamin Stephens' birth approached, it became apparent that young Shore was not going to become a married man. So when Amelia delivered a son, she was publicly thrashed, as prescribed by custom and law, and her father paid a heavy fine to the outraged community. Shore Stevenson was banished from Shrewsbury, New Jersey, and Amelia appeared alone at the parish to have her illegitimate son baptized.

Being the son of a bastard, John Lloyd Stephens could not help concur with the priest's solemn view of unwed mothers. But he also could not help being amused by the chaos that resulted from the priest's inability to explain the righteousness of marriage to the Indians. The priest understood very little Spanish; his book was in Latin, and not being able to translate as readily as the occasion required, he had secretly copied on a slip of paper, from a Spanish-language Protestant prayer book, the formal part of the baptismal service. In the utter confusion that followed, he lost the paper, and was left with the Latin text, which he translated into Spanish only intermittently. It took only a few moments to realize that this procedure was not working, so he turned to Augustin and gave him in English the questions to put to the long line of mothers in Spanish. Augustin was a devout Catholic, and he listened with great attention and respect to every word the priest said, but he did not understand a word of it. It therefore became necessary for Stephens to explain the English to Augustin in French, who then explained to one of the men in Spanish, who explained to the women in their native language.

The priest had already told Stephens about the passion of the Carib people for a multiplicity of names. One of the women, after giving her child three or four names, pointed to Stephens and told the priest to add his name to all the rest. The "honor" of becoming a godfather did not please Stephens, who stopped the ceremony and begged the priest to get him off with all possible grace. The priest understood Stephens' reluctance to accept the obligations of the honor, and promised to explain to the woman through an interpreter. But it was a very hot day, the room was crowded, the doors choked with waiting mothers, and by this point the priest, with his Latin and English and French and Spanish, was confused and in a perspiring and disheveled state. He forgot to talk to the woman, and just as Stephens was making his way back to the steamboat, she intercepted him and, thrusting the baby forward, she called him by a name he did not understand at first. So without wanting to offend the woman, he smiled meekly and lightly touched the little brown body. "Este-bans," the woman said again and again with pride as she smiled and nodded her head to the young American lawyer. "Estee-bans!"

From Punta Gorda, the *Vera Paz* proceeded to Guatemala and

Entering the Rio Dolce

entered the narrow Dulce River. On both sides of the steamboat was a barrier of vegetation, rising perpendicularly into the air three to four hundred feet. Stout exotic trees grew from the water's edge, with dense unbroken foliage, sending from their highest limbs long tendrils which descended into the water. The ocean was lost from view as Stephens and Catherwood watched the scene from the deck. Now they were enclosed on all sides. Stephens wrote in his diary, "Could this be the portal to a land of volcanoes and earthquakes, torn and distracted by civil war?" The land was so overburdened by jungle that it seemed impossible that it could be inhabited. The shade surrounded them and sometimes they were so encircled by jungle that the river seemed to disappear and the boat appeared to graze among the shrubs and trees. Occasionally, however, the green wall would sink and the sun struck the river with scorching force. But in a moment they would be in the deepest shade once again.

Stephens gazed at the tangled network of branches overhead,

but despite fanciful accounts and expectations he heard and saw no exotic creatures. No monkeys gamboling among the leaves, no parrots flying in the humid air, but only silence—a deep, pervading stillness as if every living thing had abandoned the forest. Except for the pelicans, the stillest of birds, that sat placidly on the water and rocked gently to and fro as if they were made of wood. These silent birds were the only living things the explorers saw. And the only sound they heard was the unnatural bluster of the steam engine.

For twenty-five miles the *Vera Paz* continued through the narrow passage, then suddenly the river opened upon a large lake, Lake Izabal, encompassed by mountains and studded with tiny islands. Stephens and Catherwood lingered until very late on deck, looking out into the moonlit night where ghostly herons stood against the black water and sleeping iguanas laced themselves among the vines.

They awoke the next morning in the harbor of Izabal. There was only one frame building in the tiny port composed entirely of huts and banana trees. This lone building was the establishment of Messrs. Ampudio y Pulleiro, whose business it was to unload the cargo of the *Vera Paz*, consign it to the indifferent muleteers and send it on mules over the perilous Mico Mountain Trail, the main route by which the interior of Central America could be reached. In front of the cargo office the muleteers, stinking, ragged and mud-splattered, slept sweetly on great heaps of sweaty mule blankets swarming with thousands of metallic-colored horseflies and gnats. Eventually Stephens and Catherwood would have to face the muleteers and the mountain, but for now they were hungry and dirty and wanted to think of nothing more complicated than a meal and a bath.

After eating and visiting the port's customs officer, who looked after them in his second occupation as the harbor's only barber— Stephens went off to pay an official visit to the Commandant. A soldier no older than fourteen, with a big bell-shaped straw hat falling over his eyes, stood at the door as sentinel. The troops, consisting of perhaps thirty men and boys, were assembled in front, and a sergeant was trying to drill them while he puffed with annoyance on a big cigar. The Commandant of this barefoot militia was Don Juan Penol, a young man of good family whose dangerous position in the region's unsettled political life had already marked his face with anxiety and fatigue. He regretted that he could not provide Stephens with assurances that his passport and other numerous credentials—all marked with the large seal of the United States of America—would be respected by the various warring groups clashing in his country. "Yes," Commandant Penol explained, "the conservative faction in Guatemala might be willing to recognize your authority and your passport, but the opposition's troops definitely will not. We are in a very poor political situation here, the Señor Stephens, and I cannot offer you much hope of protection. If you are here to make contact with the head of our government, you will have a difficult task, for we are a divided land."

*   *   *

The trouble had started in 1821 when Central America and Mexico—under the name of the Mexican Empire—declared independence from Ferdinand VII of Spain. This Mexican Empire soon turned into a constitutional confederation of five republics of which Guatemala was given the responsibility and expense of maintaining a central government. The years that followed, between 1825 and 1835, were filled with revolutions and counterrevolutions. Two major military personalities emerged from this period of conflict: Francisco Morazan, a liberal born in Honduras, the son of a French white man; and Rafael Carrera, a conservative half-breed Indian born in Guatemala.

Morazan quickly became the leading liberal and was elected President of the Central American Federation in 1831, and again in 1837. But he lacked a sense of timing and persuasion. His reforms were launched too quickly, and his efforts to break the power of the clergy, whom he considered dishonest and oppressive, met with strong public disfavor. North America, Great Britain and France recognized the Federation, but King Ferdinand and the Pope refused recognition. By 1837, civil war was rampant, and when cholera broke out in Guatemala, Morazan was accused by the clergy of poisoning the wells in an effort to annihilate the Indian populations.

This brought about the rise of the Indian conservative Rafael Carrera, whose troops—contemptuously known as *cachurecos*—counterfeit coins—marched against the Federation of Morazan. Carrera and his guerrillas had entered Guatemala just a few months prior to the arrival of Stephens and Catherwood, who walked right into the thick of things. In a series of bitter battles, Morazan managed to disperse the army of Carrera, and he announced the end of the revolution. But no sooner had Morazan retired into Salvador than Carrera came out of hiding, reassembled his army and began a frantic reign of terror throughout Guatemala. The countryside was devastated. Would-be generals of operatic proportions tramped through Central America. Their barefoot soldiers pillaged every settlement, and, except for a few soldiers of fortune and deserters from Napoleon's Italian troops, the liberators behaved like pirates. The roads, the cities, the smallest jungle settlements were swarming with the ill-trained, ill-paid and power-hungry soldiers of both factions. Reports of atrocities against civilians and clergy were widespread. And death was on the rampage in the very region where Stephens and Catherwood naïvely hoped to discover fabulous "lost cities."

Death and sickness were not new to Central America. The local white population—called *criollo*—feared the night air. Sickness was epidemic and white men seemed unable to survive it. The British engineer of the *Vera Paz* had been taken off the ship in a terrible state. Catherwood, being his countryman, went around to pay him a visit. He found the sick man in one of the miserable huts, lying almost unconscious in a hammock with all his rumpled, sweaty clothes still on. Though a huge man, easily six feet four and powerfully built, the engineer was completely helpless with raging fever. A single candle on the dirt floor gave a gloomy yellow light, and a little group of nervous crew members stood around the sick man, whose hellish malaria was a dreaded and entirely mysterious ailment of the tropics.

Fighting the depression of civil war and the illness of the land, Stephens visited the forlorn grave of his predecessor in office, the Minister to Central America, Mr. James Shannon, who had died in this sickly harbor town of Izabal and had been buried here. Behind the village on a desolate knoll was the improperly inscribed grave of the late Minister. Stephens stood staring at the dank ground where James Shannon was interred, overcome with a sense of death and loneliness. He hurried away, putting his hand over his nose and mouth as he stumbled toward the harbor, dreading the unshakable feeling that some subtle agent of death had already entered his body, where it would await its moment.

At daybreak the muleteers began to load the cargo for the ascent of "the Mountain." By eight o'clock Stephens and Catherwood mounted and looked back at their caravan—nearly a hundred mules and twenty or thirty muleteers. The two explorers were armed with pistols and knives tucked in their belts. Augustin carried a sword and pistols, while the principal muleteer wielded a murderously sharp unsheathed machete. On his naked feet he wore a pair of monumental spurs.

Then the command to start was heard up and down the caravan, and the nearly naked Indian carriers staggered under their burdens and fell into line with the heavily loaded mules. At the last moment, Stephens secured a mountain barometer over his shoulder, unwilling to entrust that weighty but invaluable mechanism to anyone. Then almost at once they were engulfed.

The mule trail was a quagmire. A solid gloom surrounded them, shimmering with white Morpho butterflies and pulsating with the throbbing of tiny tree frogs. At every step the mules slushed and sank to their bellies in dark blue mud. The naked roots of giant matapalo trees and rusty mahoganies clogged and broke the path. The trees interlaced and wove a dank shade, and the mudholes got larger and deeper. Stephens tried to keep a watch on the equipment, but he had all he could do just to stay mounted. In desperation he called to one of the muleteers and thrust the barometer into his arms. "Take care of this," he muttered as his mule very nearly lost its footing. Now all conversation came to an abrupt end, and each person in the caravan concentrated on keeping as close as possible to the track of the lead muleteer, in the hope that he would blaze a safe trail in the mire. But there was no possibility of safety on the Mico Mountain. Even the experienced head muleteer was carried into vast mudholes by his stumbling mule, which crawled out snorting and drooling, its legs and flanks coated with thick blue mud.

The main body of the caravan was by now some distance ahead of Stephens and Catherwood's immediate group. Through the black dripping forest they could hear the sharp crack of whips and the boisterous commands of the muleteers, urging the mules on. By the time they overtook these sounds they discovered that the whole caravan had left the trail and was sloshing up the bed of a stony stream, the water turning gray with the mud bleeding from the mules' flanks. The muleteers, stripped to the waist, and with their large trousers rolled up to the thighs, were scattered among the mules, trying to keep them on the move. They splashed and shouted and waved their arms. They cursed and cracked their whips and chased after strays. Mules bolted and the muleteers raced after them and grabbed hold of precious luggage which was just about to slip off into the water, bracing their feet against the mules' sides, straining at the girths.

The stream was a scene of absolute confusion and panic. Stephens felt certain that not a single instrument and not many of their supplies would make it over the mountain. In desperation and annoyance he and Catherwood let the caravan pass, and then crossed the stream carefully and managed to reach a road on the other side. But the mud was terrible and the low-hanging branches made it impossible to sit upright in the saddle. After a short distance on this impossible road, they decided to try the stream again and descended to the bank into the middle of the whole crazed caravan of angry men and frantic animals.

The stream was no better than the road. The trees shut out all light and the stream was so stony and rutted with boulders that the mules constantly stumbled and fell, tossing both the mounted muleteers and the cargo into the water.

The full impact of their impossible situation became clear when, after an hour of staggering through the stream, they found that they had just reached the foot of the mountain and that the *real* ordeal still lay ahead.

Stephens gazed up into the clouds that concealed the shoulders of the huge earthwork which rose before them. For a moment he closed his eyes. Then with a grim smile he sat up tall, released the reins and started the precipitous ascent, entering a narrow gulley which was worn to a slick clay finish by the steps of countless mules and countless torrents of rain. The passage was so narrow that the mules could barely pass through in single file without scraping the oozing walls.

The muleteers ran among the tramping hoofs of the animals, shouting and lashing them on. If one mule hesitated or fell, the entire column was blocked—unable to go forward and unable to turn. Any sudden start panicked the mules ahead and slammed Stephens and Catherwood, who had remained mounted, against the sides of the gulley, nearly crushing their legs. Finally the passage widened and the embankments fell away, but the ascent was still very steep. The mud deepened and was filled with jagged rocks and the roots of great mahogany trees. The caravan's only good fortune was the fact that at least it had not rained in several days. But no sooner had they congratulated themselves on the weather than the sky turned black and solid sheets of rain cascaded down upon them.

The mountain path ceiba tree

They could barely see the path before them. The woods were by now almost impenetrable. And as they struggled through the sea of vegetation, rain-drenched branches lashed against them and nearly knocked them off their mules. For five long hours they were dragged through mudholes, squeezed into gulleys, knocked and bashed against trees and tumbled over ruts and roots. Every step was exhausting, every turn demanded a tremendous exertion.

"It looks to me, Mr. Catherwood," Stephens called back to his stoic partner, "as if we will do a good deal better on our own two feet than on the bony backs of these mules." And as Stephens slid to the ground and stretched his damp, numb legs, he exclaimed mockingly, "My epitaph, Mr. C, may very well be something like this: *tossed over the head of a mule, brained by the trunk of a mahogany-tree, and buried alive in the mud of Mico Mountain!"*

Walking proved even worse than riding. The rocks and roots were so slippery, the mudholes so deep and the climb so steep that it was impossible for Stephens and Catherwood to continue on foot. So again they climbed onto their mules and clung to the saddle pommels in fear that the poor creatures would break down from fatigue. Stephens' mule fell first. Realizing that she was going down and that he could not save her with the rein, he strained every muscle and managed to fling himself clear of rocks, roots and trees, coming down in a thick bath of black mud with a tremendous belly flop.

Catherwood was thrown next. He struck the ground so violently that he lay unconscious for a moment before sitting up in the deep mud and staring into the air. All this time, through all these discomforts, he had not said a word; his face had remained absolutely expressionless even when torrents of rain came pouring off the brim of his tattered hat. For a long moment there was not a sound from him. Then, without moving from the mudhole where he lay half buried, he muttered, "If I had known, Mr. Stephens, about this bloody Mico Mountain before I agreed to accompany you, you may be certain, sir, that you would have come alone to Central America." Then he quite elegantly got to his feet and remounted the pathetic mule, and the caravan moved forward.

During this horrendous journey they had not encountered a single person. Then abruptly at a turning in the trail they met a tall wild-looking horseman wearing a battered wide-brimmed panama, a fringed poncho, plaid pantaloons, large spurs and an enormous sword. His appearance was indeed fearful, but there was also something sadly amusing about this lone rider entirely encrusted in muck. To the explorers' amazement, he addressed them in impeccable English. It seems that he had lost his muleteers and supplies somewhere among the terrible trails of the mountain. He had been twice thrown from his mule, which had rolled over him on his second fall and very nearly crushed him. He was thoroughly disgusted and totally exhausted.

After asking for something to drink, he slipped from his mule and trudged through the mud as he exasperatedly explained that he had just come from Guatemala City, where he had been negotiating a bank charter for nearly two years. Stephens smiled at the muddy man with disbelief but was soon convinced that this disheveled fellow was really a bank president when shown the charter. This banker explained that he was en route to England to sell shares of stock in his new bank. He also informed the explorers that Carrera had already marched on San Salvador and that a battle was expected at any time between the forces of Carrera and Morazan. The situation was perilous on both sides of the Mico Mountain and the travelers had no time to lose. So they parted as abruptly as they had met—the solitary rider disappearing at once into the twisted terrain while the caravan continued its terrible ascent.

It seems unbelievable that this could possibly be the great highway to Guatemala City. Almost all travel and merchandise from Europe had to pass over this hellish pass. Yet there was no effort to improve it or to divert travel by some less arduous route. Catherwood found such neglect barbaric, but Stephens, almost playfully, said that he envied a people who were so content with nature that they were not forever trying to improve upon it.

In two hours they finally reached the banks of a wild river which tore its way through the side of the mountain, foaming and breaking over great rocks. It was called *El Arroyo del Muerto*—"The Stream of the Dead," and it seemed ideally named for the mountain from which it plummeted. Even before Stephens and Catherwood had dismounted, the muleteers were scattered among the rocks and shade of the trees that lined the turbulent river, quietly eating their humble lunch of corn cakes. The mules stood placidly in the shallows, their bodies utterly motionless except for the sharp twitching of their ears and tails.

The turmoil and anxiety of the mountain vanished at once as Stephens and Catherwood sat on the ground under a large tree. But just as suddenly they became aware of the losses caused by the journey. Of particular concern was the barometer that Stephens had given to one of the muleteers. This man also carried besides the barometer a small white pitcher of which he was very proud. And on several occasions during the ascent, after a stumble or a narrow escape from falling into the mud, he had turned around to his friends and held up the pitcher with a wide victorious smile. This gave Stephens some hope for the barometer, and, in fact, the muleteer had managed to carry it through that terrible trip without its being broken. Unfortunately, however, the quicksilver had escaped, making the instrument completely useless.

There were other losses which, though less important to the scientific aims of the expedition, were far more depressing. When Augustin placed a well-filled napkin in front of the hungry explorers they found its content completely ruined. Their food supplies had been carefully stored in the napkins—enough boiled eggs, bread and roasted fowls for three days. Augustin had forgotten to pack salt, but, for some curious reason, he had placed in each napkin a large envelope of gunpowder, which had broken and spread throughout the precious food supply. All the natural beauty of the scene, all the travelers' gratitude for rest, everything except their tremendous appetites, vanished as they sat by the river, under a tree and stared at the gunpowder-soaked morsels of food. The only thing to do was hurry ahead to their encampment.

Toward dark they finally reached the rancho of Mico. After ten hours of the hardest riding they had done in their adventurous lives, they were informed that they had only traveled twelve miles. When they trudged into a room filled with the other guests of the little settlement, they were a very picturesque pair—plastered with mud, smelling like mules and barely able to bring a sound from their parched throats.

The other guests were travelers from Guatemala City and were on their way down the terrible mountain en route to the harbor at Izabal. Among them was a French merchant on his way to Paris, and the other guests consisted of a Canonigo Castillo, his secretary and two Pavons who were fleeing the religious persecution of the civil war.

The *canonigo* offered a very friendly welcome to Stephens and Catherwood, as if they were done up in impeccable dinner dress, and immediately invited them to the table, where he offered them chocolate and a dish called *frijoles*—black fried beans. Despite their outrageous appearance, Stephens and Catherwood unhesitatingly accepted the hospitality. After eating as quickly and as much as decorum permitted, they felt overwhelmingly sleepy, but agreeable company had been as rare as food on their journey, so they sat up with the other worldly guests and talked of travels and exploits, of politics and God, fashions and ladies, late into the night.

When at last they had hung up their hammocks, Stephens and Catherwood decided to use their last bit of energy to bathe and change clothes. They found, however, that their luggage had not been unloaded by the muleteers. And they were obliged to climb into their hammocks just as they were, mud, stench and all.

When the candle was extinguished, the guesthouse was instantly cast into a dense blackness. John Lloyd Stephens slowly raised his hand to his face and happily wiped the dried mud from his forehead. With the Mico Mountain behind them, he sensed a marvelous adventure opening before him. He was finally standing in the world where he had dreamed of standing. He was finally in the land of the "lost cities"!

In the utter stillness of the tiny sleeping room at the Rancho Mico he could hardly breathe with the excitement churning within him. From somewhere among the childhood relics of his life there lingered a stupendous exhilaration as he envisioned himself walking among the fabulous ruins. Then fatigue gradually mixed with the visions. For a moment his thoughts raced on *. . . ancient cities . . . ruins lost in eternal time . . . never seen before by modern man. . . .* Then, with a marvelous sense of pride in having passed over the Mico Mountain, he fell asleep.

Before daylight Stephens was out of doors, grateful for the air and the muffled sounds of twenty or thirty men, the muleteers and carriers of the other guests, sleeping on the ground, lying on their backs with their black woolly jackets, called *char-mars*, wound around them.

Daylight came slowly through the colossal labyrinth of boughs and vines, glowing among the leaves and making whole trees turn gradually transparent. As the day broke, the men reluctantly arose. Soon the Parisian merchant assembled his carriêrs, took some chocolate and, after saying good-bye, set off with a grim smile over the awesome mountain which rose between him and the sea. The churchman, Canonigo Castillo, set off next. He had crossed the Mico Mountain twenty years before, when he first arrived in this country, and he still vividly remembered the horrendous journey. He sniffed the morning air disdainfully and stepped into a *silla*—a chair with a high back and a little canopy to protect him from the sun. This chair was perched on the back of an Indian who was bent almost double under the weight of the stout *canonigo,* who was in high spirits, smoking a cigar and waving his handkerchief in farewell until he was out of sight. Now Stephens and Catherwood were alone.

None of their muleteers or carriers had arrived and it was getting on into the morning. Already the ground was glowing with the heavy assault of the sun. Stephens and Catherwood sat sullenly in the shade and stared into the distance, hoping to catch sight of their carriers. They were beginning to worry that they had been abandoned like the muddy banker they encountered on the trail, when finally at about eight o'clock, Augustin and a single carrier appeared and sheepishly explained that instead of staying with the other carriers of the *canonigo* and merchant in the encampment at the Rancho Mico, they had slept at a nearby rancho. "And what," demanded Stephens, "has become of the other muleteers?"

They also had slept at the rancho and had already gone ahead.

"But our clothes! How are we to bathe and change clothes?" Catherwood intoned in a quiet rage.

"Oh, the clothes are safe, very safe," Augustin said proudly, gesturing far into the distance. The caravan had left hours earlier, taking all the luggage with it.

Stephens could not speak he was so annoyed. He had hoped to change clothes before embarking on yet another day's travel. Looking down at his mud-covered trousers, he could barely tell where his cuffs left off and his boots began. But just as he started to curse, Catherwood cleared his throat officially and smiled. "I once knew a very attractive young lady," he said, "who was absolutely fascinated by gentlemen in soiled apparel." Stephens managed to laugh, and Catherwood suggested that they saddle up quickly and set off if they hoped to every catch up with their clean shirts.

Stephens was not easily daunted. He had traveled with Turks

and Arabs through primal countries and he understood the problems of trying to keep order in a caravan of men who at any moment might get it into their heads to quit and go home. He grinned with renewed determination and, brushing the dust from his beard, mounted his mule and faced the craggy countryside. "Come along, Cath. We had better hurry, because my underwear travel's at a gallop!" he shouted.

The countryside which lay ahead was dramatically changed from the jungle trails of the Mico Mountain. The distant horizon was jagged with the outline of mountain peaks, and the land immediately before them was dry and dusty, buttoned by smooth stones and covered by a forest of enormous candelabra cacti, miles of spiny giants standing singly with their bulbous appendages held stiffly upward to a cloudless sky. Beyond the cacti were dark pines, and beyond the pines were elaborate thickets of mimosa, whose winsome yellow blooms sent a rich musk into the air.

The road wound through this craggy country. After two hours of trudging along silently they arrived at a collection of ranchos called El Posos. The expedition's sole remaining carrier immediately rode up to a hut and dismounted very much as if he had arrived at his home. The woman of the house came out and chided him for failing to come the night before, which he gruffly blamed on Stephens and Catherwood. It soon became evident that the explorers stood a very good chance of losing this man to his girl friend.

Catherwood for the moment was far too hungry to worry about manpower. Most of their supplies had been spoiled by Augustin's gunpowder and what little food remained had gone ahead with the caravan. So they had to try to buy provisions. The people of El Posos lived almost exclusively on tortillas and black beans. The carrier obliged his employers by buying a basket of beans, but informed them that unfortunately they required many hours of soaking before they could be cooked and eaten. So Stephens urged Augustin to go back out into the village and try to find something—*anything*—which could be eaten immediately.

The lagoon

He succeeded in buying a single squawking, emaciated chicken, which he proudly held out to the hungry travelers with a wide smirk. Then he promptly wrung its neck, ran it through with a stick, and smoked it over a frail fire. It made a grubby meal, but there was little time to bemoan the poverty of their dinner, because it now appeared, as they had feared, that the carrier was unwilling to tear himself away from his lady-love. But like a dutiful husband he sent, by Augustin, the only carrier left to the explorers, a loving message to his wife at the town of Gualan.

Again the road lay over the ridge of a high mountain, with a handsome valley on either side. In the distance were tall green hills scattered with grazing cattle. The sun blasted the land obsessively. There was no winter here, no time of cold winds and snow, but endless summers.

No sooner had Stephens complained about the ceaseless scorch of the sun than it began to rain, a heavy, hot rain. Then, in less than an hour, it cleared abruptly. Rainwater dripped luminously against the sunlit sky and the ground steamed. From the high ridge on which they made their way they could see the Motagua River, one of the great waterways of Central America, rolling in unbroken torrents through the deep silent valley. Descending by a precipitous and jagged trail, they reached the river's bank. It was a place of astonishing beauty.

Stephens climbed from his mule and stood silently gazing at the scene. All around were great mountains; and the vast river, broad and deep and pale green, rolled through the gulch with a violence of motion and a thunderous sound which roared into the surrounding canyons and fell back upon them again and again like a tidal wave of watery echoes.

On the opposite bank of the river were a few houses, and two or three canoes tied to the shore, but not a person was in sight. Stephens decided that the settlement looked too recently lived in to be deserted, so he and Catherwood sent up a bellow. Finally a small man cautiously approached the riverbank and stared at the strangers. He blinked his large almond eyes and inspected the unkempt members of Stephens' little party and at length seemed satisfied that they were not some of the mercenaries who were out to plunder every village in the region.

The man climbed into one of the canoes and set it adrift. He was immediately swept far downstream by the swift current, but by taking advantage of an eddy he managed to bring the little boat across the river to the place where Stephens and his companions stood. Once he was told that the strangers were seeking hospitality for which they were willing to pay, he smiled and suggested that they come with him to the village. So the baggage, the saddles, bridles and other mule trappings were loaded into the canoe and then they cast off. Augustin sat sullenly in the stern, trying without much success to keep hold of the halter of one of the mules, pulling the animal along after the canoe in an effort to entice the other mules into the water. But they hadn't any intention of doing so. Augustin went ashore, where he managed to drive the mules into the water up to their necks. But they soon panicked and splashed and whinnied as they struggled back to the shore again. By this time Augustin was furious. He pelted the stubborn animals with sticks and pebbles and shouted and cursed, but they would not plunge into the swift current. Finally in exasperation he stripped and, wading to his armpits and threatening the mules with a long stick, he succeeded in getting them to swim.

Soon the men in the canoe could see nothing but the ears and snorting nostrils of the frightened mules. The current was stronger than anyone had imagined and the pathetic animals were quickly being carried downstream. One was swept far below the others and when she saw that her fellow creatures had made it to the opposite bank, she raised a terrible cry and very nearly drowned herself trying to swim back upstream to her companions rather than going directly ashore where the river had carried her.

During all of this commotion, Stephens and Catherwood sat silently in the canoe, the sun blasting down on their heads. The heat was terrific. Their clothes, already rigid with several days' mud, were saturated with perspiration. They longed to strip and join Augustin in the river, but they had no time for swimming. The humidity was worse than the heat. They could barely see through the sweat which rolled into their eyes.

After nearly an hour of trying to drive the mules across the Motagua River, they finally succeeded. At once their annoyance vanished. They gratefully accepted the use of a little house where they were invited to spend the night. It was plastered and whitewashed and handsomely if simply decorated with strips of bright red paint in the shape of festoons. The floor was very clean and the thatched roof offered a shelter from the sun.

Stephens was much impressed by the courtesy of the people of this village called Encuentros. Along with hospitality the Indians possessed a curious kind of dignity which had been noticeably missing in the people of the harbor town of Izabal. Though food was scarce, they unhesitatingly offered their guests everything they owned and were offended when the explorers told Augustin to give them money. Their little supper consisted of corn tortillas, which Stephens had never tasted prior to his arrival in Central America. These corn pancakes were the major food of the Indians, along with black beans fried with garlic in grease, an occasional bit of wild meat and thick black coffee sweetened with native brown sugar. These simple rations were gladly shared with the strangers, and as Stephens and Catherwood downed the dinner the children and women sat on the ground and drew up their knees, delighted by the appetites of their guests. After eating, Catherwood went in search of the luggage. "Oh, lord!" he groaned.

"What's the matter?"

"The luggage," he muttered as rage overtook him, "our bloody luggage isn't here! They have gone and taken it ahead to a rancho fully three leagues from here!"

Augustin shook his head fearfully, backing away from the enraged Catherwood, whose face turned absolutely crimson.

"Augustin!" Stephens barked sternly, "you are going to get on your mule right now, and you are going to go fetch our luggage . . . is that perfectly clear?" But Augustin, despite his fear that Catherwood was about to punch him in the nose, shook his head with a resolute no.

By now Catherwood had regained his British composure, and a cynical smirk flitted about his pale lips. "It is a rare pleasure," he said to Stephens, "to be one of the first of my kind to acquire on his person the permanent stench of mule piss!" Stephens tried desperately not to laugh. "And furthermore," Catherwood said, on the verge of shouting, "it may very well be the most permanent souvenir of this whole bloody misadventure of yours!" And the Englishman, whose explosive temper was a periodic calamity in his career, stormed from the room.

Stephens, who had been amused by the outburst, was now perturbed by his friend's tantrum, and he turned to Augustin with an angry glance. But Augustin still refused to leave the comfort of Encuentros. He also wouldn't guide Stephens to the distant rancho where the rest of the caravan was camped with all the cargo, and he wouldn't go alone and get their baggage and bring it back. Stephens was too hot and irritable to argue about it any more. All he could think about at the moment was the cool water of the beautiful Motagua River. He gave Augustin a look of disdain and sent him away. Once he was gone Stephens found the sulking Catherwood and, to cheer him up, suggested that their only salvation was a luxurious bath. And without another word they hurried to the riverbank.

The current, however, was much too swift and they didn't dare wade far from the bank. Then Catherwood called to the canoe man, who gladly returned the explorers to the shallows on the other side of the river, where they unhesitatingly pulled off their reeking, filthy clothes and plunged into the marvelously cool green waters of a shallow. It was a luxury so excellent that it could be properly appreciated only by those who had crossed the terrible Mico Mountain and had trudged through soggy terrain and had fallen again and again from their mules into pools of muck. As much as they loathed that mountain and as often as they would talk about it as the most horrible obstacle of their lives, nonetheless they gloried in having survived the great ordeal and—what is more—done so in the same set of clothes.

Now they settled like contented hippos in the sparkling water. It was the end of the day and the sun, a great furnace, was growing soft and golden—a great orange globe just above the mountainous horizon. Then, very suddenly, the heat seemed to vanish from the land, and the shadows gradually overtook the jungle and the village like an eclipse.

They stood to their chins in clear water. On both sides of the river were towering mountains, with their loftiest peaks still dazzling in the setting sunlight. Just above the bathers, on the embankment, was a palm-leafed hut, and in front of it a naked Indian sat staring at them with the softest eyes they had ever seen, while waves of parrots, hundreds upon hundreds of these garish, boisterous green birds, flashed and fluttered over their heads, filling the river valley with their shrieks and the beating of their wings.

Stephens was on the verge of becoming poetic when Augustin, recovered from their rebuff, shouted to them from the opposite bank that dinner was ready.

When they returned to their clothes which they had laid out on the bank while they bathed, they fully realized for the first time how hideously seamed with mud and filth they were. They had only one alternative to getting back into those reeking clothes— they could go native. But Stephens and Catherwood were very much concerned with proprieties and felt that they singlehanded- ly carried the good example of Christian civilization into the jungle. Besides, they agreed that they would look ridiculous in the bit of white fabric the Indians wound between their legs to make a loincloth. So very reluctantly they crept into their filthy clothes. A little later, however, they questioned their decision when their host, a don of some refinement and means, presented himself at dinner in a one-piece garment, loose, white and very brief, not quite reaching his knees and apparently requiring utterly noth- ing under it but the human anatomy. This fine gentleman didn't seem in the slightest apologetic about his dress, nor did his elegant wife, who was dressed in a similar manner, a flimsy sort of petticoat with nothing worn above the waist but a string of beads with a large Christian cross at the end.

The explorers found themselves in still another awkward situation a few hours later when they discovered that their room was a communal bedroom containing three low beds made of strips of interlaced rawhide. The don slept in one of these beds. When he came in to retire, he had little undressing to do. He said a courteous good night and simply pulled off his cotton tunic. Stephens glanced at Catherwood with a shrug and waited a moment before deciding that it was safe to slip with some degree of privacy into bed.

Stephens was just dozing off in his hammock when he heard a noise and opened his eyes. A girl of about seventeen was sitting sideways on the small bed at the foot of his hammock. She was humming very softly and smoking an enormous cigar. The girl was extremely beautiful: a deep russet color, sitting in the half- light, dressed only in a strip of transparent cotton fabric tied around her waist. Other than this flimsy covering, she was as naked as the don's wife, except for a string of colorful beads which lay upon her handsome young breasts.

John Stephens opened and closed his eyes several times but this marvelous dream girl would not go away. Then she noticed that he was watching her and so she smiled very meekly and offered her cigar. When he declined with a gesture, still astonished by her nakedness and nearness, she delicately drew a cotton sheet over her shoulders. Still continuing to gaze at Stephens, she took a few more quick puffs on her cigar, and then lay down to sleep.

Stephens closed his eyes and tried to do the same, for he was completely exhausted. But he could still hear every now and again the sound of her quiet puffing. He half opened his eyes and saw the glowing orange specter of her cigar moving in the darkness. Then he fell asleep.

The next morning Stephens, Catherwood and the sullen Augustin started out very early. The road lay along the banks of the Motagua River for some miles. But then, after about an hour's journey, they started to climb the spur of a mountain, and when they reached the top they followed along the ridge. It was quite high and narrow, commanding a boundless view on both sides. For hundreds of miles in every direction was a primeval land without any sign of fences or villages or men. A few wild cattle wandered over the great expanse, but their alertness to every sound and their extreme shyness made it clear that unlike their domesticated kin in the United States these cows of the Spaniards wanted nothing to do with mankind.

The explorers tracked along the ridge for another hour and then entered a woody country which looked as if it had recently been cleared of much timber. Soon they came to a huge gate which stood alone in the unfettered land like a grotesque monument. It was the first sign they had seen of any form of barrier or enclosure. But it made no sense standing without purpose in this vast landscape. On both sides of the massive mahogany gate, which would have been a suitable entrance for a princely estate, there was *nothing*. Just a thick forest where, even in the shade of the lush trees, it was hot and humid. There wasn't the slightest breeze and the ground itself seemed to thunder with heat and throw dust into the faces of the strangers as they rode on their lathered and dripping mules. Stephens clutched the reins and shook his head. Abruptly his brain began to turn and he was confused and a bit ill. It was the heat, he was certain, and he feared that he was in danger of sunstroke. At that same moment Catherwood's face went momentarily pale. There was an odd rolling sensation and then a terrifying thud. At the same moment branches above them rustled in the totally windless air. "Good Lord," Catherwood muttered with a quiver, "it's an earthquake!"

It was as if this great rugged land were still being created beneath their feet. As if these towering peaks were visibly rising into the sky. "Are you all right?" Catherwood asked his friend.

"What do you mean . . . *all right?* It felt like the end of the world!"

The earth became solid once again and the jungle hummed with life. The branches enclosed everything which did not move faster than they grew. The sky itself was obliterated by vegetation for hours upon hours as the explorers continued their journey through the tangled forest. At times they suspected that it was already night, or that the sun had somehow disappeared, that behind the tiers of leaves and boughs were only more leaves and boughs—an endless succession of foliage.

The entire green world around them pulsated with hunger. Everything grew and everything ate. Hunger was epidemic here. The birds ate the insects and the insects ate the grass and the grass ate the earth—it consumed everything. The vegetation swallowed up whole mountains and surrounded and ingested everything in its path, even the ancient cities for which they were searching. "The heat is terrible! I'm only just barely conscious," Stephens moaned. Even in the forest the heat of the hidden sun followed closely behind them.

And the sun was the most mysterious thing of all, for the sun fed upon itself.

At last they caught sight in the distance of the house of Donna Bartola, a gentlewoman of the town of Gualan to whom they had a letter of introduction. It was with the greatest satisfaction that the small caravan tied the mules under a motley tree and stepped into the cool patio of the hacienda, where Stephens instantly threw himself into a hammock. The shade and the quiet of the tiny house surrounded him and he smiled happily. Then, sitting up and softly pressing his fingers to his head with a grin, he looked at the luggage piled at the door and realized that for the first time since leaving Izabal he would be able to change his clothes. This ecstatic experience was immediately followed by the privilege of sitting at a refined table and dining on the excellent cuisine of Donna Bartola.

Toward evening Catherwood and Stephens strolled through the little town of Gualan. It stood on a plateau of breccia rock, at the junction of two great rivers, and was snugly placed within a vast cordillera, a fierce bristling ring of protective mountains. There was just one street in the town and it was lined with squat one-story houses with tiny piazzas in front of each. At the end of the street was a gravel plaza and at the center of this spacious meeting place stood a Gothic church which was astonishingly grand for such a small village. In front of this classic of Spanish Colonial style architecture was an austere and monumental cross, at least twenty feet high.

After looking into the church, they turned from the plaza and walked down to the Motagua River, where on the bank a boat was being constructed of mahogany. Nearby was a group of men and women laughing as they forded the stream and carried all their clothes on their heads with complete nonchalance. Just beyond and around a bend in the river, three girls were bathing. Stephens and Catherwood sat under a tree and grinned at one another. Catherwood was too exhausted to make any sketches despite the beauty of the girls. So he simply leaned back peacefully and gazed at the handsome naked limbs while a tumult of clouds gradually filled with the colored fires of the setting sun.

Soon it was dark and the two friends had some difficulty finding their way back to the house of Donna Bartola. Considering the unorthodoxy of recent nights, the explorers were curious to find out about their sleeping arrangements at the hacienda. Tonight they were finally given a room to themselves. Except, as they later discovered, for the companionship of thousands upon thousands of great black ants that darkened absolutely every-thing, including the candles, which they completely covered, up to the flame.

Their hammocks gave them protection from the ants and they managed to sleep soundly. Very early in the morning a servant awoke them with a good breakfast of chocolate and small rolls of sweet bread. While they were making a feast of these delicacies, the head muleteer of the caravan who was responsible for the absence of the luggage and supplies, arrived and stared at his employers contemptuously. He paced around the table sullenly for a long while before they could prompt him to say what was on his mind.

"*Dinero*—money," he said. He wanted an advance against his fee despite Stephens' insistence that he was to be paid after his job was completed. "Look here," Stephens reminded the mule-teer, "you vanished with all of our baggage as if it didn't even matter to you. Do you hear me?"

The muleteer ignored the criticism and continued his com-plaint by claiming three dollars more than was owed to him.

"I say," Catherwood muttered, "but he does go on. Don't give him a penny until the journey is over."

"If necessary," Stephens barked, trying to sound official in his faltering Spanish, "we will go on without any of you! I have already told you more than once: you will be paid when the journey is completed and not a day before. Now I really do hope that I have made myself quite clear."

The muleteer went away in a fury. It was a bad sign and both the explorers knew it. Less than a half hour later a constable appeared at the house with a summons to the *alcalde*, the town's mayor.

"This is utterly preposterous," Stephens said as he eyed the document. Catherwood, who was at the moment cleaning his brass pistols, laughed with mock bravado. "Don't worry, my dear

friend, if they put you in prison, I will bombard the entire town!"
With this he displayed both pistols with a flourish, making the
little constable very nervous.

The town hall of Gualan was located on one side of the central
plaza. Stephens followed the constable into a large room in which
the *alcalde* and his clerk sat very formally, despite the fact that
their shirttails were out and they were barefooted. The angry
muleteer was seated arrogantly among a cluster of the fellows
who were to be his witnesses.

The explorers soon learned that their treacherous muleteer—
after all his poor service as their guide—had reported them as
debtors. Stephens was shocked by the accusation and thoroughly
annoyed to be put in such an unbearably embarrassing position.
Obviously it would have been simpler to pay the troublesome
muleteer and be done with him, but Stephens looked into that
fellow's foul face and saw such smugness there that he decided
not to pay him a cent even if it meant going to jail.

And so the hearing began in the little courtroom. Attorney
Stephens defended himself in English, though no one had the
slightest notion of what he was saying. The *alcalde* was nonetheless impressed by Stephens' eloquent manner and decided in his
favor almost at once. The muleteer was in a rage and did not stop
cursing all the while he was rushing out of the room.

Stephens thanked the *alcalde* for his wisdom and legal expertise
and then showed him several official letters of introduction as
well as his passport. The wrinkled little official was astonished by
all the signatures and seals and ribbons. And when he discovered
that Señor Stephens was a representative of the Presidente de los
Estados Unidos he gallantly pushed aside the inquisitive town-
folk and invited the foreign visitors into the bar for a drink and a
cigar.

"Well, dear me," Catherwood joked as he stepped forward like
a dandy, "don't mind if I do."

That evening the town was in commotion over the ceremony
of Santa Lucia. The firing of muskets, petards and rockets had
announced the arrival of an unexpected but very welcome visitor

in Gualan, one of the holiest saints of the calendar—Santa Lucia, the most marvelous of the miracle workers introduced to the Indians by the padres.

During past months not a single priest had come to Gualan, because of the anti-religious campaign of the civil war. The arrival of Santa Lucia was therefore like a blessing to the villagers in troubled times. Morazan's rise to power had been signaled by an attack upon the clergy. The countryside was overrun with priests, friars and monks of different orders who were desperately trying to escape Morazan's troops.

Stephens was sympathetic toward the frightened clergymen, but he was also appalled that the largest buildings, the best cultivated lands and a great portion of the wealth of Central America were in the hands of the clergy. Morazan had decreed the end of the Church's power, and from the Archbishop of Guatemala down to the poorest friar, the clergy were in great danger. Some padres immediately fled, others were banished, and many were hurried by mule to seaports and shipped off under sentence of death should they return.

Many of the enormous churches of the region had fallen into ruin. Of those which still stood, their doors were rarely open, and the practice of religious rites was quickly fading away among the people who had only recently been converted to Christianity.

Matters were quite different in the areas where the troops of Carrera were powerful. A half-breed Christian fanatic, Carrera had gained a strong hold over the people by trying to restore the Church and the exiled clergy. The tour of the Santa Lucia was regarded as proof that Carrera was keeping his promises.

All day Stephens and Catherwood had heard of nothing but the miracles of Santa Lucia. At the dinner table Donna Bartola admitted that she too had once prayed to the saint and that her prayer had been answered. The explorers were curious about the ritual so they locked the house and accompanied Donna Bartola, her servants and a flock of noisy children to the house of the saint to pay their respects.

The sound of a fiddle and the firing of rockets helped them

find their way. The saint had taken up residence in the hut of a poor Indian in the outskirts of the village, and for some time before Stephens and his friends reached it they encountered crowds of people of all ages and in every degree of dress and nakedness, smoking and laughing, talking and dancing. When they arrived at the sanctuary, a path was politely cleared for the visitors so they were able to enter the little hut.

The roof and walls were thatched with dried cornstalks and the door was a simple opening in one of the walls. Inside was a crowd of kneeling men and women. On one side was a simple little altar, about four feet high, covered with a very clean white cotton cloth. On top of this altar was an elaborate pedestal, and on top of that was a glass case containing a large waxen doll dressed in faded blue silk and heavily ornamented with gold leaf, spangles and paper flowers. This was the great Santa Lucia who had come to Gualan to save the people and the Church.

Over her little head was a canopy of red cloth on which a gold cross was embroidered. Near this waxen *santa* was a sedan chair trimmed with red cotton and gold leaf. This was the litter on which the saint was carried from village to village.

Donna Bartola, who was a widow and a very handsome, mature lady, fell at once to her knees. The ceremony of praying had already begun, and the music of a drum, violin and flageolet filled the small hut and entwined with the earnest murmurs of the faithful Indians.

Stephens, who towered above the kneeling crowd, felt self-conscious, but he could not sink to his knees and pretend to pray. This world of the jungle, though he admired its intensity and honesty, was not his world. And so he tried to be as quiet and inconspicuous as possible while he studied the faces of the people around him.

He watched the eyes of one young girl in particular. She beamed with vitality as she gazed at the saint, and her lips moved in rapid prayer. Her manner was different from that of any Christian he had observed in worship, for her fervent concentration was more like a trance than devotion, and her movement was highly sensual, though she addressed herself to a saint who epitomized disembodied spirituality. Her breast heaved and her head rolled and her eyes flashed so excitedly that Stephens was embarrassed by the feeling that he was invading her privacy. A trace of saliva hung from her full lips, and when she took a breath a low moan came from deep within her chest. Finally Stephens looked away in dismay. This was devotion of a sort which entirely evaded him.

When it was time to leave the hut, Stephens and his friends found themselves surrounded by a wild bunch of naked boys setting off fireworks and shouting with delight among the elders who kneeled in little groups across the entire landscape. Beyond the barrage of fireworks, bounded by a wall of darkness, was a group of young men and women dancing frantically by the light of blazing pine torches. In the frenzy of the dance Stephens recognized the same trance which he had seen in the hut of Santa Lucia. He knew that this was a ceremony of far greater antiquity than the rites of Christianity; and gradually as Stephens watched, he began to enjoy the unbounded freedom of the young dancers, and as he walked past them he wistfully nodded to the throbbing, archaic drumming.

Excusing himself to Donna Bartola and Mr. Catherwood, he strolled aimlessly by himself for many hours, passing through the alternating darkness and flashing fires which surrounded the jubilant dancers. They made him feel hopelessly old at thirty-four and helplessly solemn. Finally near dawn he returned to the hacienda.

The sound of prayers faded away as the explorers lay in the darkness of their room and quietly made plans for the next day. They wanted to reach Guatemala City in the hope that Stephens would locate the political leaders of the Central American Federation and be able to present his credentials. They also knew that they were in the locality of one of the "lost cities." An eighteenth-century writer named Francisco Fuentes had claimed that an old and well-preserved architectural complex was to be found in the region known as Copan, just beyond the Guatemala border in

Honduras. Fuentes called this intriguing ruin the "Circus." And Stephens and Catherwood eventually wanted to search for this "Circus," but for now politics came first.

The morning was so hot and humid that the travelers decided not to go outside. Instead they pressed themselves against the coolness of the thick walls of the house and tried to doze. But it was impossible for Stephens to sleep, and so he sat for hours gazing through half-closed eyes at panting dogs rolling in the dust under the shade trees.

In the evening they paid a visit to the local padre. He was a short fat man wearing a curious white nightcap, a blue-striped jacket and huge pantaloons. He was peacefully swaying in a hammock and smoking a very large cigar when they entered his home. After offering his guests refreshments and cigars, he invited them to enjoy the coolness of the night air on his patio, where they talked about local customs and history.

"Have you ever heard," the padre asked offhandedly "of a place called Copan?"

Stephens explained that it was the very place for which he and Catherwood were searching.

"Ah," murmured the padre, puffing intently upon his cigar. And then he sat in silence and nodded thoughtfully.

The padre was more interested than most of his clerical colleagues in the pre-Columbian history of the Indians. He was familiar with their history and probably understood more about the ruins than anyone else in the region. "The Indians are devout. They are very religious. They have a great respect for the faith of other men. They love all the saints. It is a pity that so few white men understand them." With this he hitched up his enormous pantaloons and lighted another cigar. As for Copan, he said quietly, he knew only what rumors and folklore told him—and that was very little. "Yes, there is probably such a ruined city somewhere out there in the jungle. But where it is and how it might be found is another question."

The padre's skepticism about the existence of Copan did not diminish the curiosity of the explorers. To the contrary, the very fact that rumors existed about such a ruined city made them all the more hopeful. They believed that with luck they might find the city they felt certain was located somewhere in the jungle near the Copan River.

"But, gentlemen," the padre said indulgently with a smile, "do you know the jungle of the lowland? My dear friends, you cannot imagine the ordeals you will face if you are determined to travel to the Copan River."

The next morning Stephens and Catherwood awakened early and by seven o'clock were already on the road, more anxious than ever to complete their diplomatic duties in Guatemala City so they could search for the mysterious ruined city of Copan. Soon they were tracking along the banks of the Motagua River, which by this time had become a familiar traveling companion to the caravan. The surly muleteer led the way, tugging at his mule as he muttered curses and Spanish maledictions, spitting into the dust with open disdain and glowering through his thick black eyebrows at his employers. Next came a string of dutiful mules carrying high loads which swayed to and fro. Between the mules were the silent Indian carriers as well as two noisy mule drivers whose sniggers and tall stories never ceased. Then came the nimble-stepping little mule of the slumbering servant Augustin, who was luxuriously slumped over his saddle, where he jiggled and wiggled like a great sack of jelly, and snorted, wheezed and purred contentedly in an unperturbable sleep.

Behind this dusty little party of travelers were Stephens and Catherwood, riding side by side and deeply involved in conversation. When they were not chatting they were enjoying the exquisite landscape brilliantly lighted by ferocious sunlight. Beyond the river was a great range of mountains, six or eight thousand feet high. The trail began to rise, and within an hour the caravan had left the Motagua. Soon they found themselves in a wilderness of flowers. Every bush and shrub was covered with purple and red blooms, and on the slopes and in the ravines leading down to the river were large trees so covered with red blossoms that they appeared to be on fire.

By two o'clock they had reached the village of San Pablo. There

Stephens hired a local guide who knew the way to the town of
Zacapa, where the caravan planned to spend the night. The head
muleteer was utterly offended by the intrusion of a local guide,
and insisted under his breath that he knew the road to Zacapa
perfectly well. But Stephens and Catherwood had no patience
with the muleteer in view of his attempt to extort money from
them in a court of law, so they ignored him and ordered the
caravan to resume the journey.

By four o'clock they had a distant view of the great plain of
Zacapa, bounded on the far side by a mountainous barrier at the
foot of which stood the town. After a long descent they crossed
the flatland, which was very green and well cultivated, fording a
stream and entering the town of Zacapa, which was the finest
place they had seen since arriving in Central America. The main
plaza, landscaped with scarlet hibiscus and numerous palm trees,
was dominated by an impressive church with a facade rich in
Moorish detail.

Stephens and Catherwood rode up to the house of a certain
Don Mariano Durante, the largest residence of the town, where
Augustin was told to knock at the grand front door while his
employers brushed away some of the dust of the road and tried to
make themselves presentable.

The door was opened by a French-speaking black from Santo
Domingo, who told the visitors that Señor Durante was not
presently at home but that the house was entirely at their service.
So they gratefully entered a large elegant courtyard filled with
fountains, trees, flowers and a lush atmosphere of green-tinted
shadows and fragrant air. The mules were put in the hands of the
servants. Meanwhile, Augustin, the muleteer and his helpers
were so overwhelmed by the opulence of this grand house that
they self-consciously crushed their hats in their hands and bowed
repeatedly as they backed into the street, where they set up their
camp.

Stephens and Catherwood were in their element. Standing
erect and filled with composure they entered the grand *sala* with
its broad windows and iron balconies entwined with flowers. The

handsome room was furnished with sturdy tables, a European bureau and upholstered chairs. In the windows of this lovely *sala*, in hanging cages, were dozens of beautiful songbirds as well as two canaries from Havana.

This rich home was the residence of two bachelor brothers who willingly provided hospitality to distinguished travelers in the lack in Zacapa of any inns or hotels. Stephens and Catherwood unhesitatingly entered into the luxury and comfort of the house. While Stephens was sitting at a writing table collecting his travel notes, he heard the tramp of mules in the yard, and soon a gentleman entered, took off his sword and spurs, and laid his pistols on the entry table. Supposing him to be another traveler like themselves, Stephens and Catherwood graciously asked him to take a seat; and when dinner was announced they invited him to join them at the table. It was not until bedtime that Stephens and Catherwood realized that they were doing honors to one of the masters of the house, Señor Durante.

Slipping into a clean soft bed, Catherwood laughed softly at their presumptuous error. "Well," Stephens said in his droll manner, "we can flatter ourselves that he certainly has no reason to complain for our lack of attention."

 The next morning the town of Zacapa was thrown into commotion by the arrival of a detachment of Carrera's shabby soldiers, on their way to Izabal to receive and escort a cargo of muskets. The house of the brothers Durante was a traditional gathering place of the town's dignitaries, and as always the conversation turned upon the revolutionary state of the country. Some of the townspeople, when they realized Stephens' official position, urged him to go at once to San Salvador, the headquarters of the Morazan party, rather than trying to continue along the road to Guatemala, which they assured the travelers was occupied by the barbarous troops of Carrera.

Stephens understood the partisan fervor of civil war and accepted this advice with skepticism at the same time that he tried to change the subject. But the topic of war was too urgent to be avoided, and Señor Durante innocently asked Stephens whether America had ever been engaged in great wars. Durante said he knew that the North Americans had fought a revolution, for he had read about it in *La Historia de la Revolucion de los Estados Unidos del Norte*, but he said that he knew little about the other wars of the United States. While Catherwood looked on with a wide grin, Stephens assured Señor Durante that the United States of America was a civilized nation which avoided war at all costs.

"Ah," Señor Durante asked naïvely, "but didn't you also avoid at all costs a war in 1812?"

Mr. Catherwood waited for Stephens' reply. "It seems to me," the American explorer said rather dryly, "that after such a long day we would all prefer sleep to politics."

"Yes, of course," Señor Durante said politely.

"Of course," Catherwood said with a smile.

The next day the muleteer and his men did not make an appearance until very late. In the meantime, Stephens had an opportunity to obtain information about the state of the country. From what he could make of the warnings and cautions given to him by authorities and peasants alike, it seemed unnecessary and unwise to go directly to Guatemala City. In fact it was better, Stephens decided, to wait out the military convulsions of the region. And meanwhile there was no reason, officially or otherwise, to delay the search for the ruins of Copan.

When the muleteer finally appeared, alternately stuttering and cursing in his effort to explain his lateness, Stephens stopped him cold and told him to forget his improbable explanations and try to tell at least one truth. "Do you or do you not know the road to Copan?" Stephens demanded.

The muleteer opened his arms in a gesture of theatrical astonishment. *"Of course,* señores," he assured them. "I know the road to Copan as other men know the palms of their own hands!" Almost without a pause for breath, the muleteer immediately made a new contract with his employers to conduct them to Copan within three days, mapping out the entire trip in stages, and from Copan onward to Guatemala City. "Of course, señores!"

he said again and again, rubbing his chin and smiling with an oily grin which Stephens had come to dread.

At seven o'clock the next morning the caravan continued its journey. By the following day they had reached Chiquimula, a little town near the border of Guatemala that the troops of Morazan had devastated the prior year. Passing the village, the travelers came upon the bank of a stream. Here the muleteer made a gallant gesture, indicating with a great show of authority the direction the caravan was to take. And so Stephens and Catherwood followed the stream until they came upon an old Indian. The muleteer wanted to ignore this man but Stephens insisted upon asking him if they were on the right road.

"No, señores," he told them. "I know the *camino real* of Copan. But it is not here, señores. It is on the other side . . . far away, on the opposite side of the river and across the great mountains. You have come the wrong way, señores, if you are going to Copan."

Stephens gave the muleteer a dark look, wondering if he had deliberately taken them out of their way because he had lost his court claim against them. They had come a long distance since morning, and now they would have to return to the river and start all over again.

The next day, after a great deal of difficulty they managed to find a pathetic little cowpath and began to wander along it for an hour or more before they finally found the *camino real*. But this "royal road" was little more than a stony trail suitable for a single mule. Stephens was more exasperated with the muleteer than ever. By now it was obvious that the man didn't have the slightest knowledge of the whereabouts of Copan and had lied to them in order to strike a bargain for additional money. It was also clear that they were entering a region which was so wild and uncharted that it was unwise and unsafe to follow the cunning muleteer. But they had no other choice.

By eleven they had reached the top of a mountain, and looking down, they could see the town of Chiquimula. They had come full circle to very nearly the same place they had been the previous morning. The situation began to seem hopeless.

Stephens and Catherwood were not certain where they were or

if they would ever succeed in finding Copan or Guatemala City or any other place they intended to visit. Now, however, they had other problems. Clouds abruptly gathered around the towering mountain, and for more than an hour the caravan rode sullenly and silently in a crushing rain. When at last the sun broke through they could see the mountaintops still towering far above them, and on the right, far below, a deep valley piled to the brim with a lush abundance of vegetation. It was a stupendous sight, more rugged and boundless than any view either of the explorers had encountered anywhere else in the world. As they began to descend along a perilous, jagged path, the great mountains rose higher and higher around them. Then the terrain gradually began to spread out into vivid colors, rising several thousand feet in every direction and turning from pink to red and orange, barren and craggy and stripped of vegetation except for the gigantic black and green pines which clustered here and there among the rocks, growing upward directly from the iron core of the mountain.

Far below, they could faintly see the village of Hocotan, which they hoped to reach by nightfall. From this distance all they could discern of the little town was a ramshackle cluster of huts lying flat upon the ground and the gigantic Church of St. John the Hermit rising like a monolith from the floor of the valley.

They continued with effort down into the valley and along the dry riverbed. Heavy clouds clung to the peaks above them and soon it began to rain again. By four o'clock they could see the massive church of Hocotan rising peculiarly out of the desolate plain. And finally they entered the cobblestoned streets and encountered farmers leading mules piled high with hay. According to the travel plan agreed upon with the muleteer, Hocotan should have been the end of the day's travel. That was agreeable to Stephens because his companions were very weary and because he had been told that the *cura*, the Indian priest of the village, knew much about the ruins of Copan. The muleteer, however, refused to stop and spurred on the entire train of mules, which took off toward the open plains at a trot.

Stephens shouted furiously and tried to overtake him, but he couldn't get his mule to gallop. Suddenly, in a fury, Stephens jumped to the ground and began to chase the muleteer on foot, bellowing at him as he ran. He put his hands on his pistols as he was running to steady them in his belt. The muleteer took all of this in, first with delight and then with considerable dismay when he saw Stephens reaching for his pistols. He came to an abrupt stop with an expression of panic on his face and clutched his murderous machete. He was convinced that Stephens had gone mad and was about to shoot him on the spot. *"Ayuda!"* he sobbed. What could be more frightening than a mad American with two pistols?

Now he carefully slipped to the ground with his hands up. "Señor," he stammered with a frightened smile, *"estoy muy nervioso! Si, si . . .* whatever you say, señor!" He was more than willing, he insisted, to come to terms, but he had good reason for insisting upon continuing the day's journey. He said that if they wanted to reach Copan by the following day, they would have to continue and make an encampment farther along the trail. Stephens and Catherwood had no faith in the conniving mule driver, but they wanted to give him no excuse for abandoning them or leading them on another wild-goose chase, so reluctantly, after a quick conference, they agreed to his plan.

At six o'clock in the evening they climbed through a rocky pass which opened upon a great mesa crowned by another gigantic church. It was the seventh such church they had seen that day. Coming upon these immense buildings in desolate regions accessible only by mountain trails was astounding.

After exploring the church, the two travelers rested momentarily and gazed around this dusty, desolate place. The grass was tall and untouched by the wind; the soil unbroken by footprints, not a human being anywhere; and even the windows in the little prison near the church were devoid of faces, the door swinging to and fro with a steady groan. The village was deserted. Not even a dog lay asleep in the shadows.

Stephens and Catherwood slowly rode up to the town hall, which bore an old battered sign indicating the name of the

Imprisonment

village: Comatan. The door was fastened and barricaded, apparently to prevent stray cattle from entering. After searching the empty street, Stephens tore away the fastening, broke open the door with some difficulty and peered into the dusty room.

"This is as good a place to spend the night as any," he said. "Let's unload the mules."

Augustin was sent off to forage for dinner, ambling through the deserted village aimlessly, scratching his head and muttering. In half an hour he returned with one egg. Though he managed to find little food, he discovered that the town did have a population, which he had awakened. The *alcalde*, an Indian with a gold-headed cane, and several of his assistants, *alguazils*, with long slender wands of office, came to stare at the intruders in the town hall.

Stephens showed these barefooted officials his passport and explained that his caravan was going to Copan. Stephens suspected that they could not read the passport and so he made efforts to impress them with the awesomeness of the seal.

As the other officials examined the broken locks of the town hall with some misgivings, Catherwood nonchalantly asked them for eggs, chickens, milk and other food, to which they answered, without as much as a glance at him, *"No hay*—There is none." Then they left without a word.

Stephens and his friends stood staring after the town's officials, trying to grasp the significance of their visit. The town hall contained nothing but a large dusty table and two benches. Stephens shouted insults at the muleteer, abusing him for insisting they forgo their overnight stop at Hocotan as planned, and for guiding them to a place where they could get nothing to eat and no hospitality. While the muleteer grumbled in a corner, Stephens and Catherwood made their meager dinner on bread and chocolate, taking special care not to offer any to the rogue who had put them in this hungry predicament.

Fortunately there were pegs in the walls for swinging the hammocks, and in a disgruntled mood they prepared for the night. Catherwood was already in his hammock and Stephens was half undressed when the door suddenly burst open, and thirty men rushed in, the *alcalde, alguazils,* soldiers, Indians and townspeople, ragged and ferocious-looking men, armed with staves, swords, clubs, muskets and murderous machetes, and carrying dozens of blazing torches which threw fearsome huge shadows on the walls. At the head of this angry mob was an arrogant officer of perhaps twenty-eight with a patent-leather hat and a sword and an expression of unbridled contempt on his face as he glared at the aliens. Stephens later learned that this insolent soldier was a captain in one of Carrera's companies of liberators.

The *alcalde* was extremely drunk, and he stumbled forward and demanded to see the passport once again. Stephens assumed his most authoritative manner, much practiced in the courts, and presented the document to the drunken man, who in turn handed it over to the Captain, who rocked back and forth on his feet and puffed up his chest as he glanced at the passport. Then he looked up very coolly and said that it was not valid.

In the meantime, Catherwood and Stephens had hurriedly

dressed so they would feel on a more equal footing with the young braggadocio. For the first time during their journey they were exceedingly unhappy that they didn't speak fluent Spanish. Through Augustin they tried to explain the official character of their travels. Stephens called the officer's attention in particular to the endorsements on the passport of Commandant Penol of Izabal. But it was maddening to attempt to use diplomacy when Stephens knew that every subtlety of his debate would be lost in the translation by Augustin. He could see the rising anger in the Captain's face, though he could not comprehend what was being said by either Augustin or the officer. Through all of this the *alcalde* tried to intrude, telling the officer that the passport Stephens had shown him on his earlier investigation was printed and not written and that it was printed on a very small piece of paper, whereas the document Stephens was now offering to the officer was written by hand on a very large sheet.

"I promise you," Stephens insisted annoyedly, "that this is exactly the same document I showed you before!" But the Captain smirked and glanced away with an arrogant blink of his eyes and turned his back on them. Both Catherwood and Stephens did their best to remain calm while they argued with the crowd, but it came to no good. Having heard enough, the officer told the intruders flatly that they could not proceed on their journey, but would have to remain at Comatan until information was sent to Chiquimula and orders were received for the handling of their unlawful entry into the country.

Stephens was outraged, but he understood the danger of the situation and tried to keep his temper. He had no intention of staying the night as a prisoner. He would turn back rather than face that disgrace, but when he agreed to abandon his journey to Copan altogether, and return by the road on which he had come, the officer smiled unpleasantly and told him peremptorily that he could not leave Comatan under *any* condition.

Then the officer hostilely extended his hand and told Stephens to give up his passport.

"This passport, sir, was given to me by my own government. It is evidence of my official character, necessary for my personal security, and I will certainly not give it up to you or to anybody else!"

For his part Catherwood delivered an impassioned lecture to the stunned *alcalde* in a mixture of Spanish, French and English which the man could not possibly comprehend. But Catherwood was not in the slightest daunted by this; he spoke at some length on international law, on the prescribed treatment of diplomatic visitors, and on the consequences of disregarding the special passport and endorsements obtained by Washington for Stephens from Commandant Penol and General Juan Cascara of the toppling federal government of Central America. But Catherwood's legal harangue, like Stephens' U.S. credentials, didn't make the slightest impression on the barefooted assembly, which had gradually grown into a mob.

Stephens repeated that he would not under any circumstance give up his passport, offering instead to go with it himself, under guard, to Chiquimula and straighten out the entire mess. The young officer responded with unrestrained arrogance, saying that Stephens would not go to Chiquimula or anywhere else, neither forward nor back, but would remain where he was. Again the officer thrust out his hand and intoned threateningly, "The passport, señor. Now!"

For a long moment Stephens glared at the young man and his icy stance. Neither of the men moved. Stephens considered relenting to the demand, but his sense of freedom, his dignity and his official status as a representative of the United States of America had been abused. His face set into an expression of defiance. And with deliberate gestures he placed his passport inside his vest, slowly buttoned his coat, and said, "If you want the document, sir, you will have to come and take it."

The officer, with a gleam of triumph flushing his face, declared theatrically that he planned to do just that if the document were not immediately surrendered.

During all of this time, the mob stood with their hands on their swords, and two soldiers sat on a bench with muskets trained on

Stephens and Catherwood. Augustin had been superficially cut across the head when the crowd burst in and now he was in a rage. Holding his hand to his bleeding wound, he began aimlessly shouting again and again in French, "Fire on them! Kill them all!"

The officer got the gist of Augustin's outburst and instantly raised his hand. All weapons in the room were positioned for attack. But before the officer had the chance to give the order to attack, another officer—older, better dressed and better disposed—stepped forward and asked to examine the passport. Stephens hesitated and then reached into his pocket. He was so angry by now and so determined not to let the document out of his hands that he insisted upon holding it up before a blazing pine stick while the second officer read it aloud.

This reading produced an effect on the *alcalde* and his citizens which was completely unexpected. It seems very unlikely that even the young officer had actually been able to read the passport, because now, as the official words were read aloud, the crowd backed away from the aliens, humbly pulled their hats from their heads and glanced at the ground in an expression of shame.

Stephens and Catherwood asked again if they would now be permitted to leave. "We would be grateful," the older officer said politely, "if the señores would remain in custody until this unfortunate matter can be cleared up."

"There is nothing to clear up!" Stephens retorted. "Although General Cascara may very possibly have some clearing up to do with those of you who illegally detained us!" Stephens was not inclined to be polite, and demanded a courier to carry an urgent letter to General Cascara at once.

"But señor . . ." the officer started; Stephens, however, turned away from the man with a glowering expression, saying, "The courier, if you don't mind!"

The *alcalde*, feigning authority despite his drunkenness, promised that Stephens' letter would be sent to the General if Stephens paid for the expense of sending it.

"Shocking," Mr. Catherwood intoned with disdain, *"positively* shocking!"

"Never mind," Stephens muttered, "let's get on with the letter and have this farce over with as soon as possible."

The letter was hastily written to General Cascara. Not to mince matters, Catherwood signed the document as "secretary" of the expedition, which at the moment seemed like the most effective thing to do. But they were at a loss for a means of properly sealing the letter. Then Stephens smiled brightly as he had a theatrical impulse and, while all present solemnly observed him, sealed the letter with a new American half-dollar and then ceremoniously handed it to the *alcalde*. All gathered around to examine this impressive document. The ferocious eagle spread its wings and the stars glittered in the torchlight. There were numerous awed signs and considerable mumbling among the Indians and officials, although the arrogant young officer wouldn't even glance at the letter.

Finally everyone left, locking the explorers in the town hall and stationing twelve able-bodied men with swords, muskets and machetes at the door. The young officer smirked as he strutted out, but the older officer told the *alcalde* to be extremely careful with his prisoners. "For," he said in a husky voice, "if the prisoners are harmed or if they manage to escape during the night you may be certain that your head will answer for it."

The excitement was over, and Stephens and Catherwood were exhausted, although Augustin was still cursing wildly in French and insisting madly that they should have opened fire on the whole bunch of them and killed them to the man. Eventually Augustin, his head wound treated, bundled up in a corner and fell asleep. But Stephens and Catherwood got little rest that night. The soldiers had camped at their doorway, where they brawled, yelled and drank endless quantities of *aguadiente*. The prisoners sat glumly at the big table and opened a basket of wine which Donna Bartola had given them as a farewell gift. They drank a toast to their narrow escape from the machetes, and then, fastening the door as best they could from the inside, they once again climbed into their hammocks.

Not more than two hours later the door again burst open and the whole ruffian mob marched back in, with swords, muskets, machetes and blazing torches as before. In an instant the two weary explorers were back on their feet. Stephens, half asleep, was certain that they had come to take the passport by force. But to his surprise the *alcalde* handed Stephens back the letter with the big seal of the eagles and the stars and said there was no longer any reason to send it to General Cascara since they were now at liberty to leave and continue their journey if they desired to do so.

But Stephens was not going to let the matter pass that easily. Realizing he had attained a position of power, he swore to those assembled that the matter of the imprisonment in Comatan would not be forgotten. "So you will please send my letter by courier as agreed, sir, and you will please do so immediately," Stephens barked, pulling on his trousers as arrogantly as the awkward situation permitted.

The *alcalde* naturally objected to this plan, but after being threatened with extreme political repercussions he gave the letter reluctantly to an Indian and sent him on his way to the General. Then the *alcalde* pounded three times on the floor with his gold-crowned cane and in a very few moments the guards withdrew, the onlookers vanished and Stephens and his friends found themselves alone.

It was already daybreak. The travelers had not managed to get any sleep. But they decided to leave Comatan at once. They ate some chocolate, loaded the mules and started back on the wretched little path by which they had come upon this terrible human settlement. As they left the village it was as desolate as when they had arrived. Not a person had been there to welcome them, and now there was no one to bid them good-bye.

"Shocking," Augustin said in imitation English, "*absolument* shocking!"

After a difficult two-day march from Comatan the travelers finally descended to the banks of the Copan River, hardly able to believe that they had reached this remote place of myths and lost history. Augustin lumbered along on foot, whistling and smiling to himself, his backpack filled to overflowing with pineapples. The Indian bearers trudged silently along in each other's footsteps. And Stephens and Catherwood were absorbed in the wild beauty of the river valley, until their reverie was interrupted by the thunderous shouts of the head muleteer, ordering them to wait for him.

"That man is impossible!" Stephens complained.

They dismounted and sat on the bank to wait for the muleteer, who was somewhere hidden in the underbrush, shouting at a helper he had taken on at Zacapa: a boy, no more than fourteen years old, to whom he had given the worst task of the expedition, that of chasing the wayward mules. "That little fellow is in danger of running his legs off," Stephens remarked as he peered into the foliage for a sign of the boy.

The breach with the muleteer had not improved, even during the crisis at Comatan, which at first Stephens suspected was somehow his doing. The mule driver had not lifted a hand to protect them. "None of that craziness at Comatan would have happened," Stephens reminded Catherwood, "if we had stopped where we wanted to camp for the night."

Almost as if he were disappointed that Stephens and Catherwood had not been executed on the spot by the militia of Comatan, the muleteer had been gloomy all day. He was particularly angry at the mules, and they in turn were particularly perverse. Finally the animals had gone astray, and the muleteer spent so much time abusing his young helper for permitting their escape that he did nothing to reassemble the beasts. For an hour Stephens and Catherwood sat impatiently on the bank of the river listening to the muleteer's spiteful voice as he cursed the mules, the boy and his employers.

After an hour they were finally back on the trail, and by four o'clock they saw a hacienda at a distance. It stood alone in a wide valley and promised a quiet resting place for the night. Despite the disagreement of the muleteer, who always wanted to go in the opposite direction to that indicated by his employers, the caravan turned off the *camino real* into a wild pathway, stony and overgrown with bushes and so steep a descent that everyone was forced to dismount, letting the mules go ahead.

The site of the hacienda of San Antonio was wildly beautiful and its owners perfectly hospitable. While the supper was being prepared by the señora of the house her husband arrived, a swarthy, rather grim-looking man, with a broad-brimmed sombrero and huge whiskers. When he realized that the men in his house were foreigners asking for hospitality, his harsh expression immediately vanished, and he bid the travelers welcome.

During a fine dinner eaten mainly with fingers, Stephens

learned from Augustin that their boy herdsman was ill. The muleteer had paid no attention to the child and left him to groan with a violent fever. Catherwood angrily left the table and made the child a comfortable bed on the piazza, dosing him with medicine and giving him a bit of kindness and attention. The rest of the evening was passed very pleasantly with the host and hostess, who were a kind and simple couple, much honored by the visit of the foreigners. It was the first time they had ever met men from another country, and they asked countless questions and examined the travelers' apparatus, particularly their metal plates, cups, knives, forks and spoons—objects they had never seen before. The woman clasped her hands together as if she were seeing a royal treasury and said that her guests must be very rich and possess *"muchos ideas*—much wisdom."

The woman asked her guests how many wives they had, and in this way Stephens and Catherwood learned that their humble host had a second wife who lived at Hocotan, and that he passed alternate weeks with each of them.

Catherwood shook his head. "In England, sir," he said with an expression of impatience, "you would be transported."

"And in North America," Stephens added with a grin, "you would very likely be imprisoned for life for such indulgences."

Their host stared at them for a moment, trying to decide if they were joking with him or if what they told him could actually be true. "If that is so," the man said politely, "then I am afraid you come from barbarous nations." With that he smiled pleasantly and offered to assist his guests in swinging their hammocks. It seemed like a very good idea to Stephens, who was finally feeling the shock and exhaustion of the prior night's incident at Comatan. So at nine o'clock they drove out the dogs and the pigs, lighted cigars and went to bed. Including the servants, women and children, there were eleven people in their room. All around in the dark were tiny balls of fire, shining and disappearing with the puffing of numerous cigars. One by one the orange embers went out, and one by one they fell asleep.

In the morning the muleteer's young helper was much better,

but Catherwood insisted that he was not sufficiently recovered to travel. His master, annoyed by Catherwood's intrusion, insisted that the lad get up at once and prepare for their departure. Both Stephens and Catherwood objected loudly, but the muleteer ignored them and led his young assistant off by the nape of the neck.

The hosts of the hacienda refused to charge them for their hospitality, so the explorers in appreciation distributed among them various trifles, and when bidding them good-bye, Stephens saw with regret a ring which he had given the woman sparkling on her husband's finger. But the good woman was obviously happy with her spouse and only left his side long enough to chase after her departing guests with a piece of fresh sugar cane.

Everyone left the hacienda of San Antonio with warm good feelings for its exceptional hospitality except the surly muleteer, who was indignant, as he said, that Stephens and Catherwood had given presents to everybody but him. Even his young helper was beaming despite poor health, for he had been given a knife. Unfortunately for him this trifling object made the muleteer more jealous than all the other gifts.

Somewhere on the pine-covered slopes, unmarked by any sign, the caravan shortly thereafter crossed the boundary line between Guatemala and Honduras. And at two in the afternoon, they reached the village of Copan, which consisted of half a dozen dusty huts thatched with cornstalks. Their arrival caused a sensation. The entire settlement flocked around the strangers and gazed at them with open mouths, touching their clothing and peering at the equipment loaded on their mules. Augustin immediately asked about the famous ruins, but none of the villagers seemed to know anything about *ruinas*, and told the travelers that they should go to the hacienda of Don Gregorio, since he knew everything there was to know about the village of Copan.

The villagers were unpleasantly reminiscent of the people of Comatan—dirty, ill-mannered and stupid-looking. Stephens and Catherwood had no wish to stop at the village and told the muleteer to continue to the hacienda, but he refused and said that

his agreement was to conduct them to Copan and this, unquestionably, was Copan.

"I have no patience left for this fellow!" Catherwood exclaimed,
but Stephens placated him, and after a long wrangle the caravan
finally resumed its journey, riding through a wooded area,
fording the Copan River once more and coming out upon a
clearing on one side of which was a handsome hacienda with a
tile roof, lavish outbuildings and stables. It was obviously the
residence of a rich landowner.

As the caravan approached, it was met by a pack of barking
dogs, and every doorway was filled with women and children,
utterly amazed by the appearance of the strangers. Though no
men were home, the women welcomed the strangers with kindness and explained that Don Gregorio would return soon and
would surely conduct the guests to the *ruinas* or whatever else
they had come to see.

At once the fire was rekindled in the kitchen, and the sound of
patting hands meant that tortillas were being made. In half an
hour dinner was ready. During an excellent meal a young man
arrived on horseback, very flamboyantly dressed, with an embroidered shirt, fancy breeches and a lavish vest. He was accompanied by several men driving a small herd of cattle. An ox was
quickly selected, a rope thrown around its horns, and the animal
was drawn up to the side of the house, where another rope was
thrown around its legs and it was thrown to the ground. Its feet
were tied together, its great head drawn back by a rope tied from
its horns to its tail, and with one thrust of a machete the throat
was opened and the large frightened eyes rolled. The pack of
dogs, growling and snapping at one another, lapped up the blood
as it poured from the beast. Without delay the ox was skinned,
the meat separated from the bones, and in an hour the whole
animal was hanging in long strings on a line in front of the
hacienda doorway.

At the climax of this ritual the master of the house, Don
Gregorio, arrived, staring at the strangers as he galloped over the
bloodstained ground. He was a large man with black whiskers

and a beard of several days' growth, and from the humble manner of the household it was easy to see that he was a domestic tyrant. Almost at once Stephens disliked him, sensing in him the same petty arrogance the travelers had encountered at Comatan.

Before dismounting, Don Gregorio glanced indifferently at the visitors and then, without a word, he turned his back on them and entered the house. Stephens and Catherwood waited somewhat nervously until he had finished his dinner and then, hoping it was a favorable moment for introductions, Stephens entered the hacienda alone. In a few moments he came back out looking both sheepish and annoyed. "What did he say?" Catherwood asked anxiously.

Stephens leaned against a tree with a sigh and gazed blankly into the wild landscape. "In my travels and in my business affairs," Stephens said very quietly, "I have sometimes found people to be cold . . . but I must tell you, Cath, I have never experienced anything quite so cool as the don's behavior."

"But what did he say?" Catherwood whispered, so that the muleteer and Augustin would not overhear him.

"I told him that we had come a very very great distance in order to visit the ruins of Copan. And though he never responded to my comment, his manner made it quite clear how he felt. He might just as well have said: *What's that to me?* But instead he said nothing at all for a long while and then he told me that the ruins were on the other side of the river. So I asked him whether we might procure a guide, and again he said that the ruins were on the other side of the river. He said that the only man who knew anything about the ruins lived on the other side of the river."

Catherwood and Stephens looked helplessly at each other for a long time, and then they both sighed. "I'm afraid that I was rather slow," Stephens said at length, "in coming to the disagreeable conclusion that we are not particularly welcome here."

The don was not pleased with their looks. He was not pleased by their manner. And he was also not about to believe that they had marched halfway across Central America in order to look at a pile of rocks and ruins.

In a quiet rage, with utter indignation, yet feeling a need to keep up some appearance of civility, Stephens ordered the muleteer to saddle the mules and prepare to leave. But the rascal instantly sensed the vulnerability of his employers and was thoroughly enjoying the situation. He positively refused to saddle the animals again that day and commenced a loud, theatrical diatribe of foreigners in general and Americans and Englishmen in particular, debasing their morality, accusing them of withholding wages, of being irrational and arrogant, and generally letting the don of the hacienda know that his judgment of these strangers was absolutely accurate and just.

For the first time since employing this traitor and scoundrel, Stephens felt an uncontrollable desire to knock him down. He was just about to satisfy that impulse when Don Gregorio came into the yard. Catherwood appealed to the don, offering payment for the loan of just two mules on which the explorers could ride back to the village of Copan. The master of the hacienda obviously took great pleasure in the predicament of the strangers, listening like a magistrate to the accusations of the muleteer, the denials of Catherwood and Stephens, and the French fury of Augustin, who had come to have a deep loyalty for his employers and detested the muleteer's treason.

Finally Don Gregorio consented to the loan of two mules. Leaving the muleteer still shouting curses and complaints, Stephens and Catherwood hurried back to the village. But it was of little use, for the guide they sought was away. A cockfight was under way and no one wanted to be disturbed by the strangers and their futile attempts to speak intelligible Spanish. *"No, no, señor, imposible,"* all the men said when asked if they would go to the hacienda and bring back the explorers' luggage. "You must talk to Don Gregorio."

"Don Gregorio is the only one who can help you."

And so they learned to their annoyance and distress that Don Gregorio was the great man of Copan—the richest man, the most powerful man, a petty tyrant, and absolutely nothing happened in the village unless Don Gregorio ordered it to happen. It was a disaster for the travelers that they had made a bad impression on him, and it was essential that no one in the village realize that they had not been well received at the hacienda.

Again Stephens and Catherwood gazed blankly at one another. Distastefully and reluctantly, but hoping at the same time to somehow make a more favorable impression, they decided they must return to the hacienda.

The don sat on a chair, with the detestable muleteer at his side, a half-concealed smirk on his ignorant face, talking about *ruinas* and glancing with ridicule at Stephens. By this time eight or ten men—sons, servants and laborers—had come in from their day's work, and all stood around Stephens and Catherwood as they dismounted. No one offered to take their mules or made the slightest effort to show some sign of welcome. The women turned away, as if they had been reproved for receiving the guests in the first place, and all the men, taking their cue from the lordly master of the house, looked on so insultingly that Stephens wanted to throw all the expedition's cargo into the road and curse them for their barbarous inhospitality. But Catherwood warned him against angry actions, explaining that if they had an open quarrel with the don, after all their trouble getting to Copan, they would be prevented from seeing the ruins.

The don grasped the utter irritation of the strangers and suspected that they might, after all, have the ear of the military. So he smiled and coldly pointed to a chair, telling Stephens to sit down. It was only with the greatest effort that the American smothered his rage and sat down. There the two silent men sat staring coolly at each other while the assembled population of the hacienda milled around Catherwood and the expedition's cargo.

Augustin was thoroughly enraged by the treatment of his employers. On the road he had often swelled his own importance by telling the story of the flags hoisted and the cannons fired when the expedition had left Belize, and so now, in this unfriendly company, he hoisted more flags and fired more guns than usual, beginning his story with forty guns and elaborating as he went along until the salute had become a cannonade. But none of this made the slightest impression on Don Gregorio. He did not like the strangers.

They were not asked to stay but they were also not asked to leave. Without a word the don got up and left Stephens sitting alone. Catherwood eventually took the don's chair and again the Englishman and the American looked into each other's faces with an expression of dismay.

Toward evening a cowskin was spread in the piazza, ears of corns were thrown upon it, and all the men, with the don at their head, sat down to pick the kernels. During the entire evening no notice was taken of the strangers, except when the wife of the don sent a message by Augustin that supper was being prepared for the visitors. Their wounded pride was somewhat relieved by this good news, and their annoyance was somewhat abated by the additional message that the hacienda possessed an oven and flour and that the women would bake some bread if the strangers wished to buy it.

After a silent supper everyone prepared for sleep. The don's grand house was not opened to the travelers. The master and his family went indoors, leaving the yard to the strangers. All along the wall were wooden frames from which hammocks could be hung. But Stephens and Catherwood had so little space that they had to sleep as if plunged into a sack, with their feet as high as their heads and their rumps almost touching the ground. It was a ridiculous situation, one in which Don Gregorio obviously took great pleasure.

By morning Stephens and Catherwood had made up their minds to persevere until they had seen the ruins, no matter how ugly the don might be. Fortunately, one of the don's sons, a very civil young man who was embarrassed by his father's treatment of the strangers, brought a man named José from the village. He was the guide who knew about the ruins. This was the first bit of good luck they had had since arriving at Copan.

It was quickly arranged for José to take the explorers to the ruins. The muleteer was openly disappointed that his employers managed to secure a guide. He shouted at his young helper; he beat the mules; and he wasted so much time loading the cargo that they did not leave the hacienda until midmorning. But at last they were on the way to Copan!

Stephens was a realist. He had traveled the most remote regions of the world and he knew that civilizations simply did not exist in the kind of hostile climate and terrain which he and Catherwood had found in Central America. The farther they got into the terrible labyrinth of greenery, the less faith they had in the existence of the remnants of a great civilization. Both Stephens and Catherwood were very skeptical by this time, and when they finally arrived at this site where the ruins were said to be, it was with the hope, rather than the expectation, of finding wonders.

 The jungle reverberated with the drone of crickets, a sound so intense and persistent that it made their heads whirl. They pressed themselves into the solid barrier of vegetation, following a slender path butchered into the foliage by José's machete. They were blinded by leaves and the translucent green shadows which shimmered in the air like neon filigree in the depths of a sea. Great lazy drops of moisture dripped slowly through a mountain of foliage and then oozed over the layered mossy floor of the jungle. Parasites clung to the branches, and festoons of crimson and orange flowers draped themselves in the limbs high above. One plant grew upon another, staggering to reach higher toward the remote treetops where the sun radiated like a furnace whose light was barely visible in the humid depths of the vegetable world. Crickets droned and water dripped.

Then suddenly the dense thicket vanished at a river's edge. Stephens and Catherwood sank to the bank, withered with fatigue. For a moment they could think of nothing but their panting lungs and the sweat flowing into their eyes and down their necks.

"Señores," José was saying to them, trying to call their attention to the opposite bank of the river.

Stephens was certain that all he would see when he wiped the sweat out of his eyes would be a barricade of greenery on the other side of the river, more horrendously tangled and impenetrable than the jungle through which they had slashed a miserable trail. But what he saw was far more startling. Amidst the roaring foliage and just beyond the brown stream which rolled lazily past them was a high, wide and unbelievably massive stone wall, perhaps one hundred feet high, with vines and furze sprouting from between every crack and crevice. It seemed to be alive, for the droning which infused the whole jungle grew louder and came like an emanation from this incredible huge wall standing on the river's edge in the middle of a green labyrinth.

"My God! What the hell can it be?" Stephens muttered.

"*Ruinas,*" José chanted knowingly with an entranced nodding of his head. "*Si, si . . . ruinas . . . ruinas.*"

A chill shot through Stephens and a short involuntary burst of laughter poured out of him before he shook his head cautiously. "My God, it looks absolutely fantastic, Cath!" he murmured; but it might be anything. He couldn't possibly tell what this great wreck of stone had once been. He couldn't tell how old it was or what kind of structure it was. In some places the wall had collapsed into the river like an avalanche and some of the stones had been swept away. But there were other wide sections of the wall still standing intact though covered with thousands upon thousands of roots and vines. But there was simply no question that whatever else it was, it was clearly something of magnitude and mystery.

"Let's not jump to any conclusions," Stephens warned Catherwood, who had not said a word but stood dumbstruck by the huge wall which rose up in front of them. "It could be anything, Cath. In this damn rotten jungle it could look like it's been here a million years and it could really be nothing but the ruin of a Spanish fortress or something. It could be anything," Stephens repeated several times, more to quell his own excitement than Catherwood's. "It could be anything."

Catherwood did not answer but splashed blindly into the river and staggered forward without taking his eyes off the massive wall. Stephens hurried after him while José calmly forded farther upstream where the river was narrow. But the explorers did not wait for him. They rushed to the foot of the wall and searched in every direction for some kind of entrance or stairway. There was none. So they began to scramble up an embankment of stones where the wall had crumbled into the water. As they scampered over the rocks on all fours, pulling themselves upward by saplings and bushes, they both began to talk at once. But when they suddenly reached the summit they fell silent, and the drone of the crickets rose into a roar and then stopped.

There was nothing there.

From the top of the wall there seemed to be nothing more to this "ruined city" than a ridiculous massive wall standing along a precipice which bounded one side of the Copan River. From the top they could see nothing. Nothing but trees, ficus, vines and the underbrush of centuries. Their hopes sank. They had been fools to believe in the superstitious tales of Indians. This place was exactly the same as the miles of woodland and jungle they had encountered everywhere else in Central America, landscapes in which it was unthinkable that a great civilization could possibly have existed. The whole expedition was nothing but a ridiculous wild-goose chase.

Stephens had hoped to discover a great clearing in the middle of the jungle, a vast plateau, an Eden amidst waterfalls and secret lakes and caverns. But everywhere around him was the same terrible forest piled high against the river wall. Whatever the purpose of this huge structure, it obviously had nothing to do with an ancient civilization. The only real curiosities of this place were the monkeys—thousands of them rushing through the trees and screaming at the intruders from every direction. It was the first time they had seen these strange mockeries of man in Central America. And as the monkeys shrieked and crouched on the summit of the wall and among its nooks and crevices, staring down upon the strangers, they seemed like fearsome spirits guarding their ancient sanctuary. They raced overhead, cracking dry branches, which broke under their weight. They soared through the treetops in long, swift processions, forty or fifty at a time, making an eerie noise like rushing air, like a gust of wind which retreated in the shimmering leaves and echoed into the depths of the forest.

José had shown them all that there was to see, and he was ready to return to the village. But Stephens and Catherwood insisted upon seeing whatever lay beyond the wall, and they threw themselves into the dense thicket that bounded the ruin and crashed into a maze of branches, tendrils and roots. They fought their way forward until José reluctantly answered their calls for assistance and hacked into the foliage with his machete. But even with his help it was almost impossible to penetrate the thicket, which grew more dense as they pushed forward. José wielded his machete with fast wide strokes, throwing up a storm of twigs and mutilated leaves.

Then suddenly they broke into a clearing and found themselves at the foot of a mound of earth and stones in a curious shape, which Catherwood's experienced architect's eye quickly scrutinized while Stephens began to laugh with delight. Spider monkeys lunged through the air and hid above them in the leaves, screaming warnings and cringing from the invaders who had found their secret. The explorers exchanged a quick excited glance. They both instantly knew what the other was thinking—there was no question of it, this mound was the ruin of a pyramid! A pyramid in the middle of a wilderness! Without another moment's hesitation they bounded up the tiered structure. At the top they wheeled around and surveyed the structure.

Some of the stones had been thrown down by the roots of saplings, and others had been wedged apart by large trees which burst from the mysterious masonry structure which rose from the floor of the jungle, but enough of the stone steps remained in position to make it absolutely certain that Stephens and Catherwood were standing on the top of a pyramid.

This was no Spanish fortress; this was something unexpected and marvelous! But what was it? Catherwood's heart pounded with excitement as he stared down at a row of skulls carved into the stones—designs unlike anything he had seen anywhere in the world. Stephens took one look at the sculptured rock and then they both hurried ahead, climbing over the ruins to the edge of the pyramid, where they saw a wide terrace overgrown with trees. It was almost lost among the foliage but it was definitely some kind of magnificent and grand ceremonial terrace.

It was the Eastern Court of the acropolis of Copan. It had never before been seen by white men. But Stephens and Catherwood did not grasp what they had found or its significance. In their tremendous fascination they bounded down the stone steps into an area so covered with vegetation that at first they could not make out its form. But after quickly clearing the way with José's machete, they could see the outline of a square with rows and rows of steps on all sides almost in the form of a small Roman amphitheater. But it could not possibly have been Roman, for the steps were highly ornamented with sculpture—exquisite in craftsmanship, but like nothing either of the travelers had seen in Rome, Greece or Egypt. Whoever had made this mysterious place, one thing was already certain to John Stephens, they were not savages and they were not one of the known cultures of antiquity.

On the south side of this "theater," about halfway up the side of the embankment, was a colossal head, perhaps the sculpture of some forgotten hero or ruler. Its face was a startling mixture of grandeur and fearsomeness. It evoked a sense of destiny and dominion entirely remote and alien.

In the distance was another temple enveloped in the tentacles

Fallen idol, Copan

of rampant fig trees. On its broken stairways stone jaguars reared up on their hind legs and clawed the air. Above them a great stone head, the symbol of the corn god, fought with an imposing tree for its ancient place among the ruins. Everywhere, locked in the grip of foliage and hidden under centuries of debris, were the most startling and wondrous sculptures.

Carried by their enormous agitation and energy, Stephens and Catherwood rushed down the steps into a broad terrace a hundred feet high, perched on top of the massive wall they had first seen and overlooking the river. The entire terrace was covered with trees, and even at this height were two gigantic ceibas, perhaps twenty feet in circumference, extending their half-naked roots a hundred feet in every direction, binding the ruins, and shading the grotesque sculpture with widespread branches which cast a deep shade that made the scene look like a long-forgotten cemetery. Stephens, overcome with a sense of doom and finality, sat down exhaustedly on the very edge of the great wall and gazed into the deep shadows of this sacred place. Was it a strange citadel from which some unknown people had sounded the trumpets of war? Or was it a temple for the worship of some long-lost god? Whatever the ruins were and whoever had made them, one thing was very clear: it would require a great deal of exploration and clearing away of vegetation to get even the slightest glimpse of the magnitude of this marvelous lost city which they had rediscovered.

Now even the monkeys had deserted the ruins, or perhaps they had fallen silent and lurked behind the shadows of the ceiba trees, staring with their enormous eyes at the terrible white strangers who had uncovered their riddles of time. There were no answers. In Egypt, where the explorers had traveled, the colossal stone skeletons of the temples stood in the sand in naked desolation, but here an immense forest shrouded the ruins, hiding them and slowly burying them in roots and dead leaves which filled the nostrils with the reek of centuries of relentless decay. If these once great builders had suddenly perished in some calamity, it seemed certain to Stephens that it was right here, in this dead city, that the last of their marvelous race had been lost forever in time.

The mysteries which lay hidden beneath the foliage captivated them entirely. Though they had planned to spend only a few days making drawings and measurements of whatever ruins they might discover, they were now determined to overcome the difficulties provided by Don Gregorio and, after hiring workmen, to search everywhere among these ruins for clues to their lost history.

Late in the afternoon Stephens, Catherwood and their guide José exhaustedly worked their way back to the mules, which they had left at the water's edge. Silently, unable to speak in the shadows of this awesome place, they bathed in the cool river at the foot of the great wall, gazing up at the ancient stones which held centuries of secrets. Then as it grew dark they returned in a state of amazement to the hacienda of Don Gregorio.

The next morning Stephens and Catherwood carefully kept silent about their discovery. Don Gregorio was the type of man who would snatch up anything he suspected to have value. And though the explorers were feeling very exuberant and wanted to celebrate, they did not dare show their delight for fear of rousing the don's shrewd interest.

The discovery of the ruins made it more essential than ever to

win the friendship of the people of the hacienda. Mr. Catherwood's reputation for *remedios* was fortunately on the rise, much
helped by the boy mule driver's stories of his own miraculous
cure. In the course of the day almost every member of Don
Gregorio's household sought the medical advice of Mr. C. By
degrees the explorers dispelled the antagonism against them and
became friendly with every member of the household except the
master, who wanted no part of the *remedios* or the intruders, and
kept exclusive company with the surly muleteer in whom he
found a congenial spirit. Don Gregorio was not the kind of man
who reversed his judgments of people; he had taken his ground
and was far too obstinate to change his attitude about the
strangers.

Catherwood stopped at nothing to intrigue the don's entourage. He showed the men the percussion caps of the pistols as
well as the compass and the expedition's other apparatus, which
fascinated them. Stephens meanwhile found a unique means of
astonishing the women: by brushing his teeth, an operation
which they were witnessing for the first time. While he was
brushing away violently and trying to produce a maximum of
suds, the door of the hacienda opened and the don appeared. He
willfully turned his head away, taking no notice of the delighted
laughter of the women or the sight of Mr. John Lloyd Stephens
frothing at the mouth.

Stephens threw his toothbrush to the ground in exasperation
and resolved not to sleep another night on the land of this
pompous, humorless tyrant. "That is absolutely the last straw!"
he exclaimed to Catherwood, who was busily passing out medications to the don's sons. "We are going to take our bloody
hammocks to the ruins and even if there is nothing to shelter us,
we'll simply hang them up under a tree!"

Hearing this, the muleteer nearly fell down with laughter. Each
disappointment of his employers was a source of renewed pleasure for him. And he took special delight in the fact that the don
favored him while disdaining Stephens and Catherwood.

"I'm glad that you are so amused," Stephens barked. "But if

you don't mind, you can perhaps stop laughing long enough to load the mules so we can leave this place immediately!"

"No, no, Meester Estebans," the muleteer said gravely, explaining that there was no agreement for the use of his mules during the stay in Copan. He said that he definitely would not load the animals. And he added that he also would not carry the hammocks to the ruins. Then he smiled arrogantly, knowing that his employers would have to try to persuade him to assist them, for there were no other mules for hire within two days' journey of Copan.

Stephens was about to launch a full-scale assault on the ears of the muleteer when Don Gregorio gestured to him in his arch manner, indicating that he wished to speak to him. Stephens got hold of himself, told the muleteer not to take a single step until he returned, and approached the don, who was sitting with another gentleman with whom he had been conversing for some time.

This man, Don José Maria Asebedo, was about fifty, tall for the people of the region, and well dressed. He was rather ignorant but polite and was one of the most respectable inhabitants of Copan.

"I wish to explain to you," Señor Asebedo said, "that I am the owner of the idols which the guide José has told me you much admired."

Stephens was absolutely astonished by the news. The notion that anybody could actually *own* the ruins was so ridiculous that he could hardly keep from laughing in the man's face. Meanwhile José Maria Asebedo quietly explained that the land on which "the idols" were located belonged to him and that no one could go on that land without his permission. And with this he handed Stephens his title papers and smiled politely.

Stephens examined the documents, suspecting that Señor Asebedo was on the verge of telling the explorers to stay off his property. But fortunately that was not the reason he had come to see Stephens and Catherwood. Instead, the owner of the ruins had come to ask a favor. Catherwood's fame as a physician had reached the village, and Señor Asebedo wanted to have *remedios* for his ailing wife. It was a stroke of luck, and Stephens and Catherwood immediately set about winning the confidence and friendship of the polite landowner as an ally against the despicable Don Gregorio.

After very fast negotiations it was arranged that the expedition would retain the services of the damnable muleteer and his mules at an exorbitant fee; it was also decided that Mr. C. along with several workmen would go directly to the ruins to make camp there, while Stephens and Augustin went to the villa of Don José Maria Asebedo in order to pay a visit to his ailing wife. As they departed, Don Gregorio looked thoroughly annoyed by their success with Señor Asebedo and he smiled unpleasantly. The muleteer, at the prospect of having to do an honest day's work, was more sullen than ever. But Stephens and Catherwood were positively jubilant.

Don José Maria lived in one of the best huts of the village of Copan, made of poles thatched with corn leaves, with a wooden frame on one side for a bed, and furnished with a few pieces of pottery for cooking. A heavy rain had fallen during the night, and the ground inside the hut was wet. The don's wife was suffering from rheumatism, and so, without wasting any time on niceties, Stephens advised her to take her feet out of a puddle of water in which she was standing, and promised to consult his colleague Mr. Catherwood, who was an even better *medico* than he, and to arrange to send her a special linament with which to bathe her neck.

These words seemed to delight the don and his wife. And so, with this duty over, Don José Maria accompanied Stephens to the ruins, where they found Catherwood and his Indian workmen in a state of disorder. "It is utterly mad, my dear fellow," Catherwood told him at once, "to think of hanging our hammocks under the trees! Utter madness, I tell you!" The branches were still heavily saturated with rain from the prior night's downpour, the ground was muddy, and there was a good prospect of another rain.

But Stephens was determined not to return to Don Gregorio's hacienda under any circumstances. He gazed into the forest trying to imagine by what means they could devise some kind of shelter. Don José Maria was a charitable man, and grasping the strangers' problem, he came to their rescue, offering the use of a hut near the ruins, which was already occupied by a workman, his wife and his grown son but was sufficiently large to accommodate two more people. It was a humble shelter but it was dry. There was room enough for only one hammock, and, in fact, the cross-supports of the hut would not have supported two men even if there had been more room. There was, however, a pile of dried corn which had been consumed down to a shape just high and broad enough for a bed. Catherwood hung up his hammock and Stephens chose the corn pile, where he opened his bedroll. Both explorers were so happy to be rid of Don Gregorio and to be so near their precious ruins that they smiled widely at one another and felt very much at home in their shack.

After a noonday meal at which Stephens and Catherwood celebrated their liberation from the grip of Don Gregorio and the discovery of "the idols," it was decided that Stephens would return to the hacienda for the purpose of bringing over the luggage. He mounted the one mule which they had and, accompanied by Augustin on foot, set off. The heavy rains had swelled the river, and Augustin had to strip in order to ford it and pull the frightened mule after him.

When they reached the hacienda the muleteer said that it was impossible to cross the river with cargo that day. After insisting upon daily payments of his fee, rather than payment upon completion of his job, the muleteer finally agreed to carry their cargo to the other side of the river if he were paid a bonus. In the meantime it began to rain again. Almost at once the paths were flooded and Stephens urged the cunning muleteer to get under way.

Taking a bright-colored umbrella and a blue bag which Catherwood had particularly asked Stephens to bring back for him, they started toward the ruins. Augustin had a tin teapot in one hand and his reins in the other. No sooner had they entered the dense woods than Stephens' umbrella struck against the low-hanging branches and startled the mules. Stephens tried desperately to close the umbrella, but his mule bolted and ran out of control while he bounced hectically on her back. She raced through the woods, knocking him against branches and tree trunks, splashed into the river, missing the fording place, but not stopping until the current was up to her nostrils. The river was a torrent and the rain poured down. While trying to control his mule, Stephens lost Catherwood's blue bag. In a rage he very nearly broke the umbrella over the mule's flanks, driving her to the shore from which he saw the bag floating toward the rapids.

Augustin had already stripped to the skin, and with his clothes in one hand and the teapot in the other was making his way downstream toward the precious bag, which he assumed contained some indispensable drawing materials essential to Catherwood's work at the ruins. For his part, Stephens dashed among the thickets on the bank in the hope of overtaking and intercepting the bag. The branches and vines formed a sturdy barrier and it took several minutes for him to work his way down to the riverbank, where he saw Augustin's clothes and the teapot but no sign of Augustin himself. With the rapids roaring below he had horrible apprehensions about his loyal servant.

It was impossible for him to continue along the bank; so he jumped to a sandbar in the midst of the swollen river and, running to the end of it, he could see the whole face of the river and the rapids, but Augustin had vanished. He shouted again and again. Finally he heard a very faint answer over the roar of the rapids. Then Augustin appeared, working himself through the bushes and waving at Stephens, who was much relieved to see him alive.

All this time the rain was pouring down. Augustin's body was dripping wet. Stephens had forgotten in the excitement where he had tied the mule. When they finally found her Stephens climbed into the saddle in total exhaustion. Augustin, principally because he could carry them more conveniently on his back, put on his clothes and tried to look heroic.

Reaching a little shack, Stephens took shelter while poor

Augustin, being so soaked it little mattered, continued through the pouring rain toward the ruins. When the rain abated for a moment Stephens followed after him. He crossed another stream and rode along a flooded road which twisted through a snarl of branches. Soon the clouds became blacker and Stephens could hardly see where he was going. Great flashes of lightning illuminated the old stone quarries of Copan and thunder rolled through the air so loudly that he could feel the earth tremble. The rain was blinding, and while his mule was slipping and stumbling through the mud Stephens somehow lost the road. There were cattle paths in every direction. He continued on without any sense of where he was going. Several times he thought he saw the prints of Augustin's feet, but soon these were lost in puddles. At last, completely confused, he came to a standstill, sitting astride his whimpering mule in the cascades of rain.

It was very nearly night. He did not have the least notion of which way to turn. And so, feeling utterly abashed at his inability to behave with dignity when faced with the immensity of nature, he began to bellow at the top of his lungs. To his very great joy he was answered by a roar from Augustin, who had been lost even longer than he. After several volleys of shouts, the loyal servant came splashing half-naked through the thicket—the teapot clutched in his hand and the dripping stump of a cigar in his mouth. He was plastered everywhere with thick black mud except for his large eyes, with which he looked blissfully at Stephens.

They compared notes, selected a path and, shouting as they went, marched toward the sound of barking dogs. Soon they met Catherwood, who being alarmed by their delay, had come out with some Indians to search for them.

Stephens dashed into the shelter of the hut. He had no change of clothes but was grateful to be out of the downpour. Being the kind of man who loved any excuse for bizarre behavior he stripped to the skin and rolled himself up in a blanket in the style of a North American Indian. And he felt absolutely marvelous.

All evening he and Catherwood were surrounded by great

explosions of thunder. Frenzied sheets of lightning burst in the dark forest and flashed through the open hut, and the rain continued to fall in uninterrupted torrents. Their humble hosts, the workman and his family, said that they would surely be cut off from the opposite side of the river if the storm continued— which meant that the luggage might not arrive for several days, especially if the muleteer had anything to say about it.

Wreathed in thick cigar smoke, naked except for a blanket, Stephens lay in his warm bed of dried corn and brooded over the ruins of Copan. All day his mind had returned again and again to the title deeds of Don José Maria Asebedo. Gradually the notion that someone could own the ruins seemed less and less absurd. "Cath," he whispered into the darkness, "are you awake?"

"Yes," came the answer from the darkness.

"I have a fantastic idea!" Stephens exclaimed with hushed excitement. "I have an absolutely gigantic operation in mind, Cath."

"What the devil is it?"

"I'm going to buy Copan!"

Then without another word Stephens drew the blanket around his shoulders and fell asleep.

In the morning, Catherwood left early in an exuberant mood to climb among the ruins while Stephens in a more cunning frame of mind remained behind to try to negotiate for the title deeds of Don José Maria Asebedo. He explained to the naïve landowner that he wanted to hire a large crew of men and build shelters where these laborers would live while working among the ruins. He also told Don José Maria that he wished to import many spades, ladders and crowbars to excavate the ruins of Copan. But all of this was very expensive, and obviously Stephens could not possibly undertake such elaborate plans unless he held title to the land. "So, to get directly to the point," he said coolly, "how much would you take for the ruin of Copan with all of its idols?"

The don smiled very politely and nodded. He was trying to

imagine why anybody would possibly want to buy a piece of worthless land and a pile of rubble. But he was not as naïve as Stephens thought, for he understood that the American was very anxious about the land even if he pretended otherwise and even if Don José Maria could not grasp his motives for wanting the idols.

After a moment Don José Maria Asebedo smiled politely once again. He said that it was very generous of Meester Estebans to offer good money for worthless land. He said that it was a subject of interest to him and that he wished to give it a great deal of careful consideration. With that he bowed humbly and excused himself, leaving the befuddled Stephens standing alone in the hut, wondering what had gone wrong.

It seemed to John Lloyd Stephens that it was his duty to archeology and to the United States of America to save the ruins. He hoped to remove the monuments from this desolate region in which they were buried and to set them up in "a great commercial emporium" in New York, an institution which would be the nucleus of a national museum of American antiquities! The idea enthralled him. After all, the idols were located on the banks of a river that emptied into the same sea by which the docks of New York were reached. Even if the river were impassable the idols could be cut up and removed in pieces, or perhaps casts could be made of those which were too large for transport. Stephens recalled the relics of the Parthenon in the British Museum and envisioned what a precious acquisition the casts of Copan might be to a New York museum. Very soon the existence of these dispossessed ruins would surely become known and their value appreciated. The Europeans would probably get possession of them. But Stephens sincerely believed that the ruins unquestionably belonged to the United States. And so he resolved more firmly than ever that "ours they shall be!" And with visions of glory and fantasies of reward flitting before his eyes, he hired two mestizos named Bruno and Francisco and went in search of Catherwood among the ruins.

The clouds still hung over the deep forest, but as the sun rose

Stone idol

higher the sky cleared and the workmen assembled at the hut which was to become the base of operations for the exploration of the ruins of Copan. The first project was clearing away the foliage. There was no ax and so Bruno used his machete to cut away a snarl of lianas from a tall leaf-covered object. After much arduous hacking at the vines, he pulled back the mass of foliage and pointed in awe at the tall dark object still obscured by shade and moss. Stephens impatiently took the machete himself and eagerly removed the tendrils and moss from the curious object. Gradually they found themselves standing before one of the richly carved tall slabs of stone that the Indians called "idols."

The sculptural designs were totally unlike anything Catherwood had ever seen. The cutting was in very high relief and required a strong light to bring up detail. The foliage, however, was so thick and the shade so deep that it was impossible to fully grasp the intricate shapes sculpted into the stone. Catherwood stepped forward in great excitement and began quickly cutting back the vegetation surrounding the idol, working with such urgency that Stephens and the two workmen enthusiastically joined his effort, and soon a strong circle of sunlight shone upon the tall mysterious object for the first time in centuries.

In sheer sculptural artistry there was nothing in Europe or Asia to match the unique beauty and craftsmanship of this strange object. The brilliance of design was staggering and the ornamentation that entirely covered the great stone was mystifying and magnificent. The idol stood about twelve feet high and was perhaps three feet wide and three feet thick, a majestic cubical column intricately covered by a network of sculptured forms, figures and designs in which a residue of the color which once decorated it was still visible in the deepest cuts made by the ancient sculptor's tool. On the front was carved the full figure of a male, solemn, stern and terrifying, its curious mood reverberating with ancient omens. The sides were covered with unique hieroglyphs, column upon column of emblems and signs.

Catherwood did not take the time to speak. He rushed to collect his art materials and set to work at once, uncertain how he could possibly capture the awesome splendor of this great sculpture. Stephens backed away from the towering idol, gazing at it ecstatically. "Come on!" he exclaimed to Bruno and Francisco, the mestizo helpers, "let's get to work! There could be dozens of these sculptures all around us! A dollar! I'll give you one dollar for every new discovery!"

For a moment Bruno and Francisco stared with astonishment at the idol. Neither of them—though they had spent their whole lives in this forest—had ever seen the idols until that morning. They had taken jobs with the expedition for the money, thinking they would tag along and laugh at the crazy *ingleses*. But now that they had actually seen the marvels that Stephens and Catherwood were seeking, they joined the search with full energy. They both possessed sharp intuition for artistic detail and as they

Idol half buried

rushed through the woods nothing escaped their notice. Francisco spied the feet and legs of a statue, and Bruno a part of the body that matched. The effect of assembling this giant work of art was electrical upon both of them. They searched exuberantly, raking up the ground with their machetes till they finally found the shoulders, and excitedly fit all the pieces together and set the entire sculpture up except for the missing head. Then they both eagerly searched for some kind of tool with which to dig and find the missing fragment.

The excitement was contagious and Stephens rushed through the undergrowth like a boy. The ground was all mystery and entirely new. The whole region was a virgin soil. They could not see ten yards before them, and they never knew what they might stumble upon next. At one point they stopped to cut away branches and vines which concealed the face of a monument, and then to dig around a sculptured corner which protruded from the earth. Stephens leaned forward with breathless expectation while the Indians worked feverishly. An eye appeared, an ear, a foot, a hand was disentombed, and when the machete rang against the chiseled stone he pushed the Indians away and cleared out the loose earth with his bare hands.

The beauty of the sculpture, the solemn stillness of the woods, disturbed only by the hooting of monkeys and the chattering of parrots, the desolation of the ancient city lost in this green tomb for centuries, and the air of mystery which hung over the place like a strong fragrance, all created an amazement greater, if possible, than he had ever felt among the greatest ruins of Egypt or Greece. As he made his way deeper into the jungle and came upon a second, third, fourth and finally a fourteenth idol, each more finished than the last, Stephens' excitement broke free of his skepticism and he knew for certain that the legendary world he had envisioned in the depths of the Central American jungle was a reality.

After several hours of exploring the forest, Stephens returned to where he had left Catherwood and announced that he had found fifty different objects for him to copy. The artist was not very pleased by Stephens' report. He was standing ankle deep in muck and mud, surrounded by bloodthirsty insects, oppressed by the insufferable heat and nearly suffocated by the humidity, drawing with his gloves on to protect his hands from the swarms of mosquitoes which attacked every exposed part of his body. The ground was littered with countless discarded sketches, for as Catherwood had feared, the designs were so intricate, the subject matter so entirely alien and unintelligible to him that he was having great difficulty with his drawings.

Though he was an experienced draftsman and an able and ingenious chronicler of the architecture and monuments of antiquity, the ruins of Copan eluded him. He had made fine scale drawings of the monuments of Memphis, Abydos, Karnak, Deir el-Bahri, Luxor and Thebes. He had even been engaged as the architectural consultant by Mehemet Ali to supervise the restoration of the Mosque of Cairo, but he was totally mystified by the style and form of the art of Copan. He had already made numerous attempts, both with the camera lucida and without, but each time he had failed to capture the tone and detail of the monumental sculpture with its peculiar blend of opulence and terror.

Both Stephens and Catherwood were despondent, though their excitement was undiminished by their problems. They returned to the hut, consoling each other. And sitting in the safety of a tent of mosquito netting, Stephens explained to his friend that the drawings had become much more important. He had already made up his mind, with a pang of regret, that they must abandon any hope of carrying away the monuments and must strive instead to make as many accurate drawings as possible. As for the idols themselves, Stephens said quietly while he gazed into the green mist of the deep forest, they must be content with having had the unique opportunity of reclaiming them from the embrace of the centuries and of having seen them for themselves.

Meanwhile Augustin announced that the mules with their luggage had not been able to cross the swollen river, but somehow the blue bag which had caused Stephens so much trouble had been recovered by one of the workmen. As for the contents of the mysterious bag which presumably contained precious art materials, upon being turned upside down all that came out was an old pair of boots, which, however, turned out to be a small treasure, being waterproof and ideally suited to Catherwood's damp, sore feet.

The following day Catherwood began to have more success with his drawings. The light fell exactly as he needed it and this greatly helped him to master his difficulties. Of equal help was the comfort of his waterproof boots. In the midst of this contented atmosphere Augustin came out into the field with a message that the *alcalde* of the village of Copan had come to pay a visit. Catherwood disliked the interruption, but since it was late he and Stephens broke off work for the day and returned to the hut.

They shook hands with the little wrinkled *alcalde* and gave him and his attendants cigars. The *alcalde*, however, was so tipsy that he could hardly speak, even with Augustin's prodding and assistance. His attendants squatted on the ground, swinging back and forth on their knee joints and whispering while they watched the foreigners.

Stephens was more patient than Catherwood and made several efforts to discover what it was the *alcalde* wanted of them. But then, for no apparent reason, the village dignitary got up abruptly, made a staggering bow and quickly left the hut, followed by his entourage. Later, while the camp was having supper, Don José Maria Asebedo paid a visit, and it was instantly apparent that he and his wife were in some kind of trouble, and, as Stephens feared, the trouble concerned them.

While Stephens and Catherwood had been busily exploring the ruins, they had caused a sensation in the village of Copan. Not satisfied with getting the foreigners out of his house, Don Gregorio was determined to remove them from the country altogether. Besides his disdain for them as strangers he was also enraged that some of his workmen had been lured away by higher wages. So the don now looked upon Stephens and Catherwood as rivals and started spreading rumors that they were undesirable characters. He insisted that their presence in Copan was illegal and that they would bring soldiers and war to the region. In confirmation of these stories, two Indians passed through Copan who reported that *los ingleses* had narrowly escaped from prison and had been chased to the borders of Honduras by a detachment of twenty-five soldiers under Captain Landaveri, the officer who had arrested them, and that, if captured, they would have been shot on the spot.

Upon hearing this, the *alcalde* of Copan, who had been drunk ever since their arrival, resolved to visit the explorers' camp and settle the doubts of the villagers one way or another. But his constabulary duties were cut short by a ludicrous situation. Stephens and Catherwood made it a practice to a carry their weapons with them to the ruins, and when they had returned to the hut to receive their guests, each of them had a brace of pistols in his belt and a gun in hand. Their appearance was apparently so formidable that the drunken *alcalde* was frightened off. No sooner had he reached the woods than his attendants reproached him for his cowardice and demanded that he send Don José Maria Asebedo to confront the dangerous intruders, since, after all, it was Señor Asebedo's land on which they were encamped.

Stephens and Catherwood got a good laugh out of this ridiculous incident, but Señor Asebedo was not at all amused. He gave them a weak smile and assured them that he had no doubts himself of their good and honorable character, but the suspicion in the village was great, the country was in a state of emergency and Don Gregorio had warned Señor Asebedo that he ought not harbor suspicious foreigners, let alone escaped prisoners. Meanwhile Señor Asebedo's distracted wife was hysterical. Her head was full of assassinations and mass murders, and though she was greatly alarmed for her family's safety she was also fearful for the strangers, whom she liked. She was certain that if any soldiers should happen to come to the village, they would ask no questions after hearing the rumors. Stephens and Catherwood would surely be murdered. And so she begged them to leave the region at once and save themselves.

Stephens and Catherwood were extremely annoyed by all of this hysteria, especially since it had been willfully caused by Don Gregorio. They had far too much at stake to be driven away by rumors and malicious gossip. So they tried to assure Don José Maria and his wife that no harm would come to anyone, that it was a false accusation and that they were completely above suspicion. But the don and his wife seemed unconvinced, though they were too polite to say so. By now such opera buffa situations were familiar to Stephens and he resigned himself to yet another performance. So he opened his big trunk and displayed a large bundle of papers and sealed credentials in Spanish which described Stephens glowingly as "Encargado de los Negocios de los Estados Unidos de Norte America."

All of these theatrics were indispensable in relieving the don and his wife of doubts and anxieties, enabling the explorers to remain quietly in their wretched little hut. The wife particularly was enormously happy to discover that her guests were tolerably respectable people, not enemies of the state, and not in danger of being tied up and shot. As for Catherwood, who had watched the charade with dismay, he was visibly vexed by the indignity of having to prove their good character at every turn and to such a miserable group of peasants.

Added to this insult was the nasty aggression of Don Gregorio and the treachery of their muleteer, who, it seems, had spread reports that they were pistol-toting villains who often threatened to shoot him. When they were finally alone Catherwood glanced with a look full of contempt after their departing hosts. "Shocking," he muttered, "positively shocking."

But by morning the entire situation had changed course again. While the workmen were gathering outside the hut, an Indian courier came trotting through the cornfield and asked for "Señor Ministro." Stephens identified himself and was given a letter direct to *Señor Catherwood, a Comatan o donde se halle,* conveying the expression of General Cascara's deep regrets for the arrest at Comatan. Stephens was overjoyed by the opportune arrival of the message. "This is my plan," he told Catherwood. "I will ask Don José Maria to read it aloud and then send him to the village for breakfast, where I know he will announce the story in every direction!"

In order not to miss the pleasure of seeing Don Gregorio's face when news of the letter arrived, Stephens decided to let Catherwood return to the ruins alone while he visited the village, taking Augustin with him so he could once again run up all the flags and fire the guns of Belize. At the village Stephens also planned to openly defy Don Gregorio by getting up a party of villagers to come and pay a visit to the ruins.

Stephens' first visit, however, was to the house of Don José Maria, where the question of the purchase of the ruins came up once again. The don hesitated. He could find no likely reason for delaying, especially now that the character of Señor Estebans was acceptable beyond any doubt, but still he was evasive.

"If you will, Don José Maria, tell me now—what will you take for the ruins?"

The question seemed completely mad to the little man. The property was so utterly worthless for any practical purpose that Stephens' still wanting to buy it seemed exceedingly suspicious.

Don José Maria was totally at a loss what to do, but promised Stephens that he would give the matter very serious thought, consult his wife and definitely give an answer by the next day.

As promised, the next morning Don José Maria arrived at the hut near the ruins in a terrible state. He was very anxious to convert unproductive land into money, but he was also afraid to sell the land to a stranger, since such an action could bring difficulty with the government. The don sat in a pitiable condition, obviously wanting to be convinced that it was right for him to turn the property over to an American.

Stephens understood the familiar situation at once, and with a flourish he opened his trunk once again. The credentials and documents of recommendation were read and reread. The letter of apology from General Cascara of the federal government was carefully examined. The bundles of documents with the seals and ribbons were brought out. Then Stephens patiently awaited the don's decision. But still he seemed uncertain. So as a grand finale Stephens opened the trunk once again and put on the diplomatic coat, with its profusion of big eagle buttons and gold braid. He also wore a panama hat, soaked from rain and spotted with mud, a checkered shirt, white pantaloons which were yellow up to the knees with mudstains, and big black boots. The outfit was absolutely ridiculous and Stephens felt like the African king who had received a company of British officers in a cocked hat, military coat and not another stitch of clothing. Ridiculous or not, Don José Maria could not withstand the impact of the marvelous gold buttons on the diplomatic coat! It was the finest garment he had ever seen, and the don, his wife and all assembled realized fully for the first time that they had in their presence an illustrious incognito! Don José Maria simply could not resist this fantastic spectacle. He gave in at once. And John Lloyd Stephens bought the ancient city of Copan.

Years later Stephens was to write, "The reader is perhaps curious to know how old cities sell in Central America. Like other articles of trade, they are regulated by the quantity in market, and the demand; but, not being staple articles, like cotton and indigo, they were held at fancy prices, and at that time were dull of sale. I paid fifty dollars for Copan. There was never any difficulty about the price. I offered the sum, for which Don José Maria thought me only a fool; if I had offered more, he would probably have considered me something worse."

The seventeenth day of November 1839 was the date on which the first systematic survey of a Maya ceremonial center began. Though Stephens and Catherwood knew nothing about the ruins they had rediscovered, they sensed that this day was to be an important moment in American archeology. The villagers of Copan, however, couldn't understand what the excitement was all about and were completely mystified by the unrepressed jubilation of Mr. Stephens and Mr. Catherwood. As far as the explorers were concerned it was absolutely necessary that this momentous event be fittingly celebrated.

Fortunately Stephens, quite by accident, had arranged just the right gala event. All the people of the hacienda had been invited to the ruins and they arrived in a procession led by Don Gregorio's wife, followed dutifully by a clutch of gasping old ladies, a string of excited servants, a gaggle of chattering children and two of the don's stately sons who had defied their father by visiting *los ingleses*. Messieurs Catherwood and Stephens received them among the ruins, seated them as well as they could and, as the first act of civility, gave them all cigars—a *cigarro* for the ladies, a *puro* for the gentlemen. Augustin, barefooted and with a smile on his scarred thug's face, politely served chocolate, and the ladies chatted contentedly under their pink umbrellas while sitting on great chunks of priceless rubble.

Meanwhile, Mr. Catherwood's drawings were much admired by all. And finally the ruins and monuments themselves were inspected. Stephens found it difficult to believe that not one of the guests, not even the don's grown sons, had ever seen the "idols" before. The lost city was not "lost" but simply dismissed as a pile of useless rubbish somewhere out in the forest. Even the Indians of the village knew nothing about the history of the ruins though they belonged to the same tribe and spoke exactly the same language as the long-vanished sculptors and architects who had created all the astonishing pyramids, terraces, monuments and great stairways.

Since John Stephens considered himself, in a manner, the "proprietor" of the lost city, he was bound to do the honors, and, having cleared a few footpaths through the foliage, he led the visitors on a little tour, showing off all the lions of his collection just as the cicerone does in the Vatican. When finally the guests departed, escorted to the very edge of the river, Stephens and Catherwood waved farewells and then smirked at each other with the acute satisfaction of knowing that these very impressed tourists would avenge them on Don Gregorio by raising endless praise of their hospitality, gallantry and many polite attentions.

Then the explorers got down to serious work. Under the deep shadows of rain clouds the new owners of Copan planned the survey of the shattered city. First the entire site was measured. Catherwood took charge of the surveyor's theodolite while Stephens and his crew of Indian workers cut the stations, using the same tape measure that Catherwood had used to map the ruins of

PLAN OF COPAN

Scale of English Feet.

300   200   100   0   100   200   300 F?

South

East

West

North

A Square Altar sculptured on the four sides and top.
B Statue erect.
C Statue and Altar.
D do.   do.
E do.   Fallen do. with many fragments on side of Pyramid.
F Colossal Head.
G Remains of sculptured figure.
H Colossal Head.
I Sepulchre and underground passage leading to the River.
J Remains of 2 circular Towers with Stairs.
K Statue and Altar, (Fallen.)
L Statue and Altar, (Erect.)
M do.   do.
N do.   do.
O do.   do.   (Fallen)
P do.   do.   (Erect.)

Q Statue and Altar, (Erect.)
R do.   do.   (Fallen.)
S Statue of Female with Altar. (Erect.)
T Beautiful Fragment, partly buried.
U Court Yard, with steps on three sides.
V Pyramidal Building, with remains of Shafts of Columns.
W Entrance with remains of Steps 10 ft. wide, and 6 ft. high
X Area, overgrown with Trees.
Y YYYYY Remains of Walls.
Z ZZZZZZ Remains of Pyramidal Buildings.

The dotted line shows the boundaries of the survey.

Indian Rubber, Mahogany, Cedar, and other large trees are dispersed over the Ruins.

RIVER COPAN

F. Catherwood.

Thebes. The mestizo tailor Bruno used his machete to fell trees, while his friend Francisco assisted Catherwood's survey by putting his straw hat on a pole and positioning it in accordance with Catherwood's bellowed instructions. As a result of two full days of clearing and measuring, Catherwood was able to make an accurate map. This first map of the ruins, however, showed only a few of the monuments because the heavy undergrowth concealed most of the city, and the explorers had no idea of its extensiveness. Not for a half century would anyone again visit Copan to undertake a scientific survey. And not for fully a century would investigation reveal the whole extent of the ruins or provide an approximation of their ancient splendor.

It now seems certain that Copan was not a "city" but a ceremonial center, consisting of main courts or plazas, dominated by grand pyramids with flattened crowns on which small rectangular temples were constructed. Around the Great Plaza were bands of stairs which covered several acres and elaborately encircled the central area on three sides, creating an elegant, sustained air of dignity. This expansive plaza, now ensnarled by trees and vines, was once the major meeting place of Copan, with its numerous flamboyant "idols" and "altars" producing a powerful ceremonial setting. The Eastern Court was apparently the most sacred and mysterious part of the vast acropolis. It was a spectacular amphitheater with tiers of stone seats looking down upon an extended stone platform guarded by two massive jaguars standing on their hind legs. Above the courtyard of this theater was a gigantic stone head, which Catherwood drew with great faithfulness. At the end of this court, though totally buried at the time of the explorers' visit, was a temple with an entrance composed of crouching human figures holding above their heads an elaborate wreath of sculptured stone.

From these eastern courtyards, masonry stairways rippled 125 feet down into another plaza, which is now called the Court of the Hieroglyphic Stairway. When Stephens and Catherwood saw this colossal assemblage of inscribed stone steps it was almost entirely buried under centuries of vegetable debris. Today great ceiba trees still rise out of the flanks of the Hieroglyphic Stairway, dropping their branches over the sides of the stately earth mound which supports the monumental staircase. It is one of the greatest achievements of Maya architecture and sculpture, rising almost seventy-five feet in height at a steep angle of about sixty degrees. The sixty-three treads of the stairway are cut with 2500 separate hieroglyphics arranged in such a manner that they "read" in horizontal lines, rather than in the usual columns. At the base of the stairway is an idol which is now believed to record a solar eclipse, an astonishing scientific observation for the date of the stele's creation, A.D. 756. The stairway is supposed to be one of the last major architectural achievements of the Maya world. The profusion of hieroglyphics are presumed to record a major saga of its creators, but not very much is known about the glyphs. Stephens guessed correctly that they were closely related to dates and the names of deities.

In 1839 the architectural form of Copan had been nearly shattered by the living encroachments of jungle and animals, yet Catherwood had a trained architect's eyes with which he could discern the main characteristics of its shape and forms. While Catherwood was led by his eye, Stephens possessed a remarkable archeological intuition. He grasped immediately that here, as in Egypt, monuments were ceremonial structures predominantly religious in function and form. The architectural imagination of Copan seemed to Stephens to be an elaboration of sculptural concepts. The structural results of this imagination were as impressive as anything the explorers had ever seen, an extraordinary achievement considering that the Maya had no concept of the true arch, were ignorant of the means of bonding corners and did not possess the formula by which to lay off a right angle— essentials of the classical structures of the Old World.

North of the Stairway Court is the Sacred Ball Court reserved for the most mysterious and famous of all sports in Mesoamerica. The game was called *pot-a-tok* by the ancients, but little is known about it or its apparent religious purposes. The court is in the shape of a capital I, with buildings on either side. These structures might have served as dressing rooms for the players, who wore lavish ceremonial regalia according to ancient reliefs and paintings which depict the game. Along the side walls of the Ball Court are structures which seem to be stone benches. The center of the court contains three square markers which might have been used to score in the game or to indicate boundaries, but no one knows for certain. It is assumed that the Maya played this ball game in a manner similar to an Aztec game which was described six hundred years later by chroniclers whose language has been translated. There were two teams consisting of three to nine players. A hard rubber ball was the object for which the teams competed, trying to keep it from hitting the floor of the court while each player tried to score. The ball could only be hit with the elbow, knee or hip. No one knows for certain how scoring was accomplished. Six tenoned parrot heads are sunk into the slanting benches of the side walls of the court, but it is unknown if putting the ball through the hole in the heads was the objective of the game.

Beyond the Ball Court the magnificent acropolis of Copan descends into the Great Plaza, which is surrounded on three sides by many tiers of stone seats. Within this vast plaza the huge slabs of carved limestone—the "idols" or stelae of Copan—are located. Pomp and pageantry once filled the Great Plaza during ceremonial occasions. At one time the floor of this expansive court was plastered and painted in a variety of bright colors, though predominantly red and blue. Today twelve mysterious stelae stand in the court. The carving of these marvelous stone monuments is in high relief almost to the degree that some of the figures are nearly in the round. Nowhere else have archeologists discovered figures carved in the manner of Copan. The quarry for the stone used for these stelae is less than a mile from the site. It is a very hard flintlike material in which the ancient sculptors managed to achieve remarkable results with only the use of stone, bone or wooden tools.

The figures depicted on these monuments are clothed in resplendent costumes, decorated with jade and the feathers of birds. Most of these dignitaries are laden with anklets, bracelets, earplugs and pendants of jade. Their opulence is depicted so formally and stylistically that their appearance borders on abstraction. The usual costume seen on the monumental figures is a breechcloth. The feet are sandaled and the heads are crowned with gigantic headdresses. The faces seem to be portraits, possessing fine differentiation and character. Despite the tendency to stereotype American Indians as beardless, many of the figures of the stelae have goatees, full beards and mustaches. In front of most of the stelae are low flat monuments that are called altars though their purpose is still unknown.

Catherwood was overwhelmed by the abundance of monuments and very nearly stymied by the uniqueness and complexity of the sculptural style. By the third day, however, he had finally mastered the means of rendering the images faithfully. Since there were no major structures still standing, Catherwood concentrated on the "idols" that Stephens and his two enthusiastic helpers had freed from the tangle of vegetation. For the first time in centuries the strange monolithic slabs were exposed to sunlight. Their surfaces were entirely incised and sculptured with images and signs, as if the ancients of this mysterious place had a dread of empty space. Yet the mastery of the materials was so complete that Maya sculptors approached a thirty-ton stone as Oriental craftsmen dealt with small pieces of ivory.

Catherwood was enthralled by his task and moved with tireless excitement from one idol to the next, drawing each with extraordinary verity. One of the monuments had been displaced from its pedestal by enormous roots; another was locked in the snarl of the branches of a tree which had almost lifted it out of the earth; and another had been hurled to the ground and bound down by huge vines and creepers. One idol was standing completely intact in a dim grove of ceiba trees, and in the solemn stillness of the woods it seemed to be a great divinity mourning for a fallen people.

The mysterious atmosphere of the ruins would never fade from Stephens' memory. "That city was desolate," he later wrote,

CATHERWOOD D.

ANDERSON S.

A curious altar

". . . laying before us like a shattered ship in the midst of an ocean of green, her masts gone, her name effaced, her crew perished, and none to tell whence she came, to whom she belonged, how long she had been on her voyage, or what caused her terrible destruction; her lost people to be traced only by some fancied resemblance in the construction of the vessel, perhaps never to be known at all."

For days the sharp blows of machetes resounded through the forest. Stephens gazed at the Indian workmen, trying to discern in their bronze faces some sign of the creative power that could account for the masterful stoneworks produced by their ancestors; for Stephens was already convinced that American Indians alone should be credited with the creation of this incredible place. The art was unique. Its style, patterns and subject matter were definitely not those of the outside world. The power of these monuments was utterly alien to anything Stephens knew or felt. Here was some galvanic aspect of nature captured in stone which was unknown to other men; here was the quintessence of a refined grotesquerie and a controlled fiendishness which Stephens could not grasp but which somehow expressed itself in masterful forms with exceptional force. Here was the power of expression rather than the expression of beauty. The ancestors of his humble workers had achieved all of this! In every stone portrait could be seen the semblance of their faces—prominent noses, high reclining foreheads, and wide almond-shaped eyes. Yet the Indians could offer not the slightest clue to the origin or purpose of these magnificent works of art which their remote ancestors had produced.

Equally mysterious to Stephens was the lavish embroidery of glyphs which blanketed every stone. What did these thousands upon thousands of signs mean? It seemed unquestionable to him that history itself was graven onto the monuments but in some utterly remote "writing" which could only be understood if by chance a Maya Rosetta Stone were discovered. Stephens' belief that the stelae spoke of both dates and events has proved correct. He made another important discovery, which became apparent to him when he returned to America and compared the glyphs of Copan with the reproduction of a rare Maya polychrome manuscript called the Dresden Codex, which had been written in the eleventh century. He decided, and quite correctly, that the people who had written the one had also carved the other.

After several days of arduous labor Stephens and his workmen had cleared enough foliage from the monuments to keep Catherwood at work for at least a month. But a month was far longer than Stephens had planned to remain at Copan. He felt compelled to fulfill his diplomatic assignment. This required him to continue his chase after the evasive government of Central America. And so a council was called at the base of one of the idols. Stephens, Catherwood, Augustin, Bruno and Francisco—perspiring, stung, bitten and muddy—assembled in the misty afternoon. Every possibility was discussed, including abandoning the ruins entirely. But that seemed an unnecessary sacrifice, since the excitement in the village had quieted down, the work was undisturbed by Don Gregorio, and Catherwood had finally gotten the knack of rendering the monuments with great accuracy.

The best plan seemed to be separation: for Stephens, in the company of the muleteer and the dedicated Augustin, to travel to Guatemala City in search of the seat of government, and for Catherwood and his workmen to remain behind and finish rendering all the monuments which had been extricated from the jungle.

John Lloyd Stephens had spent thirteen days at Copan. He was glad to leave the domain of Don Gregorio, but his departure on November 30 was rather sad, for he was not only leaving his good friend and partner in many horrendous and hilarious adventures, he was also saying a final farewell to the fantastic ceremonial world which he had helped to rediscover. He would never see Copan again.

The most difficult preparation for the departure from Copan was making a treaty with the crusty muleteer, whose insufferable pride had been further bolstered by his acquaintance with Don Gregorio. Now there was simply no dealing with him. But after a lengthy series of debates, diatribes, recriminations and apologies, an arrangement was finally reached. The mules were loaded, and at two in the afternoon Stephens and Augustin mounted. Catherwood, in a rare sentimental mood, accompanied his comrade to the edge of the woods, where he said his farewells. Then Stephens and Augustin were off into the green world.

The good will of the muleteer didn't last very long. At parting, the plates, knives, spoons and other tin utensils had been divided between Catherwood and Stephens, who put his share in a basket which was loaded on one of the mules. Unfortunately these utensils rattled around and made such a clatter that the mule was spooked and ran off with a great noise until she eventually threw herself into the bushes, where she panted pathetically. The muleteer blamed the entire mishap on Augustin, who had done a poor job of packing, and both men began to yell at each other. Stephens escaped the hoarse croaking curses as quickly as he could, riding ahead into the deep forest, where the monkeys and parrots chattered in the sunlight of the distant treetops. Eventually tempers cooled and the little caravan made a new start.

By four in the afternoon they had reached the Quadalquiver River, which was the boundary line between Honduras and Guatemala. Soon they started the ascent of the great Sierra Madre range that divides the streams of the Atlantic from those that empty into the Pacific Ocean. The climb was difficult but nothing by comparison to the Mico Mountain, and in two hours they reached the top. The view from the summit was fantastic, but it rained during the entire journey and Stephens was so busy floundering among mudholes that he didn't have the chance to give the scenery a second thought. The clouds finally lifted as they made their descent, and Stephens looked down on an almost boundless plain, running from the foot of the Sierra into the clouded distance. Standing entirely alone in the expansive, desolate plain was the great church of Esquipulas, the holiest shrine of Central America. For three hours the church was their beacon as they trekked through the glistening late-afternoon light. Finally, as the sun was setting, they entered the town and rode to the convent, where Stephens presented his passport and letters of introduction and was given a hearty welcome by the padre. The entire household of the *cura* turned out to assist Stephens unload the cargo and in a few minutes the mules were happily munching corn in the yard and Stephens was installed in the most lavish accommodation of the convent.

The *cura* was a young man of about twenty-seven, with a delicate body and a face which beamed with refinement and intelligence. He was dressed in a long black bombazet gown, drawn tight around the waist. When he introduced himself as

Esquipulas

Jesus Maria Guttierrez, Stephens was visibly shocked, for this was the first time he had ever heard the name Jesus applied to a person.

At dinner the *cura* gave Stephens a distressing report on the state of the road to Guatemala City. Carrera's troops had fallen back from the frontier of Salvador and in the process had taken over the whole line of villages along the road to the capital. "I fear," the padre said softly, "that they are ignorant soldiers ... simple Indians who cannot understand passports or official documents. They have already committed great atrocities, señor, and I fear for your safety. There is not a curate on the whole road, and attempting to travel it alone would surely expose you to robbery and murder."

Stephens accepted the advice of the *cura* though he was anxious to reach the capital. After a long night of conversation and hospitable attentions, Stephens climbed into his bed with the rare feeling of being a welcome guest. It was a striking contrast to the hacienda of Don Gregorio.

He was awakened by the sound of the bells calling the Indians to morning mass. After breakfast he set out to visit the great church of the pilgrimage, the holy of holies of Central America, where every year, on January 15, pilgrims came to pay homage to "our Lord of Esquipulas."

There was but one street, nearly a mile long, with mud houses on each side. At the top of this long street, on elevated ground, stood the great church. On the massive stone steps in front of the church several men reclined, quietly displaying their various deformities and outstretching their brown palms to Stephens. At the top of the steps was a noble platform a hundred and fifty feet wide from which the view of the great plain and the mountains surrounding it was magnificent. The church rose in solitary grandeur out of the desolation; the facade was rich with stucco ornamentation and the figures of saints. At each angle was a high tower, and over the dome a spire. Above the entire structure was the royal crown of Spain—the power that had once ruled the vast American domain for three centuries but now, Stephens noted with a certain pride, did not possess a foot of land or a single subject.

Inside the church a mass was under way. The Indians crossed themselves repeatedly as they entered, dropping to the floor at the doorway and gradually sliding forward on their knees into the vast darkness of the church. The priest quietly spun his Latin phrases, which resounded throughout the dimness of the grand colonial-style cathedral. Then bells began to ring and the large assembly of old men and brightly dressed women, with their barefooted children, knelt amidst hundreds of yellow candles which were clustered on low benches scattered among the worshipers. Some of the women covered their heads with tiny aprons. Others were threadbare and bareheaded. Their handsome dark faces were lighted by the flames of countless candles, and their reverent expressions deeply impressed Stephens. The choir of rural boys chanted in reedy untrained voices which possessed a melancholy beauty that Stephens had come to associate with the Indians of the region. In front of the altar, in a rich shrine, was an image of the Savior on the cross, "our Lord of Esquipulas," to whom the church was consecrated, and famed for its power of working miracles for the deformed and sick.

Stephens returned to the convent, and while he was enjoying the morning sunlight among the flowers of the garden the curate approached and, carefully closing the door behind him, asked in a whisper if Stephens' servant were faithful. Augustin's thuggish face constantly aroused people's suspicion. Everyone who had ever seen Augustin, from Colonel MacDonald to Don Gregorio, had distrusted him on sight and cautioned Stephens about him. Stephens, however, had come to be extremely fond of his servant and often recounted with dramatic detail Augustin's heroic behavior on several difficult occasions. But the *cura* of Esquipulas still cautioned Stephens to beware of him. Soon after this, Augustin, who seemed to suspect that he had not made a very favorable impression, asked Stephens for a dollar to pay for a confession. The padre, however, was not fond of Indians, and Stephens noticed that even after Augustin's valiant effort to change the impression he had made on the priest, the padre still avoided him.

The Indians dearly loved the padre. Once when the troops of Morazan had invaded the town, the Indians hid him in a cave in the mountains, where they supported him for six months. Lately the political difficulties of the country had greatly increased, and the prospect of a full-fledged civil war in which the clergy would play a major role in opposition to Morazan was growing greater every day.

The padre and Stephens sat discussing these gloomy matters in the embrasure of a great window. The room within was already dark. The padre lifted a pistol from the windowsill and, looking at it, said with a faint smile that the cross was his protection. Then he put his thin white hand into Stephens' and asked him to feel his pulse. It was very slow and feeble and seemed as if every beat might be the last. "It has always been like that," the young padre said quietly. Then he rose and whispered, "This is the hour of my private devotions." And he left.

The next day Stephens departed and crossed the plain, looking back at the towering church of Esquipulas. He ascended a mountain near Quezaltepeque. Heavy clouds were hanging all around his little caravan, and soon it began to rain. Stephens had the great pleasure of seeing the muleteer thoroughly drenched and of hearing him grumble and sneeze and cough, but then an unaccountable fit of good will came over him, and he lent the nasty mule driver his huge bearskin coat.

Three weeks later, when Frederick Catherwood took this same road, he heard from the padre of Quezaltepeque that a secret plan had been formulated to murder and rob Stephens on the supposition that he had a large amount of money. Only his crossing the mountain in the morning, because of his hurry to reach Guatemala City, instead of the afternoon when most travelers made the crossing, saved him from attack. But Stephens knew nothing of this, and such violence still seemed to him a gross exaggeration of the tumult of the war-torn region.

By three in the afternoon Stephens had come to the village of San Jacinto, which consisted of a collection of huts and a humble church made of poles plastered with mud. On each side of the church was an arbor thatched with leaves of Indian corn, and at the corners were makeshift belfries, each containing three rusty old bells. In front were two gigantic ceibas, a tree which Stephens had come to know from Indian mythology as the Tree of Life. There remained among the native people a story of the creation which envisioned at the center of the world a huge ceiba tree from which all life and all living things originated.

Stephens ordered the muleteer to unload the mules at the house of the *cura* of the region of Quezaltepeque who lived in San Jacinto. But before the padre had time to welcome the strangers the muleteer threw himself on the ground and with Stephens' great bearskin coat on his thankless body, began rolling in the dust and accusing his employer of trying to kill him with long marches. Fortunately the *cura* was a man who could put up with a great deal of foolishness. He hardly noticed the antics of the muleteer and immediately extended his hand to Stephens and invited him into the house to the total dismay and annoyance of the temperamental mule driver.

The padre was a sumptuous fellow: six feet tall, broad-shouldered, and with a protuberance of the belly that required a good deal of support to keep him from falling forward to the ground. His dress was decidedly unclerical—a shirt and a pair of wrinkled pantaloons. But he was a generous man. And when Stephens told him that he had ridden all the way from Esquipulas in a single day, he said that he must remain at least a week to recuperate. As to Stephens' planned departure the next day, the stout padre would not hear of it. And, as things turned out, Stephens soon realized the impossibility of his leaving, for the abominable muleteer became ill with a violent fever brought on at least in part by the grueling march through the downpour.

Stephens was determined not to linger any longer than necessary in San Jacinto despite the *cura's* exceptional hospitality. And so he tried to procure mules and a new muleteer. The village man on whom the padre often relied in such matters was pessimistic about Stephens' journey to Guatemala City. "It is too dangerous, señor, for strangers. Two *ingleses* were arrested in Honduras only the other day. They escaped but their muleteers and all of their servants were murdered on the spot!"

The padre was deeply distressed by the unwillingness of his flock to arrange Stephens' passage, and so at length he said that he himself would provide the necessities for Stephens' trip to the capital. He ordered a man to go at dawn to his hacienda for mules and to make every necessary preparation for the journey. After these unusual efforts in behalf of Stephens, the good padre was totally fatigued and threw his gigantic body into a hammock, where he swung himself to sleep.

In the morning, before Stephens was out of bed, the padre stood over him with a flask of *aguadiente*. Soon after came chocolate with a role of sweet bread. Everything was delightful except the ill health of the muleteer, which Stephens had suspected was a pretense, but his pallid color and his indifference to food soon convinced him that he was really in a bad way. So Stephens gave him some medicine, but the poor fellow was so suspicious of his employer that he was afraid to swallow it.

By noon the mules procured by the padre arrived with a strapping young Indian muleteer. The entire convent was in commotion. The padre was not used to fitting out an expedition, and many things were missing. The villagers made every effort to supply what was needed. During the bustle a single soldier entered the village and alarmed the people, who feared the military. The padre told the soldier who Stephens was and insisted that he must not molest him. And finally all the preparations were completed. A great number of people, roused by the requisitions of the padre, were at his door, and among them, for no apparent reason, were two young men with violins.

The padre meanwhile directed his gigantic energies to the matter of food for the travelers. He had packed chocolate, bread, sausages and fowl; a box of cakes and confectionery; and, as the finale, a lad came out of the house holding at arm's length over his head the whole side of an ox, with merely the skin removed and the ribs cracked. This was balanced on the back of a mule and secured with a net. Then a large pot, with the bottom up, was secured on top of another mule. The padre looked exceedingly pleased and complimented the people on their cooperation and Christian generosity to a stranger. And finally, with violins playing and a turnout of the entire village, Stephens made another start for the capital in search of the evasive government of the Central American Federation.

A low groan from the plaza reminded Stephens of his muleteer. He dismounted and at the moment of leaving exchanged a few words of kindness with this utterly nasty fellow who had given him so many problems and so much aggravation. But even with all of Stephens' malice for the fellow, he could not have wished him a worse situation. He was very nearly dead with fever and needed all the kindness he could get. His abused helper, the little boy he had bullied daily, was apparently softened by the illness of his master and sat diligently by his side, indifferent to Stephens' departure. Augustin, however, was not willing to forget the disloyalties of the muleteer and shook his fist at him and shouted jubilantly that God was punishing him at last for all of his treachery.

This was the operatic atmosphere of Stephens' departure from San Jacinto.

By sundown the caravan reached the village of San Rosalie, beautifully situated on a point formed by the bend of a river. The village consisted of only a few miserable huts. Before the door of the best of these hovels was a small crowd of people who stared at the strangers but did not ask them to stop. All Stephens wanted was feed for the mules. The provisions supplied by the padre were more than sufficient for the travelers and they required little other hospitality. But no one offered any assistance.

Ignoring the miserable villagers, the travelers made their camp. Augustin cut a few ribs from the side of the ox and his cooking soon sent a marvelous fragrance into the village as he prepared supper. Soon the wretched people gathered around his fire and gazed longingly at the abundance of food, but Augustin sent them running when he threatened them with his pistols. "Get along, you worthless villains!" he shouted. "This will teach you how to treat strangers!"

Later, while quietly feasting on their fine dinner, the travelers heard a voice of lamentation coming from the house where the crowd was assembled. After eating, Stephens investigated and found that the people were mourning the dead. Inside the hut were several women, one wringing her hands desperately and crying out, "O our Lord of Esquipulas, why have you taken him away from me?" Her prayer was interrupted when a man rode up. Stephens could not see his face in the darkness but he understood the man's words when he said that the priest wanted six dollars to bury the corpse. Someone in the crowd cried out, "Shame! Shame on the priest to make a profit on death!" and others said that they would bury the body in a field rather than pay six dollars to the priest. The horseman said that it was all the same if the body were buried in the road, on a mountain or in the river—the priest must have his six dollars. There was a great cry of rage, but the widow, weeping hysterically, agreed that the six dollars would be paid. With this she resumed her lamentation.

The corpse lay on the ground in a white cotton dress extending from the neck to the feet. It was the body of a young man not more than twenty years old, with the mustache just beginning to bud on his lip—tall, muscular and handsome. He had left his home to buy cattle and returned with a fever. In a week he was dead. Now a bandage was tied under his chin to hold his jaw closed; his thin wrists were secured across his chest and his fingers held a small crucifix made of cornhusks and flowers. On each side of his head was a lighted candle and ants were swarming across his pallid face, disappearing into his nostrils.

The widow did not notice Stephens, but the mother of the boy asked him if he had any *remedios*, if he could cure the boy, if he could bring him back to her. Stephens shook his head with astonishment and pity, stumbling out of the hut and turning into the depths of the night, which suddenly seemed filled with outcries and lamentations.

The plaza of the village was full of hogs and sewage. The huts were full of fleas and children. The women in harsh voices called out to more children. Child after child straggled home and each was piled atop the others on the filthy floor. Stephens' men were already asleep under a tree. Borrowing an undressed oxhide from one of the women, he spread it on the ground and reluctantly lay down on it.

The moon rose. Birds costumed the night and their cries filled the darkness. The woman of the most humble hut was sleepless. A dozen times she came out to smoke a cigar or to drive away the hogs. Her coarse voice sang tuneless lullabies to her whimpering babies. The song mixed with the screams from the house of mourning. Finally the morning came.

John Lloyd Stephens knocked incessantly at the door of the British Vice-Consul. But no one responded. In the dim streets of Guatemala City there was not a single person. The windows were shuttered and the doors were barricaded. Stephens knocked again. "Mr. Hall, are you there, sir?" he shouted. Still no answer. Augustin whimpered behind him in the darkness, while in the distance there was a muffled shout. Then silence. Exasperated, utterly worn out, and frightened by the curious stillness of the capital, Stephens banged with all his might at the door.

Finally a young man timidly opened the shutter of a balconied window just above them and whispered fearfully that Mr. Hall the Vice-Consul was not at home. "Nonsense!" Stephens barked. "My name is John Lloyd Stephens, young fellow, and you go tell Mr. Hall that I am a representative of the United States of

America! Do you hear?" At once the face vanished and the shutter snapped closed. Then in a few minutes the great bolt of the front door was unfastened with much rattling, and the British Vice-Consul, extremely agitated and pale, opened the doors just enough for Stephens, Augustin, and their mules to slip into the courtyard.

"My good man," Mr. Hall gasped politely, "but you gave us a terrible start." He led Stephens to his study and carefully bolted the door behind him. "We are in a bad way here in Guatemala City, Mr. Stephens. The soldiers of Rafael Carrera have not been paid and they have been in a state of revolt for days. Just yesterday these ignorant bandits who dare call themselves soldiers exacted a *loan* from my poor neighbor, a very decent French merchant who was too frightened to refuse them. The city is greatly alarmed, Mr. Stephens, and so, when you knocked, we were afraid that it was the soldiers up to some mischief. But, please, sit, do sit down, my dear fellow, and tell me how you managed to travel without being shot in this absolutely lawless city."

Mr. Hall gave Stephens no opportunity to answer, and continued his nervous explanation while he fidgeted with the buttons of his coat and paced back and forth with a delicate step. "The worst part of the whole dastardly situation, Mr. Stephens, was the outrage these brutes perpetrated against the colors of the British Empire! I was actually forced, Mr. Stephens, to bring down my staff because on their previous raid, when I had the flag flying, the soldiers dared to fire upon it, sir, calling it a *bandera de guerra!* Shocking, Mr. Stephens, positively shocking!" he exclaimed with great indignation. "These so-called soldiers are Indians! . . . barely on the fringe of the human race, my dear Mr. Stephens. Indians from the jungle . . . utterly ignorant and insolent. Only a few days ago something happened to me which I am embarrassed to mention: a sentinel the color of a copper knocked my hat off in public! . . . with the excuse that I had not raised it to him in passing! Shocking, sir, that is what it is! *Positively shocking!*"

Stephens was handed a brandy, which he drank with relish,

hoping that his agitated host would eventually realize that he had not eaten in many hours and had not slept in a decent bed for weeks. But the British Vice-Consul was embroiled in a surge of indignation and fear. "I cannot understand," he said, gulping down a draft of brandy, "how you have managed, Mr. Stephens. It is most exceptional, sir, that you were able to wander through the streets without being molested. These Indians are savages without the slightest grasp of law and order. I try to be understanding. We have all of us tried to be kindly with these natives, but it is not to be done, Mr. Stephens, as you shall no doubt soon find out. Since 1819, when they commenced their ruffian clamor for independence, they have been nothing but lawless rascals. That the subsequent history of the Central American republics has been largely a record of civil war, maladministration and financial dishonesty, is perhaps due in part to racial inferiority, but, Mr. Stephens, it is also due to the total absence of any tradition of good government as well as the brevity and artificiality of the abrupt evolution which converted a debased slave population into the so-called citizens of modern democratic states. I say this with regret, Mr. Stephens, but it is nonetheless as true as the laws of biology. You simply cannot educate an Indian. And you cannot make him a gentleman by putting him into a waistcoat."

John Stephens smiled with difficulty. Then he said, "I'm afraid that I too will soon turn into a barbarian if I don't manage to have my supper."

"Oh my, how utterly inhospitable and thoughtless of me. Of course, of course, please come with me and we will install you at once in our best guest room and have a meal prepared for you immediately. My dear fellow," he rambled on, "it is so very nice to have you here with us! How exceedingly pleasant to have a *real* American and such an illustrious traveler too . . . how exceedingly pleasant and how utterly surprising for you to drop out of nowhere in the middle of the night and you must tell us all about it!"

"Yes, of course," Stephens said rather flatly as he followed his fidgeting host into the dining room. It was two months to the day since he had embarked from New York City but it seemed to Stephens that at least a year had passed. For the first time since entering the country he had a good bed and a pair of clean sheets. It was with considerable relish that he said good night to the talkative Mr. Hall and closed the door behind him.

The next day John Lloyd Stephens began his official duties by taking possession of the American Legation—the house that had been occupied by Mr. Charles DeWitt, the late chargé d'affaires. Stephens was charmed by the handsome house of the legation. The salon was well furnished and lined with bookcases filled with books in dull yellow bindings which gave him a twinging recollection of his law office in New York. With Augustin's help he soon located the archives of the legation and, following his instructions, he prepared to ship the documents back to the United States. At two in the afternoon the mules arrived with his luggage, and he was comfortably installed in his new home.

After paying the young muleteer whom the padre at San Jacinto had secured in his behalf and sending him home with best wishes to the padre, Stephens settled down to his first duty: arranging to send a trusted escort to bring Frederick Catherwood from Copan, where he was still at work. With this accomplished, it was now his duty to look around for the government to which he was accredited. Prescribed protocol required him to don his blue diplomatic jacket with the golden buttons and present himself officially to the Minister of Foreign Affairs. But where was this gentleman? And where, for that matter, was the President of the Central American Federation? The French Minister, Baron Malelin, waved his hand in the air with a shrug. The puffy British consul, Frederick Chatfield, gave Stephens a disdainful look and stated flatly that no such government existed. As far as Chatfield was concerned, it was good riddance. Being one of those men of mettle whose singular response to everything was one of *action*, his only view of Central America was one of imperial aggression.

Since the collapse of the Spanish Empire in the early 1820s

Britain had been grasping for supremacy among the various nations struggling for control. Chatfield dreamed of a British protectorate embracing Guatemala, Honduras, El Salvador, Nicaragua and Costa Rica. The United States was determined to keep England and all other European powers from getting any additional holdings in the Western Hemisphere. But the British intended to use their base in Belize as an outpost for imperial ambitions. The presence of an American lawyer nosing around Central America as President Van Buren's confidential agent made Chatfield extremely nervous.

As for Frederick Catherwood, whom Chatfield contemptuously described as that "Yankified English artist," there was little doubt of his duplicity as far as the British chargé d'affaires was concerned. And it was for this reason that Colonel MacDonald of Belize had already sent Walker and Caddy into the jungle to discover and document the ruins of Palenque—in hopes of beating Stephens and his friend to that ancient city.

All of this intrigue bored John Lloyd Stephens. He had been in Guatemala City only three days and already the place seemed dull. The city was extremely tense, for Rafael Carrera and his Indian warriors were expected at any moment. The people were suspicious and fearful, and Stephens was the target of so much controversy that he was forced to shut himself up in the legation. Augustin fussed over him with renewed loyalty and chattered incessantly about the pompous English and the ungrateful French and the wrath of God which would destroy both Carrera and his foe Morazan, for Augustin had not come to terms with either faction of the civil war. But such conversation did not amuse Stephens.

Eventually, with the assistance of an attractive young widow who owned the house across from the legation, Stephens met many of the city's aristocrats, with whom he passed the evenings. These families had acquired under the former Spanish dominion immense wealth and rank as merchant princes. And at the time of the emancipation from Spain they hoped to take the government into their own hands. And so they did, but only for a short time. Eventually the frustrated desires of the people became fierce, and leaders like Carrera and Morazan battled for dominance in the name of the common man.

Stephens soon came to disdain the indulgences of the aristocrats and their total unwillingness to accept the needs of the people or to help prepare them for the responsibilities of self-government.

To me the position of the country seemed most critical [Stephens wrote in his journal]. At the time of the first invasion a few hundred Spaniards had conquered the whole Indian population. Naturally peaceable, and kept without arms, the conquered people had remained quiet and submissive during the three centuries of Spanish dominion. In the civil wars following the independence they had borne but a subordinate part; and down to the time of Carrera's rising they were entirely ignorant of their own physical strength. But this fearful discovery had now been made. The Indians constituted three-fourths of the inhabitants of Guatemala; were the hereditary owners of the soil; for the first time since they fell under the dominion of the whites, were organized and armed under a chief of their own. I do not sympathize with Carrera's Central party for I believe that in their hatred of the Liberals of Morazan they are courting a third power that might destroy them both; consorting with a wild animal—the people—which might at any moment turn and rend them in pieces. I believe that they are playing upon the ignorance and prejudices of the Indians, and through the priests, upon their religious fanaticism; amusing them with fetes and Church ceremonies, persuading them that the Liberals aimed at a demolition of churches, destruction of the priests, and hurrying back the country into darkness; and in the general heaving of the elements there is not a man of nerve enough among them, with the influence of name and station, to rally round him the strong and honest men of the country, reorganize the shattered republic, and save them from the disgrace and danger of truckling to Rafael Carrera—an ignorant, uneducated Indian

boy. Such are my sentiments, but, of course, I avoid express-
ing them since such ideas are detested by the aristocrats as
well as the fanatics of Carrera. As for the liberal Morazan, he
is nowhere to be found.

On Wednesday the bells sounded the alarm; the rebels, joined
by Carrera, were at the city gate, and commissioners were sent
out to try to negotiate with them. They demanded an evacuation
of the plaza by the soldiers. The military, however, responded
that the rebels would have to come and take the city square from
them. In the afternoon commissioners were once again sent out to
try to deal with the rebels, who demanded the resignation of the
chief of state, the evacuation of the plaza by the federal troops
and a free passage into the city. The Assembly of Guatemala met
in terror and agreed to all the demands. By five in the afternoon
the government troops had evacuated the plaza.

In the meantime the troops of Carrera were advancing upon
Guatemala City. Among his leaders were many known outlaws,
criminals, robbers and murderers. The rage of rebellion always
attracts outcasts and fanatics; it was true of the American and
French revolutions and it was also true of the civil wars of Central
America. The disheveled leaders of the rebel troops were on
horseback, with the stems of green bush in their hats, riding high
and shouting thunderously against a background of waving
pennants of dirty cotton cloth covered with rudely drawn pictures of saints.

In only minutes the immense mass of warriors choked up the
streets of the city, armed with rusty muskets, old pistols, sticks
formed into the shape of muskets, clubs, machetes and knives
tied to the ends of long poles. Swelling the multitude of yelling,
cursing, howling rebels were two or three thousand women with
sacks and alforjas for carrying away plunder. Many who had
never left their villages before looked with wild astonishment at
the houses and churches of the magnificent city built by the
Spaniards. They streamed in unbroken waves into the central
plaza, shouting, *"Viva la religion, y muerte a los extranjeros!"*

Carrera himself, amazed at the immensity of the army which followed him, was so embarrassed by the jubilation that greeted his entry into the city that he could barely guide his horse through the crowds.

At sundown the entire force of Carrera's troops began to sing the *Salve*—"The Hymn to the Virgin." The swell of voices bombarded the air and made the inhabitants of the city shake with dread. Then, silently, Carrera entered the great Cathedral of Guatemala. The Indians scrambled after him, in mute astonishment at the opulence and magnificence of this vast holy place. Dutifully they brushed the dust from the rags they wore and humbly set up around the exquisite main altar the primitive images of their village saints, crossing themselves repeatedly and falling to their knees in gratefulness for their victory.

Meanwhile one of Carrera's aides had broken into the house of General Prem and seized a uniform richly embroidered with gold. This stately garment was brought to Carrera in the cathedral and he wiped his nose and slipped his arms into the sleeves, still wearing his straw hat with its green bush. Another aide jubilantly brought a pocket watch, and for a moment Carrera stared at it before waving it away, saying that he did not know what it was or how it was used.

The priests were the only people who had any influence with Carrera and they tried every device to placate the rebel leader, while the people of the city waited in terrible suspense, dreading that at any moment they might hear the signal for pillage and massacre. The priests ran through the streets bearing the crucifix, and in the name of the Virgin and of all the saints attempted to restrain the Indians, whose hostility was so great that even their faith in their beloved Jesus was hardly sufficient to curb their immense rage.

John Lloyd Stephens waited for Carrera to be installed in the city hall, and then he nonchalantly requested an audience with the absolute master of Guatemala, whom his Indian rebels called *"el Hijo de Dios y Nuestro Señor*—the Son of God and Our Lord." After receiving word that Carrera would see him, Stephens put on his gold-laced diplomatic coat, glanced into a mirror to adjust the bristles of his beard and was escorted to the city hall by Carrera's guards, who were fitted out preposterously in red bombazet jackets, tartan-plaid caps and ancient swords.

When Stephens entered the immense room, Rafael Carrera was sitting at a table counting sixpenny and shilling pieces. He was short, with straight black hair, a beardless face and a dark Indian complexion. He and the several rustic officers surrounding him were dressed in very dashing uniforms which they had "confiscated" from the Morazan officers who had been killed or taken prisoner. Surprisingly, Carrera appeared to be no older than perhaps twenty-one.

He glanced with his mysterious black eyes at Stephens as he entered the stately room; and then he slowly rose, pushing aside the coins, and offered his guest the chair at his side. Stephens was remarkably calm. He was capable, whatever his personal feelings, of conducting himself with the cool confidence and control of an experienced trial attorney. He smiled cordially and sat down, and then at once remarked on Carrera's extreme youth. The rebel leader listened quietly and answered that he was indeed young but perhaps not as young as Meester Estebans imagined. Then he said, "Perhaps, señor, I have twenty-three years. In Central America that is not young, for we have too many hardships in life to be children for very long, señor." And then a subtle smirk appeared on Carrera's grave face. He sensed that he was somehow an extraordinary person, that he was the kind of man of whom others wished to ask many questions; and so, without awaiting Stephens' inquiry, he explained how he had come to be the master of Guatemala. He had begun, he said, with thirteen men armed with rusty old muskets, so old, in fact, that they had to be fired with lighted cigars. Upon recalling this story, Carrera again smirked almost imperceptibly and exchanged a remark in an Indian dialect with his officers, and everyone but Stephens laughed. Then Carrera gazed at his guest with an expression in his large black eyes which Stephens could not comprehend. And the rebel leader pointed to eight places where he had been wounded and said that he still had three bullets lodged in his body. Again the subtle grin fluttered on his lips.

Within hardly a year he had built a mighty Indian guard that carried banners proclaiming, *"Viva la religion y muerte a los extranjeros,"* which had sent foreigners running for their lives out of the country. But when Carrera eventually met the representatives of foreign nations his attitude was considerably modified, and he counted a number of Englishmen among his acquaintances. His rage was subdued by his victories. He was as mighty as a king at the time of Stephens' audience. However, his wrath was easily rekindled, as when he was shown a poster on an adobe wall which called him a bandit and an *antropófage.* *"Antropófage?"* he asked. *"Explain please."* When after several attempts the meaning—*"man-eater"*—very gradually occurred to him, he was absolutely unbridled in his rage.

Such stories made Stephens cautious of the rebel leader but did not alter his impression that Carrera was unquestionably a promising young political force. He told him that he had a long career before him, and could do much good for his country. Carrera, in an unexpected burst of feeling, laid his hand on his heart and said he was determined to sacrifice his life for his country. Stephens was inclined to believe him, for with all his faults and his many crimes, no one ever accused the rebel of duplicity or of saying what he did not mean. It seemed to the American attorney, who had a fine insight into people, that Carrera, like many self-deceiving men before him, believed himself a true patriot.

"I consider that he was destined to exercise an important, if not a controlling, influence on the affairs of Central America," Stephens later wrote. And Carrera did, in fact, remain in power for twenty-five years, until 1865, when he died in office as President.

John Lloyd Stephens had made a strong impression on Rafael Carrera, who complimented him on his diplomatic representation of "El Norte"—as he called the United States. He offered Stephens any service he might require to carry out his duties. "One day perhaps I will visit El Norte," he said, "but for now I cannot fix my thoughts on anything except the wars and my opponent Morazan." In fact, he knew of nothing else.

Stephens gazed intently at Carrera, whose ancestors had ruled the mighty cities of the civilization now lost in the jungles. And then he said a formal good-bye to the boyish general, who bowed to him very gravely and closed the door.

John Stephens was deeply stunned by his meeting with the great Indian leader Rafael Carrera who, in 1854, would be declared "*Presidente Vitalicio*—His Most Excellent Señor Don Rafael Carrera, President for Life of the Republic, Captain-General of the Forces, General Superintendent of the Treasury, Commander of the Royal Order of Leopold of Belgium, and Honorary President of the Institute of Africa."

What was most astonishing about Carrera was his ultraconservatism, born entirely of ignorance rather than a profound respect for tradition. And what was most frightening about Rafael Carrera was his absolute sincerity.

The power of Rafael Carrera was great. But he did not yet possess a formal office in Guatemala or with the Central American Confederation, although he certainly exercised an authority that meant life and death. It was clear to John Lloyd Stephens, President Van Buren's confidential agent, that he still had not found the official government of Central America. Stephens, however, had just so much patience for his diplomatic duties, and soon his hunger for adventure diverted his attention from politics long enough to undertake a tour of the country, visiting the ruins of beautiful Antigua, climbing the great volcano of Fuego, and conquering the ladies of the city of Mixco with his dashing tales of lost cities, great Indian leaders and close calls with death.

Then it was time to return to Guatemala City, for the reunion with Frederick Catherwood was scheduled for the Christmas holidays, which were only a few days away. The road lay across a peaceful wide plain where there was not the slightest indication that the region was convulsed with violence and death. Like the great volcanoes of this land, there was everywhere the impression of overwhelming beauty and tranquillity until sudden upheaval brought chaos to a world still in the process of being born.

On their sightseeing journey, Stephens and Augustin overtook a man and woman on horseback; he had a gamecock tucked under his arm, and she carried a guitar. A little boy was hidden away among the bedding piled high on a pack mule, and four lads followed along on foot, each carrying a gamecock wrapped in a grass mat, with only the heads and tails of the birds visible. The family was going to the capital to celebrate the holidays. With this festive group Stephens re-entered the gate of the city after eight days of adventures in the Guatemalan countryside.

At the American Legation Stephens found a letter from Frederick Catherwood, written from Esquipulas. It announced very bad news: Catherwood had been robbed by his servant Francisco, had become severely ill with fever, and was forced to leave his work at the ruins of Copan. To add to his misery, he had had to throw himself on the mercy of Don Gregorio. Fortunately, the don was uncharacteristically generous to the ailing Catherwood, who had slowly recovered at the hacienda and was now determined to return to the Copan ruins and complete his work before joining Stephens in Guatemala City.

All of this news greatly distressed John Stephens, who felt that he had neglected his friend since their separation. Worst of all, the messenger whom Stephens had sent to escort Catherwood back to the capital had passed through the ruins of Copan while the artist was bedridden at the nearby hacienda of Don Gregorio, and had somehow failed to find Catherwood. For the moment there was nothing which could be done, but Stephens decided that after a day's rest he and Augustin would set off in search of their English friend.

In a gloomy mood, Stephens got dressed and went to a

reception at the home of Señor Juan Zabadours, a former minister to England, where he amazed the aristocrats with stories of his great ruins. The immaculate white-powdered Spanish ladies giggled. "Surely you do not mean to tell us that these mestizos have built great cities in the middle of the jungle!" And there was laughter and many expressions of ridicule. "If that is the case"— the lady smirked from behind her fan—"then these latinos are holding out on us, Mr. Stephens, for they should be building our great mansions and cathedrals if they are such mighty architects!"

Stephens nodded slowly, and then he said, "I think not, dear madame. The ruins of which I speak are structures of the most lofty conception and not the humble Spanish imitations of your little *criollo* towns." Then Stephens excused himself and walked away.

It was Christmas Eve, the night of El Nacimiento, and the grand *sala* of Señor Zabadours was filled with the mindless aristocrats Stephens had come to disdain. Her Britannic Majesty's Consul General, Mr. Chatfield, gave Stephens the kind of lavish diplomatic greeting which normally disguises contempt. And all around him were elegant powdered ladies who possessed such a mania for a fair complexion that they constantly hid from the sunlight, for in Central America there was great pride in being *criollo*—one of pure white blood, descended from the Spanish conquistadores. And those with Indian blood made every effort to conceal it.

At one end of the *sala* was a raised platform, with a verdant covering decorated with branches of pine and cypress, filled with little birds made of paper. There was an arbor with figures of men and animals representing a rural scene, and a curiously graceless doll in a cradle. The doll was as pale as a Flemish madonna and had wide vacant eyes and bright red lips.

Always, at this season, every noble house of Guatemala had its own Nacimiento. The figure of the Christ, according to the wealth of the household, was adorned with the family jewels, pearls and precious stones. Every night the houses were opened to every citizen, without invitation, so people could admire the riches on display. The civil war, however, had dimmed the gaiety of the holiday. The houses were barred, in fear that the Indians of Carrera might enter.

The party was small, confined to the elite of the capital, who dined lavishly and then danced and smoked until midnight, when the ladies put on their mantillas, and all the guests departed for the cathedral for the imposing ceremonies of Christmas Eve. The aristocrats occupied a special platform, while the immense floor of the church was crowded with villagers. The ritual was opulent and filled with marvelous music and sounds.

But when Stephens finally reached his bed at three in the morning the bells had been long silent. He fell asleep almost at once.

The Christmas Day mass had been said in all the churches before he awoke. In the afternoon was the first bullfight of the season, and Stephens and a friend were about to leave the legation for the Plaza de Toros when there was a loud knocking at the door of the courtyard and in rode Frederick Catherwood, armed to the teeth, pale and thin, and jubilant at having reached Guatemala City alive. The two friends had an affectionate reunion almost before Catherwood could dismount, with much handshaking, embracing and sighs of relief—for each was certain that the other had been molested, imprisoned, tortured or murdered. Catherwood arrived in advance of his luggage, but Stephens insisted upon dressing him up in his own wardrobe and taking him to the bullfight. It was the first festive occasion for them since the day they had purchased the ruins of Copan. They spent several happy days recounting their adventures.

On New Year's Day 1840, Guatemala was celebrating a spring day while Stephens and Catherwood reminisced about snow, red noses and blue lips, blazing fires and piping hot beverages. Meanwhile the landscape of Central America was filled with flowers and rich green foliage. The bells of thirty-eight churches and convents tolled loudly in honor of the New Year. The shops were closed and there was no market in the plaza. Well-dressed ladies and gentlemen strolled toward the cathedral, where the elegant, festive music of Mozart resounded through the aisles and vaulted ceilings. A priest, speaking in Spanish, proclaimed morality, religion and love of country. The floor of the church was thronged with whites, mestizos and Indians—all avoiding each other. On a high bench opposite the pulpit sat the local chief of state, and at his side was Rafael Carrera, dressed in an elegant uniform. Stephens leaned against a pillar and watched the Indian leader. If he correctly read that proud brown face, then Carrera had already forgotten war and the garish stains of blood, and he was filled with fanatic religious enthusiasm, exactly as the priests would have him.

The ceremonies ended, and a way was cleared by the crowd. Rafael Carrera, accompanied by the priests and the chief of state, moved down this auspicious path, awkward in his movement, with his eyes fixed on the ground or with furtive glances at the throng that surrounded him. He breathed a sigh of relief when he came out into the open air again. A thousand ferocious-looking soldiers were drawn up on either side of the door. A wild burst of music greeted Carrera as he stepped into the brazen sunlight. The faces of the Indian soldiers glowed with unlimited devotion. A broad banner was unfurled, with stripes of black and red, inscribed *"Viva la religion!"* and *"Paz o muerte a los Liberales!"* Unhesitatingly, Carrera stepped to the front of this massive procession, and with banners flying, wild music playing and a deadly stillness among the aristocrats, he marched off to the executive mansion.

Rafael Carrera, however, was not the official head of government. If anyone truly represented the federal government of Central America it was his rival Morazan, who was rumored to still have a force in the field somewhere in Salvador. On Sunday, January 5, 1840, John Lloyd Stephens set out in search of Morazan. Frederick Catherwood agreed to accompany him as far as the Pacific Ocean, which neither of the explorers had seen before. At noon the muleteer Stephens had hired arrived, with his mules, his wife and a ragged little son. There were difficulties in getting local visas from the Guatemalan government, which feared that Stephens intended to present his diplomatic credentials at San Salvador which, in effect, would recognize the existence of the federal government of Morazan.

This political distrust of the United States was augmented by the report in newspapers which arrived that day by courier from Mexico. The papers had an account of an invasion of the northern territories of Mexico by the armed forces of Texas under Sam Houston. Stephens had had prior information on this subject, but he considered it diplomatic to profess ignorance of the entire affair. He also denied that the Texans had the support of and were being urged on by the government of the United States. No one at Government House, where Stephens and Catherwood pleaded for their visas, believed in the innocence of the United States. Most felt certain that after El Norte subjugated Mexico it would surely invade Guatemala. All these circumstances evolved rapidly into the widespread belief that John Lloyd Stephens' mission was highly secretive and had some special connection with the party of the Federalists at San Salvador. It was only with the greatest effort, and with considerable assistance from diplomats, that the visas were finally issued, and even then Stephens' document didn't indicate his official character.

When they were finally ready to depart, the muleteer had not yet finished his dramatic leave-taking of his family. His tearful wife and son accompanied him; and at some distance from the city the caravan was obliged to stop in the middle of the road in the scorching sun while the final good-byes were exchanged.

After a long march they arrived at the port of Iztapa, where Stephens was able to book passage for Augustin and himself on the French ship *Melanie*, which was sailing for El Salvador. Later, while having supper at the house where they were living prior to boarding the ship, they heard a great uproar in the street. A man ran into the dining room to tell Stephens and Catherwood that a mob was trying to murder their servant Augustin. Their dinner host and the Captain of the *Melanie* explained that the commotion was probably a machete fight and warned against leaving the house and getting involved. But Stephens felt a deep loyalty and affection for their servant, and dashed into the hall, where Catherwood immediately joined him. They were in the corridor in search of a weapon when the uproar of the crowd descended upon them. The gate of the house burst open, and a crowd rushed in, dragging with them Augustin, with his machete drawn. He was so tipsy that he could hardly stand but nonetheless wanted to fight the whole world singlehanded. With difficulty they managed to get him entangled among the saddle gear and disarmed him. He collapsed into a heap, tried briefly to rise and finally fell asleep with the most outrageous snoring.

The next day Augustin awoke with a terrible hangover, which a strong dose of *aguardiente* quickly cured. John Stephens, however, awoke with a malady which could not be cured. For the first time he had the fever. His head ached, he felt a severe pain in the small of his back, a feeling of numbness overcame his legs, and in his bloodstream millions of plasmodia multiplied at a frantic speed, bursting his red blood cells and so totally invading his body that they could never be dispelled. The violence of the fever grew. All day and night he felt like his blood was boiling. Catherwood gave him a powerful dose of medication, and toward morning he finally fell asleep; but the ailment was only temporarily subdued by the medicine. John Lloyd Stephens had contracted the "tropical kiss of death"—malaria.

At two in the afternoon he staggered, with Augustin's help, on board the *Melanie*. Though Catherwood planned to return to Guatemala City, having seen as much of the Pacific Ocean as he ever wanted to see, he came on board and remained until the ship got under way. He was deeply concerned about Stephens' health, having suffered the same symptoms himself at Copan. He tried to talk his friend out of the voyage to Salvador, but Stephens insisted that he was feeling better and expressed a heroic devotion to the fulfillment of his assignment from President Van Buren.

When the *Melanie's* Captain announced their departure, Catherwood reluctantly left his friend, urging him to finish his diplomatic chores and return to the capital as soon as possible so they could get back to the far more pleasant business of hunting for ruins. Stephens responded with an enthusiastic smile and bade Catherwood good-bye over the railing. Then the evening breeze filled the sails; for a few moments he could still see Catherwood, a dark spot on the shore. Then the waves rose high, the ship was surrounded by ocean and Stephens lost sight of his friend. He remained on deck for only a short time. He and Augustin were the only passengers. The first mate had made him a bed in the cabin directly under the stern windows. But Stephens could not sleep. Even with the windows and doors wide open the cabin was dreadfully hot; the air was thick, humid and full of mosquitoes. The Captain and mates slept on deck; and though Stephens was warned about the grave danger of the night air, at midnight he finally escaped the mosquitoes and went out into the breeze. It was a bright starlit night. The sails flapped against the mast. The ocean was utterly calm, and the dark irregular line of the coast was broken by a profusion of volcanoes. The North Star was lower in the sky than he had ever seen it before and, like himself, seemed waning. A young sailor on watch spoke to him of the deadliness of the fever and the mysteriousness of the night. Malaria was still a fabulous disease, misunderstood and without effective prevention or treatment. Stephens listened to the sailor's tale while stretching out in the freshness of the night, and eventually he fell asleep.

The next day the fever recurred and the Captain put Stephens under ship's discipline, ordering a steward to stay with him: *"Monsieur, un vomitif."* And by the afternoon, *"Monsieur, une purge."* But when the *Melanie* arrived at Acajutla, Stephens was unable to go ashore. The Captain, however, engaged a horse, mules and a muleteer for Stephens before the *Melanie* departed. All afternoon Stephens sat on the upper deck gazing at the ships in the harbor: an English brig from London and a *goélette* bound for Peru. The sailors of the *Melanie* dozed or they played cards. Six great volcanoes ringed the port, one of them emitting constant billows of white smoke, while from another came leaping flames

. and cinders. At night the volcano of Izalco was a great, pulsating ball of fire.

The next morning the mate took Stephens ashore in the launch. As soon as the boat struck the pilings, a crowd of Indians backed up against the side of the craft and Stephens was directed to mount the shoulders of one of them. Then as the waves receded for a moment the strapping Indian carried Stephens several steps toward the shore, then stopped and braced himself against the oncoming wave. Stephens clung to his great neck but, out of exhaustion, was fast sliding down his slippery sides. Quickly the Indian stepped forward and deposited his human cargo on the shore of El Salvador.

No sooner had the mate and sailors taken leave of him than Stephens had a violent ague, followed by an intense fever, in comparison with which all he had suffered before was nothing. He stumbled blindly and called out for water. An old woman with a blank expression on her leathery face poured water down his throat. He continued to beg for more, until she grew tired of giving water to him and went away. Suddenly he became lightheaded, wild with pain, and wandered aimlessly among the miserable huts, conscious only that his brain was scorching. He began to babble, asking for Augustin, who had gone off to load the mules. He could not recall a single word of Spanish, and tried in English to beg a group of old Indian women to get him a horse he could ride to Sonsonate. Some of them were laughing at him while others gazed silently at him with pity. A wrinkled old Indian, a man or a woman—he didn't know which—came slowly toward him, and as Stephens looked dimly into the stupendously old face he saw lavish feathers sprouting from the Indian's head, blooming into a magnificent headdress like those worn by the idols of Copan. This great god, this lofty ruler of the ancient cities, took his hand and slowly led him out of the blistering sunlight toward the deep shadows of an immense ceiba tree. But Stephens whimpered suddenly, for the dimness around the tree frightened him and he tugged weakly against the hand which drew him into the darkness, "I do not want to go under that tree!" he wailed.

Then suddenly he fell through an endless succession of colors into the night.

At three in the afternoon Augustin found his master lying unconscious on his face, almost withered away by the sun. He wanted to put Stephens directly back on any ship bound for Guatemala, but the half-conscious American explorer would not hear of it and begged Augustin to take him to Sonsonate, where there were a hospital and doctors. Finally Augustin consented to the trip, though he thought the plan was madness, and Stephens was lifted into the saddle and they started into the open country. Stephens was so near to collapse that Augustin had to tie him to his horse. The heat was worse than it had been for weeks and sweat poured off the animals, though John Stephens' teeth chattered and he trembled with a chill. After three hours of agony, they arrived at Sonsonate.

Just as they were entering the town they encountered a superbly outfitted gentleman, mounted on a saddle tooled in silver over which was thrown a superb scarlet Peruvian pillion. Despite the fever, Stephens glanced up at this striking elderly man and offered him a respectful nod. This gentleman, he afterward learned, was Don Diego Vigil—the "government" for which Stephens had been searching.

The next day he formally met Don Diego Vigil, the Vice-President of the republic—the only remaining officer of the Central American Federation. Stephens explained his diplomatic business in the region and told him that he was en route to the capital with credentials from the United States, but that, in the state of anarchy of the country, he was totally at a loss as to what to do. In short, he asked Don Diego Vigil if a federal government really existed.

Don Diego shook his head sadly. "I fear, señor, that your diplomatic quest is hopeless."

That night John Lloyd Stephens addressed a formal letter to John Forsyth, Secretary of State of the United States. He stated regretfully that his official mission was impossible under the circumstances of the political upheaval of the region. He indicated that he intended, at his own expense, to inspect the then-infamous "canal route" through Nicaragua which had been planned and debated in America for fifty years. He also informed the Secretary of State that he planned to continue his archeological search in Yucatan, where there were reports of lost cities which greatly intrigued him.

Then Stephens packed away his diplomatic coat and booked passage to Costa Rica, the southernmost state of the Central American Federation, determined to enjoy a quiet sea voyage and then, while returning by land, to explore the Nicaraguan canal route between the Atlantic and Pacific. Snapping his luggage closed, Stephens called out, "Augustin!" And together they descended to the harbor.

After a pleasant sea voyage southward along the shoreline of Central America and an excursion inland to San José, the capital city of Costa Rica, Stephens and Augustin finally began their overland journey back to Guatemala City on the thirteenth day of February. Their cargo was reduced to the absolute minimum, a hammock, a pair of alforjas and a poncho for the inevitable tropical rains. Augustin had packed biscuits, chocolate, sausages, sweets, and a supply of water. Gradually John Lloyd Stephens, who had a taste for exotica, had transformed himself into a rustic vagabond, collecting more and more of the wardrobe of the region, which he rolled up in an oxhide in the fashion of the natives.

Both the master and the servant were happy to be back on the road again; pleased by the lightness of their cargo, by the spirited energy of the mules, and the good humor of the muleteer they had secured in San José. Stephens smiled bravely as he looked forward to yet another terrific journey—twelve hundred miles of jungle, cowpaths and tiny villages! There had been only infrequent recurrences of the fever, and though rather weak, he felt better than he had for a week.

After a series of uneventful days, the little caravan arrived at the hacienda of Santa Rosa in Costa Rica. The sun was getting low when they came out of the forest into a large clearing. The house stood on the boundless plain, which was interspersed with groves of trees. And as Stephens rode up, a gentleman in the yard sent a servant to open the gate for the travelers. Don Juan José Bonilla met his guests on the wide porch of the hacienda, and before Stephens had time to present his credentials, welcomed him with a warm smile.

After making his guests comfortable in his handsome home, Don Juan invited Stephens to join him for dinner. While they were taking their places at the dinner table the master of the house explained that he had been an active member of the liberal party in his native city of Cartago. He had worked to carry out the principles of the liberal government, trying to save his country from the disgrace of falling back into despotism. But he was highly persecuted for his political ideals, his property was heavily taxed, and finally, four years before, he had withdrawn from politics and retired to his hacienda.

In the midst of the conversation they heard a terrible noise over their heads, which seemed to Stephens as if the roof were being torn open. Instantly Don Juan gaped at the ceiling and leaped from his chair, throwing his arms around the neck of his servant and shouting, *"Temblor! Dios, temblor!"* Earthquake!

Suddenly everyone was rushing for the doors and windows. Stephens sprang from his chair, made one leap across the room and fell into the courtyard of the house. The earth rolled and careened dizzily, pitching to and fro as it seemed to fall away from under his feet. He struggled to stay upright, throwing his arms open involuntarily to save himself from falling. His feet barely made contact with the jostling earth. Halfway across the yard he stumbled over a man who had fallen to his knees. He did not know where to run. He felt helpless and totally out of control. Just when he was about to run full speed into the open plain, Don Juan shouted a warning to him. He was leaning on his servant, crying to Stephens to come back under the protection of the trees.

The sky was pitch dark, and within the sickeningly swaying house which creaked and groaned with every roll of the earth, a single candle was lighted. Stephens and Don Juan peered into the house, calling to the servants still inside who were kneeling and praying in the dining room which could at any moment collapse upon them. The shocks continued for two minutes and then suddenly ended.

It was silent. Everyone waited anxiously, fearful that the tremor would begin again. "Mother of God!" Don Juan whimpered with a shudder, "it is over."

Exhausted and nearly senseless, Stephens went to bed. But he could not sleep. Central America teemed with insects, and riding through the woods brought so many ticks down upon him that he had to brush them off with his hand. During that day he had been in agony and twice he stripped at a stream and tore the pests out of his flesh, but this gave only temporary relief. Irritated lumps covered his body. Now in his room he plucked the insects out of his skin, leaving bleeding wounds. Don Juan, being an old hand at the problems of travelers, sent a servant to help Stephens, who, by touching the ticks with a small ball of black wax, drew them from their burrowing places without pain; yet these vermin left behind countless wounds which did not heal for weeks.

Earthquakes and insects notwithstanding, in a few days Stephens had reached Granada on Lake Nicaragua, where he was the guest of Don Federico Derbyshire. Stephens' appearance in Granada caused a minor sensation, and he was constantly congratulated for his escape from prison. "I beg your pardon," Stephens said, dumbfounded, "but, señor, I have not recently been in prison."

News had reached Granada that John Lloyd Stephens, American diplomat, had been arrested (no one seemed to know for what offense) and was in prison in San Salvador. Stephens happily reported that his only recent escape was with his life during a Costa Rican earthquake. If the tales of his arrest were humorous, the real news was distressing. Civil war had broken out again and the troops of Nicaragua had joined the soldiers of Honduras under the banner of Carrera and had slaughtered the followers of Morazan at El Potrero. After the battle, fourteen officers were shot in cold blood, and not a single prisoner survived.

The most terrible news of all for John Stephens was the fate of Colonel Juan Galindo, the soldier and explorer whose account of a visit to the ruins of Copan had been the impetus for Stephens and Catherwood's excursion to that ancient city. After the battle at El Potrero, Galindo had attempted to escape with two dragoons and a servant boy whom he hoped to save. He passed through an Indian village, where he was recognized as a leader of the cause of Morazan. He was captured and while dogs barked and women shouted curses, he was murdered by a dozen Indians with machetes. His archenemy, the British Consul Frederick Chatfield, noted his death as a casual p.s. in a letter to Colonel MacDonald of Belize: "I forgot to mention . . . Galindo was fittingly slaughtered." For John Stephens the death of Juan Galindo was an atrocity, and a devastating warning of the crisis which was at hand. More than ever it became imperative for Stephens to get back to Guatemala City as quickly as possible.

The political tension mounted as the troops of Carrera searched out the remnants of the forces of Morazan in an effort to annihilate them. As the civil war escalated, suspicion became unreasonable and the authority of local clerks and petty officials verged on despotism. Stephens' journey became increasingly dangerous.

From the war-torn city of Leon, in Nicaragua, Stephens' route led to the coast of the Pacific. Beyond the volcano of Coseguina was the Gulf of Fonseca, which made a large indentation in the coastline. It was customary to cross the gulf in a small flatboat called a "bungo," while sending mules and cargo by land, around the entire shore of the gulf—a journey which took six days or more. Stephens was warned that the Honduras troops were presently marching against Salvador and would surely seize his mules and cargo were he to send them by the customary route. So he sent Augustin ahead to El Viejo, where the owners of the bungos were headquartered, with instructions to hire the biggest boat available; for *el americano loco*, as his servant explained to the boatmen, had the crazy plan of taking his mules and cargo with him on a bungo across the gulf.

The next morning the exhausted Augustin returned. *"Oui, monsieur, vous avez le bateau*—you have the boat." But the boatman had warned that the embarkation must be undertaken at Stephens' own risk.

"And what is that supposed to mean?" he barked at Augustin impatiently.

"Please, monsieur, there is a war."

The arrangements for hiring the boat became progressively complicated. By the time the travelers reached the town of Chinandega they received word that permission to embark was required from the local chief of state because of the military situation, and no one was allowed to cross the gulf, which was the frontier of El Salvador, without such a permit.

"Merde, monsieur. We cannot wait so long," Augustin complained. "Any day the soldiers, they will start the shooting."

At noon they reached the little port of Nagoscolo, located on a narrow river which emptied into the Gulf of Fonseca. There was nothing but a single miserable hut where a woman tediously washed corn while her pathetic child groveled in the mud, its body covered with running sores. The river was nearly dry and was surrounded by mud flats baked hard in the sun and littered with several rotting bungos that had gone aground. It was a place which smelled of disease, and Stephens was relieved that he would not have to remain there long. But the miserable woman, with a hideous voice, screeched in his ears that the *guarda* had been sent direct from the capital with orders not to let anybody embark without a permit. *"Si, si,"* she yelled, following after Stephens, the *guarda* had already gone down river in a canoe to search for a bungo which had attempted to get away without a permit. He waved the wretched woman away and walked down to the bank in hope of catching the guard alone when he returned.

It was more than an hour before the soldiers reappeared. Everywhere were travelers, some who had been waiting for three days for permits from Leon. Stephens did his best to convince the guard that his boat must be allowed to leave despite the fact that he did not have a permit. The guard listened carefully and said *"Si, señor"* to everything, but when Stephens spoke about embarking, he said, "Oh, but señor, you have no permit."

The situation was becoming impossible. The road before Stephens went directly through the eye of the storm, and if he delayed as much as a day, the political situation could get so difficult that all passage to Guatemala City would be blocked. So he accompanied the guard to the hut, and with great anxiety he showed him *all* his official papers, a larger bundle than he had ever seen before, with bigger seals and more ribbons, trying somehow to give the guard an overwhelming impression of his importance. Several times he agreed to let Stephens pass and then withdrew his approval; but at length, after he was given a letter promising him the unlimited protection of the United States of America, he agreed to let the bungo go.

It was almost dark when Stephens and his crew dragged the unwilling mules aboard. To show his gratitude for their fast loading of the flatboat, Stephens invited the boatmen to supper and several rounds of *aguardiente*, which put them all in very good spirits. Stephens politely hurried them through the dinner, in fear that the guard might suddenly reverse his decision.

Then just as the whole company was about to board the bungo, a new man suddenly entered the scene and said flatly that no one would be allowed to embark without a permit. Stephens was on the verge of a rage by this last-minute interruption of his plans, and fairly bullied this newcomer out of the hut. The guard, intimidated by the official's threat to report the whole matter to the Commandant at Viejo, tried to withdraw his approval, but Stephens simply would not hear of it. He told the guard that the thing had been settled and that he would not be trifled with. "And I hope I make myself clear!" With that Stephens picked up his gun and told the boatmen to follow him. The crew was delighted by the commotion and with the surge of *aguadiente* were feeling exceedingly brave and cavalier. The guard and all the travelers who had been compelled to wait for permits followed after Stephens, who unhesitantly got on board followed by his men, who were so tipsy that they laughed wildly and pushed all opponents out of the way.

"Señor! I order you to halt!" the guard shouted.

The boatmen shoved the boat clear of the shore and it quickly moved into the current.

"Señor! You must have a permit!"

Stephens was utterly confident. Then someone from the shore cried out that fifty armed soldiers had just arrived from Leon.

"Stop or we will shoot!"

It was pitch dark and they could see nothing. Stephens suddenly envisioned a whole squad of crazed soldiers firing point-blank into the river, but the boatmen were beside themselves with laughter and shouted defiance at the shore.

The bungo was swept into the current and was moving very rapidly, whirling around and hitting against the overhanging branches. The mules tumbled down, and in the darkness and confusion the boat struck another bungo with a violent crash that knocked the entire crew into a heap on top of the mules. Stephens was certain that they were about to be sent to the bottom. But the men got back on their feet amidst enormous laughter and managed to get the bungo under control. The men sat down to the oars and pulled for a few minutes as if they were determined to tear the old bungo out of the water, shouting all the time like banshees let loose in the dark.

By nine in the morning they had reached the mouth of the

river and hoisted the sail which instantly caught a fine wind that took them into the Gulf of Fonseca. The sun was white and the heat was insufferable even on the water. They followed along the coast, and by eleven o'clock they were opposite the volcano of Coseguina. That evening Stephens stretched out on the pilot's bench under the tiller and dozed contentedly as the bungo passed the volcano of Tigre situated among an archipelago more beautiful than the lovely isles of Greece. The wind kept the bungo swiftly moving over the bright green water until at last they dropped their big stone anchor in the harbor of La Union, the frontier port of El Salvador!

The Commandant of the harbor was one of Morazan's veterans and he gave Stephens information that made him more anxious than ever about the safety of the roads. General Morazan had left the port only a few days before, having accompanied his family this far on their escape to Chile. On his return to San Salvador he intended to march against Guatemala for a showdown with Carrera's troops. Stephens was determined to overtake Morazan and complete his dangerous journey under the escort of his army, trusting that he could avoid being caught in a battle or being recognized as an acquaintance of Carrera. So at five in the afternoon on the next day Stephens, Augustin, the mules and the muleteer set out for the city of San Salvador.

In the afternoon of the second day they came in sight of the Lempa River, a vast stream pouring out into the Pacific. Stephens' caravan descended to the bank to a crossing place which was at least a half-mile wide and required a boat for transporting cargo and passengers to the other bank. Stephens went down to the water's edge and shouted for the boatman on the opposite side. Gradually other parties were arriving, all fugitives, and they soon formed a crowd on the shore. Finally the boat came, taking aboard sixteen mules, saddles, luggage and as many men, women and children as could stow themselves away amidst the cargo. The boat crossed in the dark.

On the opposite bank Stephens was appalled to find every hut and shed filled with frightened fugitives, families huddling under the trees, and men and women crawling out of hovels to congratulate friends who had put the Lempa River between them and the enemy. Stephens, at this point, was not certain which faction of the war they considered "the enemy." He and his men slept on their piled luggage, which had been heaved onto the riverbank, and before daylight they quickly loaded the mules and were again in the saddle.

The Honduras troops of Carrera were coming up quickly from the south. Already they had taken San Miguel and San Vincente, and were marching on San Salvador, where Stephens had just arrived. For four days he had been running just in front of Carrera's troops trying to overtake Morazan's forces. Now it seemed as if there would be a great collision of both armies. The muleteer would go no farther and it was impossible to engage another for the dangerous journey to Guatemala City. No one would venture on the road until the result of Morazan's expedition was known, and even to get transport as far as Sonsonate was difficult. Everywhere there was talk of the ensuing battle, and great excitement filled the city. There was no thought of flight. The spirit of resistance was overpowering. The imprisoned soldiers who were willing to fight Carrera's troops were released and furnished with guns, and drums resounded through the streets calling for more volunteers.

Though Stephens was in great danger of being caught in a frantic crossfire, he admitted to himself that he had a strong curiosity to see a city taken by assault. But he didn't have the least excuse to stay on to witness the battle. He had his passport in hand and the mules were ready. But still he lingered. At noon the city was still. Stephens lounged on the shady side of the plaza in a mesmerized mood, listening to the fearful silence. At two in the afternoon two hundred lancers assembled in the plaza and then set off with a feeble shout under a burning sun. Stephens felt let down and disappointed by war and regretted that he had not left San Salvador sooner.

Meanwhile Augustin was agonized with fear, and he smiled

with relief when his master finally told him to mount. In a few moments they were beyond the gate of silent, waiting San Salvador. Stephens glanced back momentarily and then left the capital to its fate.

From Sonsonate it was a four-day journey to Guatemala City, but the officials of the city told Stephens he was mad to leave Sonsonate at such a tense time.

"Yes, yes, I understand the danger . . . but I have an appointment," Stephens explained quietly. Frederick Catherwood was expecting him. The rainy season was at hand and by the loss of any more time the explorers would be prevented from visiting Palenque and the other ruins which they were determined to see. After all, Stephens insisted, "I have done my diplomatic duties. I have crept through more of the regions of Central America than most of you have seen. I have endured arrest and political threats and rudeness and pitched battles. But, my dear friends, I came to Central America to see ancient ruins and I shall see them."

John Stephens considered it safer to pass through the troubled countryside while the troops were in a state of suspension than after the floodgates of war were fully opened. And so he was determined to leave for Guatemala City at once. In the midst of the debates and discussions about Stephens' journey, a tall thin Spaniard introduced himself. His name was Don Saturnino Tinocha, a merchant from Costa Rica also on his way to Guatemala City, and, on the advice of his friends rather than his own judgment, he had already been waiting a week at Sonsonate for the political situation to turn less violent. Stephens told Don Saturnino that they were of the same mind exactly and that he was determined to set out the next day for Guatemala City by way of the town of Ahuachapan. At once they agreed to go together. When they finally departed, their friends were certain that they would never see either of them again. And they were very nearly right.

While Augustin guarded the door with a machete, John Stephens tried to get some sleep. There were few people in bed in the little town of Ahuachapan, for disastrous news raced through the streets as the inhabitants hid in doorways and spoke in whispers of the terrible defeat of Francisco Morazan by the rebel forces of Rafael Carrera. Morazan's troops had been razed, shattered into retreating fragments, and what was left of his valiant army was in flight with Carrera in close pursuit. Stephens and Don Saturnino Tinocha were both so tired after a difficult day that they decided to go to sleep despite the chaos of the town. So with Augustin standing at the door, frozen with fear and clutching a murderous machete, the two travelers had fallen into their hammocks without undressing.

At one in the morning Stephens and Don Saturnino were violently awakened when a hysterical colonel burst through the door and was very nearly decapitated by the fear-struck Augustin.

"*La gente viene!*" he shouted. "The men of Carrera are coming!"

Outside, the people of Ahuachapan had gone mad: swords glittered in the moonlight, soldiers were saddling horses in the courtyard and everywhere church bells began to clang. The Federalistas of Morazan were running for their lives. Stephens and Don Saturnino leaped to their feet and, grabbing the Colonel by the sleeve, urged him to tell them exactly what was happening. "Save yourselves. *La gente viene!*" he yelled frantically and pulled himself free of their grasp, too fearful to let them detain him for another minute.

Stephens cast one worried look at Don Saturnino and both of them instantly understood their predicament. "Saddle the mules!" he shouted to the trembling Augustin, who was blubbering with fright at the thought of the vengeance of Carrera's soldiers. Stephens' order jolted him into instant action and in a panic he flew from the room and out into the courtyard, where he readied the mules at record speed. Meanwhile Stephens and Don Saturnino quickly conferred and decided that it would be an error to try to escape with the refugees since this would make them appear to be enemies. Instead they would ride out of town by themselves, taking the road they intended to take for Guatemala City, and if anyone stopped them they would tell them the truth, that they were travelers who had no part in the war.

Outside, as they hastened to prepare for their departure, the streets were filled with brilliant moonlight. Women and children fled in every direction, but there were no sobs or cries of fear. There was utter silence except for the incessant, terrible clanging of the bells. On the steps of the church the sick and deformed had been quickly deposited, where they wrapped themselves in blankets and cowered in dread. Soon, except for these abandoned invalids, there was not a single person to be seen in Ahuachapan. Don Saturnino and John Stephens had been left in sole possession of the town. Now even the church bells has ceased ringing. A breeze came in off the plain, but it brought no sound of charging armies or fitful battles in the night.

So if there was to be no battle there was no reason to run. It was also possible that when Carrera led his troops into the town he might recognize John Stephens as a friend.

At dawn a little beggar boy ran helplessly through the empty street shouting, *"La gente viene! Ayudame, madre!"* Stephens and Don Saturnino followed the trembling boy, who climbed to the top of the steeple. From there they could see the *cachurecos* of Carrera at a distance, descending a hill in single file, their muskets shining in the rising sunlight. Stephens quickly scrambled down to the street and went in search of Augustin and the mules.

Stephens raced around a corner and abruptly came face to face with a single soldier moving cautiously and peering into every house as if he suspected to be shot in the back. He was in a state of shock after suddenly confronting Stephens, who, on the other hand, managed to give a semblance of composure by telling the soldier, who was a courier for his superior officer, that there was no one left in the town to oppose the forces of Carrera. Clearing his throat commandingly, Stephens forthwith surrendered the town.

Very soon the main body of the troops swarmed into Ahuachapan, led by General Francisco Figueroa. As he approached, Stephens and his party diplomatically removed their hats and the General returned the gesture and passed by. About a hundred fierce lancers followed after him, two abreast, with crimson flags on the ends of their lances and pistols in their holsters. As they passed, one ferocious-looking fellow looked fiercely at them and cried out, *"Viva Carrera!"* Stephens did not echo the declaration at once, and the soldier repeated it with sufficient rage to make clear that Stephens' life depended on his response. *"Viva Carrera, . . ."* he said flatly and turned back into the house until the soldiers had passed.

The army had hardly settled into the town when Francisco Morazan waged a frantic counterattack. Bullets flew through the streets and ricocheted off the church walls. General Figueroa, at a gallop, led his men out of Ahuachapan. The ferocity of the lancers had changed quickly into abject fear, and the arrogance of the foot soldiers turned into panic as one by one, at the crack of a rifle, they flinched, grasped at the air and fell into the road.

Stephens quickly bolted the door of the courtyard. Then the members of his party huddled behind the thick adobe walls of their house while shots burst and the cry of fleeing men filled their ears. After a momentary silence, there came the cry: *"Viva la Federacion!"* and Stephens knew that General Morazan had reoccupied the town and it was safe to come out of hiding. But it was not a victory.

General Morazan had entered Guatemala City a few weeks before and had battled for the central plaza, which he took by storm. With the arrival of his reinforcements he waited confidently. The bloody counterattack was led by Carrera. The Federalistas of Morazan lost half their number, including nearly every officer. Resistance was impossible; so Morazan stationed his remaining men to cover his retreat into El Salvador. The date was March 17, 1840.

Now in a fatalistic but orderly retreat, the defeated Morazan had forced Carrera's troops out of Ahuachapan, which provided the scant federal platoon with a moment's rest in their rush for home. Morazan's thoroughly disciplined men were bivouacked in the central plaza, where they hoped to remain unmolested until the morning, when they would continue their flight.

General Morazan was standing with several officers in the damp corridor of the city hall. A huge bonfire burned before the doorway, and he and his men were talking glumly as they drank chocolate. Morazan was perhaps forty-five years old; with dark eyes, a black mustache and a week's stubble on his tired face. The General shook John Lloyd Stephens' hand gratefully. The great soldier bowed and expressed deep apologies for the condition in which Stephens had found his country. He spoke of the treaties which had been made with the United States, about the long-discussed Nicaraguan Canal in which he urgently believed as an economic solution to his region's problems, and all the other reforms and improvements he had once planned for his people.

Stephens remained only a short time with the General and then, depressed by the utter wastefulness of war and its false promises of excitement and heroism, he returned to the house, where he prepared for his departure. The moon had risen slowly. He was anxious to set out, to put this sad scene far behind him.

John Stephens met with General Morazan one more time, in the morning before he left for Guatemala City. Without bitterness or malice the General spoke of the leaders of the Central Party, but Carrera himself he described as an ignorant and lawless Indian whom the party, now promoting him as a hero, would one day protest. "It is not the Indian whom I despise," Morazan said quietly. "You must believe me, it is not that, Mr. Stephens. My reforms are in the name of the Indians and the mestizos and the *criollos* too. But the Church has used the Indians to oppose my efforts to reduce the tyranny and greed of the padres! They have built a fortress of Indians behind which they can safely hide." Then he was silent.

General Morazan bowed politely. He was bound for Sonsonate, the capital of the straggled federation. But he did not then know that his arrival there would be greeted with the insults and invectives reserved for those who have been utterly defeated.

"I bade him farewell," Stephens told Don Saturnino as they left the silent town of Ahuachapan. "But I must admit to you, he was the most interesting of any man I met in this dreary country. Even his worst enemies admit that he has been exemplary in his private relations, and, what they consider no small praise, that he was not sanguinary. . . . The greatest outcry against General Morazan is his hostility to the Church. For his hostility to the Church there is the justification that it is at this day a pall upon the spirit of free institutions, degrading and debasing instead of elevating the Christian character. . . . I believe, Don Saturnino, and I beg you to forgive my candor in saying so, that the Central Party of Carrera has driven from these shores the best man in Central America."

These ideas were expressed by John Lloyd Stephens when General Morazan did not have a dozen allies left in Central America. His words represented an acute and excellent political insight. After little more than a century, his sentiments are exactly those held by Central Americans themselves.

The meeting with Francisco Morazan at Ahuachapan officially ended Stephens' diplomatic mission in Central America. Arriving in Guatemala City, he informed the Secretary of State that "The Federal Government was thus entirely broken up. There was not the least prospect of its ever being restored, nor for a long time to come of another being organized in its stead."

Everywhere he went friends welcomed him back to Guatemala. They considered that he had run the gauntlet for life and escaped from the most unspeakable dangers. It was difficult for him to accept the fact that these same friends would have been subjugated and defeated had Morazan fulfilled his dream of liberation. Repeatedly Stephens was stopped in the street or in a shop and asked to tell again the affair of Ahuachapan.

In the afternoon, unexpectedly, Frederick Catherwood arrived. He had spent a full month in complete peace and quiet at Antigua and had just returned from a second visit to Copan. Stephens could not have been happier to see anyone. The two friends tumbled into each other's embrace like Russian bears and resolved not to be separated again until they had explored the ruins to their hearts' content.

"By the way, Mr. Stephens," Catherwood said energetically, "the most smashing things have been happening to me. You will never guess! I have discovered a frightful lot of other ruins and I must tell you all about them! But how about you, my dear chap? You seem more than a bit bored. Hasn't anything exciting been happening in your life?"

 Stephens packed his diplomatic coat and as many other cumbersome possessions as he could spare and put them on a ship for New York. Catherwood reorganized his art materials required to render the ruins they hoped to discover. Only one project was allowed to divert their attention from the arrangements for the journey to Palenque. Stephens wanted, before leaving Guatemala, to open negotiations for the purchase of another ancient city: this time Quirigua.

Though Stephens had not personally seen the ruins of Quirigua, Frederick Catherwood's description of them convinced him to add a second ancient city to his collection of antiquated real estate. Catherwood had visited Quirigua by himself and had made some impressive drawings of what he had found in this ceremonial center, which was undoubtedly a satellite of Copan.

This was enough evidence to rouse Stephens' desire to possess it. The owners of the site were brothers, one of whom, Señor Pablo Payes, was then in Guatemala City. Stephens unhesitatingly approached this gentleman after exploring the plan of exporting the monuments of Quirigua to New York. The site was very close to the Motagua River and Stephens had the idea of transporting the huge sandstone stelae down the river and then by ship to the United States. All of these relics of the lost city, including one thirty-five-foot stele, which was probably the tallest pre-Columbian carving ever found, were to be reconstructed in New York.

Señor Payes said he would be more than happy to contribute to the great science of the United States, particularly since such antiquities were not in the least appreciated in his own country. But unfortunately for Stephens, Payes consulted the French Consul-General, who pointed out to him that the French government had paid hundreds of thousands of dollars to transport the obelisks of Luxor to Paris. If the Americans were willing to spend so much money for transport, the Frenchman slyly pointed out, perhaps the ruins were worth far more than they would admit.

Stephens had hoped to buy the monuments for a few thousand dollars at most. Payes demanded $20,000 and then sat back and confidently waited for better offers from France and Britain. Everyone withdrew from the negotiations and fortunately the ruins remained on their native soil.

While these unsuccessful transactions for the ruins of Quirigua were under way, John Stephens called upon Rafael Carrera, who, after the massacres of Quezaltenango, had established himself in Guatemala City. What the explorers wanted to obtain from the new master of Central America was some kind of document which would absolutely protect them and their caravan from all the horrendous experiences which Stephens had recently suffered in the war-torn region. He had already obtained letters from the Archbishop of Guatemala to all the padres along the route to Mexico, but one never knew for certain that God would necessarily remain on the side of those with the best artillery. For the moment the power of Rafael Carrera seemed considerably more dependable than that of the Almighty, and so Stephens shrewdly sought a passport signed in the unalphabetic hand of the former.

Carrera was enormously pleased to be of service to the representative of El Norte and sent his secretary to prepare such a document. In a few minutes Carrera was called out of the room. When he returned he brought back the passport himself, signed in his own hand, the ink still wet. It had taken him considerably longer than it would have taken to cut off a head, and he seemed far more proud of it. In fact it was the single occasion on which Stephens saw him smile.

Stephens and Catherwood had no time to lose. Palenque was almost one thousand miles distant and the rainy season was quickly approaching. And though no one in the city had ever made this precarious journey, everyone advised the explorers to give up all hope of reaching that far-distant place by land. There was little question that it would have been simpler to reach Palenque from New York than from where they were, but this fact did not discourage Stephens or Catherwood. "I dare say that I have seen more of this country than those of you who have lived here all your lives," Stephens said with confidence. "I have run about freely while your armies were attacking each other, and I have withstood your insects, humidity, and fevers. So what is another thousand miles to me?"

Not everyone was as optimistic. A countryman of Stephens', Dr. Weems from Maryland, urged him not to undertake the journey to Palenque. He warned that the whole Indian population of Los Altos was in a terrible state of excitement since the rise of Carrera, and there were constant rumors of a general massacre of whites. General Prem and his wife had been traveling very nearly the same route that Stephens and Catherwood would be taking to Mexico, and they had been attacked by a band of Indian assassins. The General was left on the ground for dead, and his wife was murdered. All of her fingers were cut off and the rings torn from the stumps. Such were the stories of the fate of travelers as the explorers were about to set out through one of the most remote districts of Central America. Then, to make matters worse, Lieutenant Nichols, the aide-de-camp of Colonel MacDonald, arrived from Belize with a report that Captain Caddy and Mr. Walker, who had been hurriedly sent out to reach Palenque in advance of Stephens and Catherwood, had been speared to death by hostile Indians of the region. Their bodies had been found nude and utterly bloodless.

Everyone in Guatemala, even Mr. Chatfield, the British Consul, urged the explorers to abandon all thought of traveling across the country to Palenque. Stephens and Catherwood seriously discussed the whole matter. They agreed that it was a very bad time to be making the long journey. And they very nearly decided in favor of an immediate return to New York, but they had set out with the purpose of going to Copan, Palenque and Uxmal and felt so determined to hold to that plan that they decided to risk everything for the unique delight of seeing what other men had not seen.

"If life isn't dangerous," Catherwood said with a casual air, "I dare say it is bound to be tedious. I have so many friends who have been careful, and I must confess, my dear Mr. Stephens, that they are among the most bored and boring men I have ever known!"

So on April 7, 1840, John Lloyd Stephens and Frederick Catherwood left for Palenque. On muleback they traveled the narrow trails that led through the high, pine-braced mountains of Guatemala, followed by the dutiful Augustin and a caravan of cargo-laden mules prodded by a young Indian muleteer and his helpers. The servant Augustin feared nothing as much as he feared his separation from Meester Estebans, whom he had come to revere as a godlike man who could face both Rafael Carrera and Francisco Morazan without fear. But the muleteers were not nearly so devoted and they would agree to a very short association with the caravan. It therefore became necessary to hire replacement mules and mule drivers at almost every village.

Meanwhile Frederick Chatfield had sent out a search party for Caddy and Walker, who still hadn't been heard from in over 140 days. Notwithstanding the reports that they had been murdered by Indians, Chatfield hoped that they had managed to beat Stephens and Catherwood to Palenque and might have a sensational report, even if it were posthumous. In his March 26 communiqué Chatfield stated: "I have no intelligence of our lost British travellers. In the midst of chaos and civil war Stephens is flying about the country to get materials for his book, and if he escapes fevers and other mischiefs he may perhaps be here soon. Personally, I never heard that there existed a road from Peten to Palenque, it might be through the Monte or bushwood, and hardly practicable. Mr. Stephens and his Yankified English artist, are gone to Quezaltenango, intending to get to Palenque across the Mexican frontiers. To go by land is in my opinion foolhardy, especially as there is little or nothing to see once you get there."

Thus far Stephens had managed to reach Lake Atitlan.

Atitlan stretched in the thin blue air between the flanks of immense volcanoes—a lake of incomparable solemnity, tinted by the azure reflections of its stupendous depths. In ancient times it had been a great center of Guatemala. Here Stephens hired an additional servant in an effort to make the duties of the faithful Augustin less difficult. But the new servant thoroughly vexed Augustin. His name was Bobon, which meant "great fool," and Augustin agreed that the description was apt. Almost at once the two servants were at each other's throats. In loading the mules for the departure from Lake Atitlan, they started quarreling. Augustin did not let up until the new servant recognized his inferior position in the caravan, and once the pecking order was firmly established, the sound of Augustin's commanding voice was virtually continuous day and night.

A rustic little lane off the main road brought Stephens and Catherwood to the ruins of Utatlan, which had already been well documented but which they wished to survey at least briefly. The ruin, lying just two miles from the village of Santa Cruz Quiché, was the center of the powerful Quiché tribes, which were considered very fierce merely because they were unchanged in customs since their days of dominance before the coming of the

*View of the Place of Sacrifice in ruins
at Santa Cruz del Quiche*

Spaniards. Their conversion to Christianity was superficial, and they still had their own idols in the mountains and ravines, where in silence and secrecy they practiced the rites of their forefathers. They were extremely cautious of strangers and had often attacked white men who defiled the ruins and sent them running for their lives.

At the end of Stephens and Catherwood's second day among the ruins their huipil-clad Indian servant, Bobon, introduced a rotund stranger who came stumbling along the stony path under a red silk umbrella, panting for breath while he chatted with Bobon in the language of the Quiché. He stopped and stared up at the explorers, who were on the summit of the ruin where Catherwood was busily making sketches. Stephens managed to recognize this stranger as the *cura* of the district, despite his most unconventional dress, and started descending to meet him. The padre suddenly laughed at the sight of the two white men awkwardly stumbling down the hill. The laughter was highly infectious, and by the time Stephens and Catherwood were at his side they too were laughing. Then all at once the padre stopped, looked at them very solemnly, pulled off his neckcloth, and wiped the sweat from his face. Then, silently as they watched him, he took out a cigar and, for no apparent reason, asked the visitors for news from Spain.

Stephens and Catherwood glanced at each other and shrugged.

"Ah, then you are not from Spain," the very large padre muttered distractedly while he searched for something in his old black coat which he did not find. "It is just as well, I expect. There is never any news from Spain anyway." Then he laughed merrily and rubbed his belly where the fabric was shiny and worn from his habitual rubbing. He wore a broad-brimmed glazed black hat, a pair of bright plaid trousers, a striped roundabout, a waistcoat, a flannel shirt, and under it a cotton shirt. He had washed when he last shaved, which was probably some weeks previous. He laughed uproariously when told that they had come to see the ruins, and said that he had laughed prodigiously himself when he first saw them. "Have a cigar," he said with a giggle, and passed them around to everyone.

This laughing padre was from Old Spain. He had seen the battle of Trafalgar, he said, and laughed whenever he thought of it. The French fleet, he recalled, had been blown sky high, and the Spanish fleet went with it. Lord Nelson was killed—all for some kind of glory—and he could not help laughing at the whole affair. He had left Spain to get rid of wars and revolutions, and now, he laughed, here he was. He had sailed with twenty Dominican friars and was promptly fired upon and chased into Jamaica by a French cruiser that didn't have anything better to do with itself. He got an English convoy to Omoa, where he managed to arrive just in time for the beginning of a revolution.

The padre's laughter was so rich and expressive that it was irresistible. Stephens and Catherwood had endured so much solemnity and anxiety that it felt marvelous to stand on a dusty hillside in the middle of nowhere and laugh uncontrollably.

Except for the Church, there were few things which the *cura* did not laugh at; but politics was by far his favorite topic of ridicule. He was in favor of Morazan. He was also in favor of

Carrera. And he laughed at both of them. Stephens and Catherwood immediately took to this laughing padre and, having
finished their work among the ruins, they accepted his invitation
to visit the convent. As they descended by a narrow path he
never stopped laughing at some greatness of folly of the world,
past, present and future. While the explorers packed their equipment, the padre sat with Bobon and Augustin dutifully at his feet,
discoursing with a keen sense of drama about Pedro de Alvarado,
Montezuma and the daughter of the King of Teepan Guatemala;
about books and manuscripts and curious old maps, to all of
which Bobon and Augustin listened without comprehending a
single word or moving a muscle, looking the *cura* directly in the
face, and answering his long low laugh with a respectful *"Si,
señor."*

While en route to the convent with the padre, he told his guests
that thirty years earlier, when he had first seen it, the ruin of
Utatlan had been standing and totally undisturbed. But shortly
after his arrival a small gold object had been found and sent to
Señor Francisco Zerabia, then the President of Guatemala, who
ordered a commission to search the entire ruin for hidden
treasure. Everything was quickly destroyed. The Indians, greatly
aroused by the desecration of their ancient palace, rose up and
threatened to kill anybody who laid another hand on the structure. "Ah," the *cura* said softly, "and but for this, every stone
would have been razed to the ground for a bit of gold."

The Indians of Quiché were highly feared and their region was
considered unsafe for whites, but the padre had no fear of them.
The Indians loved him. He had spent the greater part of his life
with them. And again he laughed. "Carrera believes we are saints
because we wear black robes. But if he decides he likes some other
color, then it will be time for Catholics to fly!" This he said with
peals of laughter until tears ran down his face. The more serious
the subject the louder the padre laughed.

At the convent the padre apologized for keeping his guests
waiting while he unlocked the thick, planked door of his room. "I
must keep it carefully secured or the cleaning women throw

everything in my chamber into a total confusion," he explained. When they entered the little room they found a table, several chairs, and two settees on which there was not a vacant place to put something or to sit down. Every spot was piled with articles—bottles, a cruet of mustard and another of oil, old bones, cups, plates, saucepans, a large lump of sugar, a box of salt, minerals and large stones, seashells, pieces of Indian pottery, skulls, cheese, books, maps and manuscripts. On the little shelf over his bed were two stuffed quetzal birds, the royal animal of the Quiché, the most beautiful that flies, whose plumes were not permitted to be used except by Indian royalty.

Amid this profuse confusion a corner was cleared on the table for dinner. The conversation now focused on the padre's extensive, if incredible, knowledge of the history of the local Indians. When this subject came up, the padre's whole manner was changed; his keen satire and his laughter were gone. "There is in the lore of these Indians sufficient interest to the mind and to the imagination," he said in earnest, "to occupy scholars and explorers for a lifetime." And his enthusiasm for the Indians' history and culture, like his laugh, was infectious.

"You will perhaps think I am telling you a fiction," he said softly, "but try to believe me if you can. There is a place in ruin beyond Santa Cruz Quiché which is inhabited by a mysterious race of Indians. Yes, it is so. Somewhere between the cordilleras of Guatemala and the flat jungle region of El Peten there exists a brown people who to this very day still live in the palaces they occupied before the coming of the Spaniards!"

Stephens and Catherwood glanced uncomfortably at one another. Could this be true? Could those whose ancestors had built the great monuments still be living in their old ways somewhere out there in the immense jungle?

"I do not believe everything I hear, but this is a world which still lives with legends and dreams, a place which is still wet with the rains of the Creation. I have seen it myself! Yes, it is so. I was told this story when I was a very young man at the village of Chajul in Vera Paz. And I was so intrigued by what I had heard that I climbed the highest peak of the cordillera—the very highest, which is perhaps twelve thousand feet! And from there, as the massive clouds parted, I saw the entire flat plain of Yucatan and a vast city spread over a great space, with temples white and glistening in the sunlight. The Indians of the Chajul say that no white man has ever reached this lost city. But it is there. I believe that it is somewhere out there still."

Stephens' eyes were fixed on the padre; Catherwood, however, was dubious. Then the *cura* took down a map and carefully pointed out the location of the city. Stephens felt a chill go through him, almost a sense of dread. Either such a lost world actually existed or the padre was quite mad. Or perhaps the whole matter was simply a mistake blown up to fantastic proportions. Today it is generally agreed that the temples towering over the jungle which the padre saw were probably the ruins of Tikal in Guatemala, which in Stephens' day were still totally unknown.

The next morning, when Stephens and Catherwood left the padre, he was calm and exceedingly kind but his irresistible laugh and enthusiasm were gone. He insisted on their accepting a gift of one of his beautiful stuffed birds as a token of their visit. Then he blinked his eyes and said good-bye.

The mules reluctantly came to life. The explorers mounted and started off, followed by Augustin, who insistently shouted at the dutiful Bobon, who carried on a long stick, like a standard, the stuffed quetzal bird given to Stephens by the padre.

Stephens and Catherwood rode along in good spirits. They were no longer easily recognizable as the dignified representatives of the much-touted civilizations of Europe and America. As their Indian carriers chanted in an alien old language, the explorers happily swayed to and fro in their saddles, gazing into the splendid otherness of the world around them. Little by little they had assumed a new and curious appearance—first with a native coat called *aguas de arma*, several undressed goatskins embroidered with rich red leather that was used as a covering in the rain; then with large straw hats which the Indians favored in the heat of the sun; and finally wearing an ever-growing number of bead and shell trinkets, feathers and handsomely woven sashes and headbands. As strange as this procession might have seemed to the city dwellers of New York, in the easy world of the jungle nobody saw anything especially unusual about the colorful dress of these strangers.

This extraordinary caravan reached Huehuetenango, almost on the Mexican border, in a dilapidated state. The backs of the cargo mules were so galled that it was cruel to continue using them. The saddle horse was not much better off. Augustin, in walking barefooted over the stony trails, had bruised his feet; and Bobon had consumed an enormous supper which gave him an unspeakable indigestion. He was always a tremendous eater and on the road absolutely nothing eatable was safe from him. Stephens was not too sorry to see him on his back, because the food-crazed servant had pilfered all the bread. However he could not help taking pity on the fellow when he rolled on the ground crying, "*Voy a morir! Voy a morir!*—I am going to die!" Catherwood, however, was not inclined to be gentle with such wretchedness, and took the patient in hand. With the use of a spoon which was unwillingly accepted by Bobon's throat, he quickly unloaded his greedy stomach. The ailment and the cure were sufficiently painful to effectively curtail Bobon's appetite during the rest of the journey. Lodging was quickly arranged in a small house and the explorers eagerly leaped into their hammocks.

The next morning, before Stephens was awake, his door was thrown open and he leaped instantly to his feet in a panic, grasping a machete in one hand and a pistol in the other—being fully prepared for emergencies after having spent some months in this war-torn land. He was flabbergasted to hear the intruder address him in English, calling him by name. It took Stephens a moment to recognize the man standing before him, for he was dressed in Guatemalan gear, his beard was long, and he looked nasty enough to have murdered half a dozen people. Then, to Stephens' great pleasure, he recognized Henry Pawling, a young American of thirty whom he had met when Pawling had been engaged as the major-domo of a cochineal concern near Amatitlan. He had heard that Stephens and Catherwood were on their way to Mexico and, disgusted with his job and the state of the country, he mounted his horse and, with all he owned tied on behind his saddle, rushed off to overtake the explorers in the hope of joining their caravan.

Catherwood was as delighted with Pawling as Stephens. His excellent command of Spanish, his ability to handle the Indians, and his rough manner with a pair of pistols and a short-muzzled double-barreled blunderbuss were welcome qualifications, and at once Stephens hired him as the general manager of the expedition.

That same day the caravan resumed its journey from Huehue-tenango. The explorers left behind an ailing mule, a horse in need of rest, a regretful Bobon and several ladies who were heartbroken at the loss of the *simpatico* Meester Estebans. The new party was reinforced by Henry Pawling and a fugitive Mexican soldier named Santiago. The whole company was under the escort of a respectable elderly muleteer who was setting out with empty mules in order to bring back a load of sugar. And the rear was brought up by Augustin, who was more loyal than ever and visibly pleased that he had survived the cannibal appetite of Bobon.

At Ocotzingo they were traveling the same route taken by the famous Captain Guillermo Dupaix, who had made a visit to Palenque in 1807 under a commission from the Mexican government. Stephens knew his famous work on Mexican antiquities which had been published in Paris in 1834, for it had greatly increased Stephens' curiosity about the ruins in the region.

Dupaix had stated that "Palenque is eight days' march from Ocotzingo." Stephens remembered those words as well as those which followed: "The journey is very fatiguing. The roads, if they can be so called, are only difficult paths, which wind across the mountains and precipices, which must be traveled sometimes on mules, sometimes on foot, sometimes on the shoulders of Indians, and sometimes in hammocks. We had with us thirty or forty vigorous Indians," Dupaix had written, "and they carried the luggage and hammocks. After having experienced in this long and painful journey every kind of fatigue and discomfort, we arrived, thank God, at the village of Palenque."

After having recited all of this to his comrades, Stephens said whimsically, "I am afraid, my dear friends, that we now have that journey before us."

Captain Dupaix, however, had not done full justice to the difficulty of the trip. Perhaps on his expedition it had not rained, but the Stephens party seemed to have rain as a constant companion. And in this region it rained with a fury they had not previously known. The conditions were so terrible that Pawling, unaccustomed to the rigors which Stephens and Catherwood had come to accept as normal, was so completely shaken that he decided to turn back and leave the caravan. Stephens was reluctant to try to persuade him to continue. So the luggage was separated. Catherwood bade Pawling a somewhat chilly good-bye—feeling as if he were deserting—and immediately rode on. Stephens, however, had second thoughts and while shaking Pawling's hand he made him an offer which was so excellent that Pawling decided to stay with the expedition. In a few moments both Americans overtook Catherwood, who acted as if nothing had happened in the first place.

There was another more serious matter than Mr. Pawling's near resignation. The travelers learned that three Belgian antiquarians had recently been turned back from their attempt to reach Palenque. An order from the Mexican dictator, General Antonio Santa Anna, forbade anyone without credentials from the capital of Mexico to visit the ruins. Pawling suggested that perhaps Stephens should visit Mexico City, where he could obtain a permit. But the waste of time seemed utterly ridiculous after all the trials they had endured to come so close to Palenque. The expedition held a council of war and there was a good deal of muttering and complaining. "I think it's uncivilized to expect someone to ride a thousand miles to Mexico City," Catherwood intoned glibly, "and then, if granted permission—"

"Which is doubtful," Stephens interjected.

"—if finally granted permission, to double back again, well . . ."

Stephens sniffed the air, indignant at the very prospect of such a situation. "To Palenque!" he exclaimed, "in defiance of General Santa Anna and all the other damn generals!"

The ruins of Palenque, buried in an immense jungle, would certainly not be guarded. And, besides, by now Stephens had not the slightest fear of soldiers or dictators or mighty generals. Palenque irresistibly drew the caravan deeper into the jungle. They had come over a thousand miles of impassable terrain and would not be stopped now by the whims of some petty tyrant who was having enough trouble fighting off the invading Texans in the north not to be terribly bothered if a few strangers wandered around his precious ruins. Besides, John Stephens had another reason for pushing ahead. He was giving careful consideration to the possibility of adding yet another antiquity to his growing list of ruined real estate.

 Early in the morning the expedition set out from Ocatzingo with an additional crew of twenty Indian workmen. Though it was only seven in the morning, already John Stephens felt faint with the heat and was overcome by the pain and fatigue of a violent headache. The fever had pounced upon him once again.

The countryside was every bit as wild and uninhabited as it had been before the Spanish invasion. The ragged road led through a deep forest so dense that it formed an impenetrable wall except for the narrow gash cut into it by the mule path. The branches jutted out at a height which barely allowed a man to travel on foot; and on the back of a mule it was constantly necessary to bend forward or to dismount. In some places the woods had been torn up and tossed into heaps by a recent tornado that had swept and battered the whole countryside.

They saw few people during the journey to Palenque. Three Indians passed them without even a glance, naked except for a piece of cloth around their groins. One of them, young, tall, swinging his arms proudly, and handsomely built, looked like a freeborn gentleman of the woods. After the sight of these Indians, they did not see another human being the entire day.

Just before ten in the morning they began the ascent of the mountain which lay between them and Palenque. Stephens felt reassured that no matter how difficult the climb might be, it would be nothing by comparison to the voyage over the Mico Mountain. He was wrong.

The day was blistering hot, the humidity so suffocating that it was difficult to breathe. The mules could barely clamber up the steep slope. And every piece of clothing, equipment and cargo seemed to multiply into great dead burdens. Stephens' headache by this time was ferocious and he could not even tolerate the pressure of the clothes on his back. He began to remove everything he could, and everyone else in the party followed suit; tossing swords, spurs and every other useless trapping into a pile which was then loaded onto the mules. Finally they had stripped down to their shirts and pantaloons, as near to the nakedness of the Indians as their self-consciousness would permit. Then the caravan moved forward.

First came four Indians, each with a large oxhide box, secured by an iron chain and padlock; then Augustin, with only a hat and a pair of thin cotton drawers, driving two mules before him and carrying a double-barreled shotgun over his naked shoulder; then Stephens, Catherwood and Pawling, who by now were drenched with sweat and so covered with fine, black dust that their color was indistinguishable from that of their workmen. Following the explorers was an Indian carrying the *silla* they had hired—a sedan chair which Stephens abhorred. Behind the *silla* were the relief carriers, and finally several boys bearing small bags of provisions.

The Indians of the *silla* were extremely surprised that the white men did not want to use their services according to the agreement and the price already paid. But Stephens would not hear of it.

Riding in a silla

F. Catherwood.

Though he was on the verge of collapse from fever, he felt a sense of degradation at being carried on another man's shoulders no matter his color or race. But Pawling and Catherwood had insisted upon hiring the *silla* in fear that Stephens might not be able to endure the trip.

The *silla* was a precaution which Stephens resisted, but when he came to an extremely steep rise in the path which made his head almost burst, he finally relented and agreed to try to ride in the *silla*. It was a large clumsy armchair, put together with wooden pins and bark strings. The Indian who was supposed to carry him was pathetically small, not more than five feet seven, very thin although highly muscular in build. A bark strap was tied to the arms of the chair, and, sitting down, the Indian placed his back against the back of the chair, adjusted the length of the strings, and smoothed the bark across his forehead with a little cushion to relieve the pressure on his skull. An Indian on each side lifted the *silla* up, and the carrier rose laboriously to his feet, where he stood still for a moment, then jogged Stephens up once or twice to adjust his burden on his shoulders, and set off with one man on each side.

Being carried was a great relief to Stephens, though he could clearly feel the carrier's every arduous movement, even the terrible heaving of his chest. The ascent was one of the steepest on the whole road, a punishment for an unburdened man and horrendous for the workmen. In a few minutes the carrier stopped and let out a sound, usual with weight lifters, which was something between a whistle and a blow. Stephens was riding backwards so he could not see where the Indian was going, but noticing that the man on the left had fallen back, he glanced down and saw that the trail was becoming progressively narrow. In order not to increase the difficulty of carrying him, Stephens sat as still as possible, but in a very few moments, looking over his shoulder, he saw that the path had become hardly a foothold for a mountain climber, with a dizzy precipice of more than a thousand feet dropping straight down.

The carrier moved with extreme care, placing his left foot first, feeling that the stones were steady before bringing up his other foot. By degrees, after a particularly careful movement, he brought both feet up within an inch of the edge of the precipice, stopped, and gave a frightful whistle and blow. Stephens sat so still that he did not breathe. He felt the rise and fall of the carrier's panting, and felt his body trembling as if his knees were about to give way.

The cliff was absolutely awful. The slightest irregular movement on Stephens' part might bring both of them down. But the carrier started again, and with caution ascended several more steps, so close to the edge that even on the back of a mule it would have been more than Stephens could endure. But he was so fearful to speak or to offer a counterorder or to beg to be put down, that he clung desperately to the sides of the chair in total silence, and hoped that the Indian did not suddenly break down and stumble into the utter emptiness of space that loomed everywhere about them.

Then, to his considerable relief, the path turned away from the precipice. But Stephens had hardly sighed with gratitude for having escaped the cliff than the trail suddenly turned downward in a steep descent. This proved to be even worse than ascending. Now if the carrier should fall, nothing could possibly keep Stephens from sailing over his head into the bottomless ravine which wound along the mountain's feet far below.

At last the Indian stopped and lowered the chair. Stephens was very nearly in tears he was so grateful to feel the ground under him again. The poor Indian was dripping with sweat and trembling like a decapitated chicken. But immediately another Indian stepped forward, ready to take Stephens back up. But he had had enough. As far as John Stephens was concerned the *silla* would not be used again during the expedition. He declared it to be a barbarous mode of travel which could only have been invented by someone totally insensitive to human dignity. Walking, climbing, stopping very often to rest, and riding when it was at all possible, the caravan finally reached a thatched shed where the explorers urgently hoped to stop for the night. But, unfortunately, there was no water.

No one knew how far away the village of Nopa was—the

expedition's intended stopping place for the night. Every time they asked one of their Indian carriers how far it was to the village, they always got the same answer: *"Una legua*—one league." Since it could not possibly be much farther, they continued. But they were wrong. For an hour more they had to climb a very steep slope, then once again there was a terrible descent. Everything that Captain Dupaix had said about this journey was true, but he had not said enough. During the thirty years since his visit the rain and the traffic of cargo mules had made the trail to Palenque even worse. It was not until the eighth day of travel that they finally reached the heights of Tumbala. Far beyond them, in the distance, some hundred miles away, was the Laguna de Terminos and the Gulf of Mexico. And directly below, smothered completely by that immensity of tropical verdure, were the ruins of Palenque.

The sun vanished, dark clouds overhung the mountain and thunder began to roll like an avalanche high above them on the obscured crown of the peak. "Oh God," Stephens muttered to himself, "it's going to rain!"

No longer caring if he remained on his feet or not, he pushed forward at an impossible speed, ordering the carriers to hurry. But their reckless descent proved almost impossible. A fierce wind had come out of nowhere and swept up the mountain so forcefully that they could barely push their way down against it. The forest around them cracked with the brutal thrusts of the gale and the air filled with dust and dry leaves. Branches snapped and plummeted to the ground, and there was every reason to fear that a violent tornado was quickly building up. "Hurry! Hurry along, all of you!" Stephens cried out over the roar of the wind. But the descent was so steep that even the mules froze in fear of the path and one of them bolted rather than continue down the mountain. The whole world seemed to be falling apart and tumbling down upon them. They could hear nothing but wind. The dust blinded them. The mules whinnied in fear and the Indians began to stagger and fall. Whole trees were uprooted and loosed boulders, which pounded the mountainside and fell crashing across the path.

It was almost five o'clock when they finally reached the flatlands. Now the mountain was entirely hidden by clouds, and the storm raged high above them. The exhausted travelers crossed a river, and continuing silently through a forest, they reached the rancho of Nopa.

This rancho was nothing but a pitched roof covered with palm leaves, supported by four tree trunks. That's all there was. All around this humble shelter were great heaps of snail shells and the ashes which were the remains of the fires used to cook the snails.

The travelers had hardly congratulated themselves on arriving at such a pathetic vacation spot before a full army of mosquitoes began to attack them.

The Indians quickly made a fire and Augustin, who was very nearly drunk with exhaustion, unpacked a skinny fowl he had purchased in San Pedro and fumblingly prepared it for the hungry company. But the meal was also attended by the mosquitoes, and while one hand was occupied with morsels of food, the other was used to beat off the biting insects. It wasn't long before it became perfectly clear that the caravan had very poor prospects for the night. In an effort to lighten the load, not one of them had packed netting. So they lighted fires all around the rancho and sat down and smoked inordinately. But cigars and conversation were of little help. And none of the travelers was in a hurry to lie down and try to sleep in the blizzard of insects. They sat up till very late despite their fatigue, and they talked about pleasant days in New York City, Paris and Rome.

The darkness around the rancho was filled with fireflies of extraordinary size and brilliance, darting among the trees. These glistening insects distracted the explorers until at length they decided to try and get some sleep in preparation for another long journey the following day.

Obviously hammocks would not be of any use, since they would leave the body exposed on every side to the attack of the mosquitoes. So they spread mats on the ground and lay down without removing a single piece of clothing. Pawling, being inventive and not put off by work, went to considerable trouble to rig his sheets into a covering for his bed, but it was so hot under the shelter that he could not breathe, and he roamed around despondently all night and occasionally splashed into the river in hopes of drowning some of the little blood-sucking monsters which clung to his flesh. And if the mosquitoes were not bad enough, the air was also filled with tiny white-winged gnats which were so numerous that one could not take a breath without inhaling and choking on a dozen of them.

The Indians did not seem to mind the heat, the humidity or the insects. They busied themselves with catching snails, which they cooked for their supper. Then they lay down to sleep on the bank of the river. They seemed completely content, until midnight, when explosive lightning and thunder brought a deluge of rain. The Indians leaped to their feet and with very courteous bows, came under the shed for protection. There they lay perfectly naked, sleeping blissfully while occasionally slapping their bodies with one hand. Stephens looked on with envy, while the incessant hum and bite of the mosquitoes kept him in a state of civilized irritation.

His body was protected by layers of wet, hot clothing, but it was impossible to put any kind of covering over his face without suffocating from the heat. He tried to sleep for hours, but it was of no use. Before daylight he finally gave up and walked to the river, which was broad and very shallow. He pulled off all of his clothes and stretched out on the graveled bottom of the shallows where the water was barely deep enough to run over his body. It was the first comfortable moment he had had for days. His heated body became cool, his fever dissipated gradually and he lay there contentedly until daylight.

The morning air was pleasant, and as the sun rose, the airborne army of tormentors disappeared. It seemed as if the new day might be easier than the last one had been.

As they traveled over an open plain, they came into a handsome region of fine pastures where herds of cattle grazed peacefully. The grass was deep and sweet. And birds sent up a chorus of songs. Continuing through this mild country, they climbed to a wide table of land from which they could see the village of Palenque just ahead. It was a collection of huts with a serene atmosphere which was very welcome after the tyranny of the mountain they had crossed.

In one of the huts lived the *alcalde* of the village, a white man, about sixty, dressed in drawers and a shirt hanging loose, quite respectable in appearance from the standpoint of the tropics, with a stoop to his shoulders and an expression on his face which was very doubtful. With what Stephens intended as a most captivating manner, he offered the *alcalde* his passport. Unfortunately, as it turned out, they had disturbed the gentleman's siesta and he was not in a very good mood. He asked what he had to do with the passport. When Stephens found that he could not answer the question, the *alcalde* went on to say that he had nothing to do with passports, and did not want to have anything to do with them. He told them that they must go to the *prefecto* if they really wanted to show somebody a passport. But it didn't matter in the least to him. Then he turned around two or three times in a circle, just to show that he also didn't care in the least what they thought of him. And, finally, conscious of what was passing through the traveler's minds, he added that complaints had been made against him before. But it was of no use. They couldn't remove him from office. And if they did he didn't care.

This extraordinary greeting at the end of a harrowing long journey was rather discouraging. It was, however, so important for Stephens and his caravan to make a good impression of this crusty official that he tried not to display the slightest annoyance. Instead he told the *alcalde* that they wished to stop for a few days of rest—which meant that they would purchase many things from the villagers. This didn't make the slightest difference to the *alcalde*. So Stephens asked if there was any bread which could be bought in the village.

"*No hay*—there is none," he muttered, scratching himself slowly and looking the other way.

Stephens asked if there was any corn.

"*No hay.*"

"Any coffee?"

"No hay."

"Chocolate?"

"No hay."

The *alcalde* seemed to get increased satisfaction the more he was able to answer *"No hay."*

Their prospects for getting any food were very doubtful, and the situation deteriorated further when it became clear that their request for bread had deeply offended the *alcalde*. Innocently, and entirely without intending the slightest offense, Stephens had looked very disappointed when he realized there was no bread to be had in the village. This thoroughly annoyed the official, who thought the reaction was a blatant smear on the reputation of Palenque. To make matters worse, Augustin, looking out for nobody but himself, muttered that he could not eat another tortilla. And to every newcomer who happened onto the scene he said with particular emphasis that he simply could not eat any more tortillas. And when no one was willing to listen, he repeated the sentence to himself.

The *alcalde* smoldered for a moment and his large nose twitched incessantly. Then he said very quietly and flatly that there was as a matter of fact an excellent oven in the village, but no flour, and that the baker had gone away seven years before, and that the people of Palenque were able to do quite well without bread.

To change the subject Stephens threw out the conciliatory remarks that, at all events, he was very glad to have escaped the rain on the mountain. Again the *alcalde* glared at him and his nose twitched, asking why they should expect the weather to arrange itself for their pleasure. And he repeated with great satisfaction an expression common to the Palenquians: *"Tres meses de agua, tres meses aguacero, y tres meses del norte!,"* which meant "Three months of rain, three months of heavy showers, and then six months of rainy north winds!" Then, while the Indian carriers were piling the luggage on the ground he turned and walked away.

Stephens sighed wearily and rode to the house of the *prefecto*, hoping for the best. Fortunately the man proved to be the local saint. He greeted Stephens with lavish courtesy and offered him a chair and a cigar almost before he was inside the hut.

As soon as the *prefecto* had seen Stephens' passport, he said that he had been expecting the American explorer for some time. Stephens was amazed but said nothing.

"Your good friend," the *prefecto* added, "Don Patricio told me that you were coming here."

This surprised Stephens still more, as he did not recall any friend by that name, let alone anybody who could possibly have visited Palenque. Soon, however, he realized that the "Don Patricio" was the Englishman, Mr. Patrick Walker of Belize. This was the first news of Walker and Captain Caddy that anyone had received since Lieutenant Nicols had brought a report to Guatemala City that they had been speared by hostile Indians. Stephens expressed real pleasure to learn that the British team was safe. The two explorers had managed to reach Palenque by the Belize River and the Lake of Peten, without any more difficulties than the Stephens party had encountered. After two weeks of research among the ruins they had left for the Laguna and Yucatan. Eventually they published a report of their findings with drawings by Captain Caddy, but the literary achievement of John Stephens and the art of Frederick Catherwood totally eclipsed their efforts.

Rather than worry about the good possibility that the Walker and Caddy report might reach print before his own book, Stephens was glad for their safety and was also keen enough to realize that the success of the British team at Palenque meant that there would be no objection to the visit of the Stephens party despite General Santa Anna's prohibition of explorations at the ruins. Stephens and his colleagues had agreed not to mention the ruins until they had a chance to determine the attitude of the officials of the village of Palenque, and up to that moment they feared that once their purpose for being in the region were known they might find that all the agony of reaching the ruins

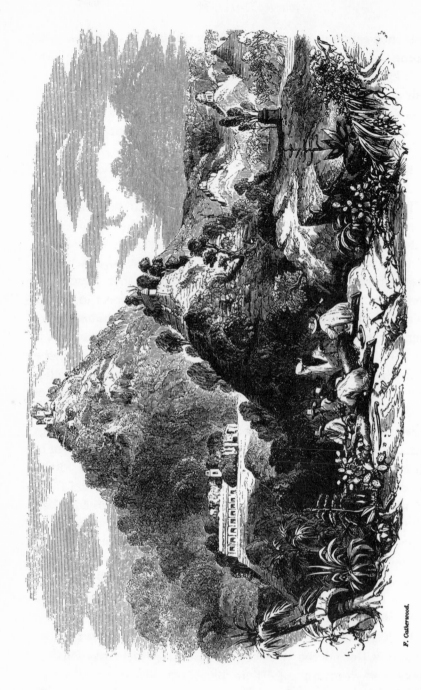

General view of Palenque

F. Catherwood.

had been in vain. So the fact that the *prefecto* already knew about their wish to explore Palenque was a great relief.

"Oh, yes, I know that the General Santa Anna does not want this and he does not want that," the *prefecto* said pleasantly. "But it is of little importance here. This is a very quiet place, señor. Revolutions do not happen in Palenque. I have been *prefecto* in this village maybe twenty years. The generals come and go, but I am still here, señor."

It seemed to John Lloyd Stephens that the prospects for Palenque were ideal. But no sooner had he settled down to supper than the sky opened up and a torrent of rain poured down on his head, ruined his dinner and very nearly washed him away.

They had reached the end of their impossible journey. At dawn, while the jungle was still translucent with vapors, Stephens and Catherwood came upon the ruins of Palenque, hidden among a succession of hills and covered by a rich network of foliage. During the eighteenth century, the Indians of the Tumbala hills had discovered these ruins, and for years tales of fabulous Palenque were told and retold and elaborated into a local mythology.

Strewn everywhere along the mule path was marvelous sculptured stone for which any museum would have been grateful. This priceless rubble stirred Stephens' imagination, for it was all that remained of a gleaming white road over which elegant people bedecked in jade and feathers had once paraded in the lavish pageantry of an empire. Above him the little Otolum River poured from a vaulted culvert sixty feet overhead where in the mist of the tropical morning he could vaguely make out the fern-veiled outline of an immense white building. The rest of great Palenque was barely visible in the tidal waves of vegetation which spilled over it. A city on the brink of time, slipping into oblivion, hanging on the very edge of the mountains.

Stephens was the first of his party to reach the top of a mound, where he found the ruins of the building called the Palace. It looked down over a wide plain, once claimed by the empire and transformed from jungle into cornfields. Beyond, some eighty miles in the distance, was the Laguna de Terminos, which gave ancient Palenque its access to the sea.

Stephens commandeered this stately wreck of a palace as the expedition's headquarters, for they intended to stay in the ruins rather than make the arduous eight-mile trek from the village each day. The structure was a fine architectural achievement, consisting of numerous chambers, divided by thick stone walls and grouped around four handsome courtyards. From the center of the Palace complex rose a curious pagodalike tower unique in Maya architecture. The tower and every other structure was completely ensnarled by roots, vines and fig trees.

While gazing at this wondrous world, the explorers turned loose the turkeys and chickens which they had brought as livestock. They selected the front corridor of the Palace as their dwelling. At one end of this corridor Augustin busied himself setting up a kitchen, oblivious to the wonders which surrounded him. The luggage was stowed among the precious stones or hung on poles reaching from wall to wall. Pawling and the Indian workmen mounted a great slab, which was at least four feet long, on stout stone legs and this became the expedition's conference table, dining table and desk. Beds were constructed of poles and bark strings with exquisitely carved stone headboards.

With night came the huge fruit bats, which lunged at the departing Indians, who feared the ruins and would not remain among them after dark. They hurried back to their village, and as their shouts dissolved into the vast silence of the jungle, the explorers were left alone, the sole inhabitants of the dark Palace of vanished kings.

Other strangers had preceded Stephens and Catherwood, and their names were written on the walls. The infamous Count Jean-Frédéric Waldeck's name came first, with a faded drawing of a lady under which he had inscribed the date 1832. Then there were the names of Captain John Herbert Caddy and Patrick Walker, who had arrived only a few months earlier; and then the scribble of Noah O. Platt, a New York merchant in search of logwood, who had come far out of his way in order to see the

Front corridor of the Palace Palenque

ruins. Also among the signatures was the doggerel written by a young Irish merchant who lived in Tabasco, William Beanham, and who was later found murdered in his hammock.

There had been other distinguished visitors. In 1773 Fray Ramon de Ordoñez y Aguilar had come to Palenque and was so impressed by the ruins that he wrote about them in his *Memoria*. José Antonio Calderon and Antonio Bernasconi visited the site in 1784 and sent a report to Spain. Then in 1786 Captain Don Antonio Del Rio was sent to the fabled ruins by royal decree. The Del Rio report, illustrated by pencil drawings, was lost in the archives of Spain, but a copy of it was found by Dr. Felix Cabrera in Guatemala City, and his much-edited version eventually made its way to London, where it was published in 1822 with the line engravings of Count Waldeck, who had not yet seen Palenque. Then in 1807 Captain Guillermo Dupaix and the artist Luciano Castañeda made their report on Palenque. This aroused curiosity about the ancient site and prompted Count Waldeck to travel to Palenque so he could see with his own eyes the ruins he had rendered from someone else's drawings. The Count took up residency among the ruins in 1831 with the aim of making drawings of all the monuments. There, in a wrecked temple not far from the Palace where Stephens and his friends were encamped, the Count, with his Indian mistress, spent two years preparing his first book, published in Paris in 1838, when he was reportedly seventy-two years old, *Voyage Pittoresque et Archeologique.*

This was the background of the exploration of the ruins of Palenque when Stephens and Catherwood arrived in 1839. Whereas their rediscovery of Copan made them unique among Central American explorers, their arrival at Palenque was the climax of a succession of several earlier visitors.

Stephens, Catherwood and Pawling were wandering around the Palace with candles, amazed by the monumental design of the building. But Augustin was not in the slightest impressed by a heap of broken-down architecture. He had more important things to worry about. He hadn't the slightest interest in old stones and monuments. After all, a man could not eat them. What good was it to be an explorer? He equally scorned the occupation of muleteers and the work of carriers. His only ambition was concerned with an art which, for him, was of the highest order: *servir a mano*—the business of the menial in the excellent service of his masters. He aspired to be the best of all servants. And for this reason he was distressed that the explorers had not remained at the village where there were provisions and facilities which could add measurably to his ability to make his masters comfortable. The camp among the ruins, as far as Augustin was concerned, was totally uncivilized. After all, how was he to manage?

To help reconcile Augustin to living in the ruins Stephens allowed him to devote himself exclusively to cooking, and this delighted the servant. At nine o'clock he called his masters to their first dinner at Palenque. The tablecloth for this festive affair was made of two very wide leaves, each about two feet long, plucked from a tree on the terrace of the Palace. There were also several flickering candles, and an immense salt shaker which held at least five pounds and was made of cornhusks. Augustin was overjoyed by the compliments of the diners. Everything was perfect until the sky became overcast and, in a moment, a sharp thunderclap announced another storm. From the high elevation of the Palace terrace they commanded a view of the sprawling treetops of the forest, and could see in the flashes of lightning the tallest trees bent by the force of a fierce wind which was very quickly making its way toward Palenque. Soon a fierce blast swept through the open arches of the Palace, bringing a cold shower of rain. Immediately the entire table was cleared by the wind, and before they could escape they were drenched. Augustin shouted into the sky like a madman as he snatched up the plates and hurried with them deeper into the shelter of the Palace, where his gentlemen glumly finished their meal standing up.

The rain continued. The wind rushed through the dank ruins. They could not keep a candle lighted. But fortunately the entire Palace was lighted up by huge fireflies which shot through the corridors, circled the tower and crawled slowly over the entire surface of the ruin. They were the same curious, shining beetles which they had seen at Nopa, famous among the early Spaniards as wonders of nature. Pawling caught several of these glowing insects and brought them into the shelter. They were more than half an inch long, with a sharp horn on their heads. Behind the eyes were two round transparent organs full of highly luminous matter. Four of these beetles threw a light so brilliant it illuminated the entire alcove, which was several yards across. To test in earnest the rumor that it was possible to read by the light of just one of these insects, Catherwood emptied the pockets of his shooting jacket and found a Broadway omnibus ticket on which he could clearly and easily read, "Good to the bearer for a ride. A. Brower."

This little souvenir of the United States brought vivid recollections of home, of comfortable dining rooms, soft beds, elegant parlors and beautiful ladies.

With these nostalgic thoughts in mind, the travelers went to bed with the wind and rain sweeping through their cold shelter all night. By morning everything—bedclothes, wearing apparel and hammocks—was wet through, and there was not a dry place to stand or to sit in order to put on their wet boots.

At about ten o'clock the Indians from the village arrived with fresh tortillas and milk. A local guide came with them. He was the town's butcher but he knew the ruins and had been employed by Waldeck, and also by Walker and Caddy, and was recommended by the prefect as a responsible man with knowledge of the layout of the ruins in which he took a peculiar interest from the viewpoint of the other Indians of Palenque. Under his escort they set out for a survey of the ruins.

Ancient Palenque looks up toward the wooded hills which surround it and looks down over a wide plain below. The hills in which it is hidden do not roll gently toward the Laguna but fall abruptly into the flatlands which spread out toward the sea. The fern-covered slopes and dripping forest that circle the ruins form a shimmering green screen behind the white temples and monuments. Palenque is a stone nest in the foliage-dominated escarpment, built by those who wished to live like eagles. From a conceptual point of view, Palenque is the most beautifully designed city of the Maya. The architecture is highly inventive and well suited to the wet climate. The delicate stucco decoration of the buildings has great sophistication. This art is highly disciplined and portrays a peaceful world rather than the violent scenes often depicted in the art of other Maya areas. The Palace, like all the buildings at Palenque, has a mansard-type roof which was originally completely stuccoed in bas-relief. The structures were given added grandeur and height by the addition of extremely high roof combs. Today these combs are blank and perforated, but during ancient times they were entirely covered with carved and plaster ornamentation which was brightly painted, as were the buildings themselves. The complexity of detail which had befuddled Catherwood at Copan was not found at Palenque, where a quite different style of design and detail was produced by the artists and sculptors of El Peten.

The architecture of Palenque has aroused much speculation

since the time of Stephens and Catherwood. A curious type of arch is found there. The shape is reminiscent of those in the Islamic world. The builders of Palenque also indulged freely in the unique use of curved lines, creating entirely new forms distinct from those of the entire region. Stucco cartouches decorated with tropical leaves and flowers in a rococo style are also unique to this site, as are several human figures shown seated in the lotus position. The relationship of these forms to elements of Far Eastern art baffles experts and continues to be the source of debate. Some authorities advocate the so-called trans-Pacific theory and insist that Asian mariners reached Central America long before Columbus and the Vikings and had an impact on the cultures of the region. Though most aspects of this theory are contested, it is generally agreed today that an elaborate and sophisticated art of pottery, for instance, was introduced from Japan to coastal Ecuador in South America approximately five thousand years before the arrival of Christopher Columbus. Researchers are constantly discovering more and more unexplainable links between the arts and languages of North Africa, Japan and the Americas.

John Lloyd Stephens, however, was one of the first explorers to insist that the cultures of Central America were American and not the achievements of Egyptians, Phoenicians or the survivors of lost continents. There is little doubt that he was substantially correct in crediting the cultures in the Americas to natives rather than accepting the notion that was popular in his day that American Indians were incapable of producing the cultures which surrounded them.

Stephens and Catherwood soon realized that Palenque was not a city of great pyramids and monumental stelae. The decorations carved in stucco were the major style and medium of Palenque. These were highly individual and very technically advanced. The refinement and subtlety of the stuccos was vividly expressive in comparison to all other sculpture of Mesoamerica. It was essentially a linear style, very different from the flamboyant, fierce and robust style used by the artists of Copan.

Stephens and his friends had an exhausting day, having chased after their speedy guide, who wanted to get back to his shop.

In the afternoon the storm arrived punctually as it did every day at Palenque. The explorers had rearranged their sleeping setup so that their bedding was better protected, but discovered a new problem in the attack of mosquitoes. In the middle of the night Stephens awoke from the buzzing and biting of the insects. The rain had finally stopped, and the moon, breaking through the heavy clouds, lighted up the ruins. He picked up his sleeping mat and climbed over a mound of stones, where the wall had collapsed, and stumbling along outside the Palace, groped in the dark along a low damp passage, where he spread his mat in the hope of escaping the mosquitoes. Bats were whizzing through the entire moldy corridor, making a sinister noise, but Stephens knew that these creatures ate mosquitoes. The dampness of the passageway was cooling and helped him relax. But he did not sleep well because of the apprehension of snakes, lizards and scorpions.

At daybreak Stephens returned to the front of the Palace and found Catherwood and Pawling sitting on carved stones, half dressed and in a rueful frame of mind. They had spent the night worse than he, and after consoling each other, utterly weak with sleeplessness, they set to work.

They lived in this way among the ruins, not at all the romantic adventure which Stephens had pictured in New York City when he was dreaming of his explorations of Central America. Each morning the Indians arrived with provisions. They were always late and they always left early, and rarely did the same men show up on two successive days, so it was always necessary to reteach each crew of workmen the jobs which others had learned the day before.

Somehow the work progressed. As at Copan, it was Stephens' job to prepare the different objects which Catherwood was to draw. Many of the stones were so obscured by dirt and fungus that they had to be scrubbed and cleaned like crockery. Stephens' health was steadily declining, and fortunately Pawling was on hand to relieve him of a great part of the work. In the first ten days at Palenque the entire site was measured, drawn and fully explored despite the constant bombardment of rain, the lash of wind and the insatiable appetite of insects. Besides all these hazards, the explorers suffered from another and worse infestation, called by the Indians "niguas." These terrible vermin ate their way into the flesh, under the toenails, and laid their eggs there. Gradually the infested feet swelled and the infection gave off the sickening reek of decay. Until Palenque, Stephens had somehow escaped these niguas, but soon after reaching the ruins he noticed that his right foot was swelling. He had carried the parasites in his flesh, conscious that something was wrong but not knowing what, until the nits had been laid and began to multiply. Pawling instantly understood Stephens' problem and picked the vermin out with his penknife, which left a terrible infected wound. Finally the infection became so great, and the swelling increased so much, that Stephens became seriously alarmed, and decided that he must return to the village and try to find some kind of medical attention. It was no simple matter to get there. The foot by now was so swollen that there was no possibility of putting it in a stirrup; just to keep the infected limb in a hanging position made it feel as if the blood would burst through the skin. But after a very careful trip on a mule with his leg on a pillow over the pommel of the saddle, he finally reached the village.

As Stephens ascended to the plateau on which the village was located, he was surprised to see an unusual amount of excitement. A crowd of people came running into the street, and they seemed very roused at the sight of Stephens. He began to feel a bit nervous, especially since he was alone, when two men on horseback came to meet him. As it turned out, the town's population was anxiously expecting three padres and had somehow mistaken Stephens for all three holy men. The people were exceptionally disappointed to find that the approaching figure was only the *americano*.

Feeling rather downcast, Stephens rode on to the door of the old hut he had occupied on first reaching Palenque village.

Almost at once the crusty *alcalde* appeared at the door with his keys in one hand and his other outstretched for the rent. Surprisingly he was in full dress, i.e., with his shirt tucked into his pantaloons. Stephens was gratified to find that the *alcalde* was in a worse frame of mind at the coming of the padres than he had been at the time of Stephens and Catherwood's arrival. In fact, he seemed rather friendly, and became quite concerned about the infected foot as soon as he saw Stephens' condition. The swelling had become so great that the flesh had turned dark and the smell of decay was overpowering. "Señor Estebans," the *alcalde* said in a kindly tone, "you must go at once to the bed. The foot, she is not good. I do not understand how it is with men of intelligence and wealth who are coming from the great city of New York. You are eaten by our little niguas, while we poor uncivilized peasants living here in the wilderness are not troubled by them. How is this possible, señor?"

Stephens gave him a dark look and said nothing.

The patient was soon on his back, lying perfectly quiet for two days while remedies and medications and sundry concoctions which would have horrified any self-respecting physician were poured, rubbed and smeared on his grotesquely deformed foot by midwives and old men. By the third morning the inflammation was gone and he could stand. The padres had finally arrived and the village was very excited when they made their triumphal entry, escorted by important citizens and a train of more than one hundred Indians, carrying luggage, chairs, hammocks and also carrying the three rotund padres who were perched on their shoulders. They had been carried in this fashion all the way from Tumbala, for being a padre in this country was a glorious thing, and next to being a padre oneself, the next best position was being a padre's friend.

When Stephens paid a visit to the padres he was warmly greeted and asked to take a seat. After some very general conversation about the importance of religion among the Indians and the great strides which had been made in their conversion, cups of chocolate were passed around, and one of the padres went to his luggage and produced a pack of playing cards, which he placed on the table. "I always carry them with me," he explained to Stephens, who was rather shocked, especially since it was Sunday. "It is very pleasant," the padre continued, "to travel with companions, and wherever we might stop to do the work of God, we can have a little game at night."

The cards had apparently provided a good many games, for they were well worn. Then, without saying another word, all three padres systematically cleared the table and took their positions while an old Indian servant laid on the table a handful of grains of corn and a new bundle of cigars. "The grains of corn," the padre next to Stephens explained politely, "are valued at a medio each." Stephens nodded in disbelief.

Very soon the players became very involved in their game of *monte*. Stephens left them playing as earnestly as if the souls of countless unconverted Indians were at stake. Before he left, the padres invited him to come back to dine with them, and he gladly accepted.

When Stephens returned he found that dinner had to be delayed because one of the padres was missing. While they waited for their colleague, the mammoth *cura* of Tumbala, who weighed at least 240 pounds, picked up his violin and played a few folk tunes which charmed everyone. In the meantime, the missing padre finally made an appearance and it seemed as though they would finally sit down to a sumptuous dinner which Stephens had been much anticipating after eating tortillas and tough chicken for almost two weeks. But the padres continued to talk and laugh and to make jokes at the expense of the late-arriving priest, who, it seems, had lost sixteen dollars at their game. He insisted that he was a ruined man, which brought on more laughter, and they offered him a chance to get his revenge. At once the table was cleared of bowls and bread and all the other utensils which had promised a lavish meal, and the cards and grains of corn were once again spread out before the priests. And while the padre of Tumbala played the violin, his two friends played *monte* and Stephens' stomach growled.

Feeling a bit offended at being kept waiting for dinner, Stephens said as politely as possible, "Señores, in my country were you to be seen playing cards on Sunday you could be thrown out of the Church."

One of the priests replied quietly, without looking up, "Yes, that may be so. An Englishman once told me very much the same thing. He also went into some detail about the fashion of observing Sunday in England. You will I hope pardon me, Señor Estebans, but it seems to me quite stupid."

With that they fell under the spell of their game. Dinner was obviously going to be much delayed, and so Stephens, after watching for a very long time, wandered out into the street, where a breeze cooled him.

Then a mournful procession made its way past the house. Stephens, who had a peculiar fascination for funerals, followed the mourners. The corpse of a young Indian girl was borne on a rude bier, without coffin, in a white dress, with a shawl over the head, and followed by a meager procession of old women and children and no one else. Stephens walked beside them and gradually realized by what he could pick up from their conversation that the body was that of the mistress who had once lived with Count Waldeck on top of his pyramid at the ruins of Palenque. She had been the pride and beauty of the village whose portrait Waldeck had used to embellish his book on Palenque. Her life had been cut short once Waldeck deserted her. Ignorant and innocent, she was persuaded to marry another man, who mistreated her. Soon she was dead. Now her bier was set down beside the little grave, and when the attendants lifted the body the head turned on one side and the hands dropped and swung freely. The miserable grave was too short, and as the corpse was laid into it the legs buckled and the knees came up in a grotesque posture. Stephens gazed at the girl's face, which was thin and wasted. But he thought that the mouth had a sweetness of expression which made him believe that she had died contentedly and without malice toward the men who had abused her. He could not turn away from her placid face, which was so touching in its beauty that he almost wept for her. The old women around the grave seemed to think she was better dead. She was poor, without friends or family, and her husband loathed her impurity. The men who had put her in her grave mumbled and went away. The women and children remained and with their hands began to scrape up soil and throw it on the corpse. The body was very gradually covered, so slowly that Stephens became mesmerized by the dreadfulness of the scene. At first the feet stuck out, and then all was buried but the face. A small piece of muddy soil fell upon one of the eyes, and another on her smiling mouth, changing the whole expression in a moment so that death took possession of her. The old women stopped for a moment and commented upon the terrible change which had come over the corpse. Then the dirt fell on the face, covering everything but the nose. And then she was gone—as if she had never existed and as if her life had meant nothing.

Shaken by the burial, Stephens hurried back to the padres' dinner, which was already in progress, and quietly took his place at the table. It was a marvelous meal.

By the next day Stephens was ready to return to the ruins. At eleven o'clock he arrived and found the Palace filled with activity. But there was a marked change in the place and in his friends since he had left. The walls were damp, the corridors wet, the moldy smell lingered and the roof and walls could no longer resist the mildew which crept over everything. The saddles, boots and bridles were green and mildewed, and even the guns and pistols were covered with rust. Frederick Catherwood's appearance startled his friend. He was extremely gaunt. He was lame from the infestation of niguas. His face and hands were swollen from mosquito bites, and his left arm hung nearly paralyzed from rheumatism. Everywhere among the ruins was the dreadful stench of decay.

Late in the afternoon the storm again set in with terrific thunder, which rolled and rumbled with fearful crashes through the corridors and against the walls. Every day life at the ruins became more difficult. To the explorers it seemed as if the world

Palenque. Temple of the Inscriptions.

of Palenque were coming to an end, though the ancient walls had suffered the wet season for centuries. The work became nearly impossible, yet Catherwood insisted upon continuing until he had completed drawing all the structures.

Against the constant spray of a windy drizzle, they cut their way through the underbrush, slowly climbing the stones of a pyramid until they came upon the temple at the top. Plants wound through the perforations of the roof comb and trees with great naked roots dug into the masonry and tried to dislodge the stones. Though the building had suffered greatly from the invasion of creepers and roots, this marvelous structure, the Temple of Inscriptions (which Stephens called "No. 1 Casa de Piedra"), was the most awesome and best-preserved of the outlying temples of Palenque.

The front of the Temple, facing north, was entered by five doorways and was decorated by four handsomely crafted stuccoed reliefs, though all the figures had lost their faces. Yet the elegance of the art was unmatched for its detail in the fanciful garments of the figures—delicate designs which had withstood a thousand years of great rains and intense sunlight.

The stucco mosaic had once been brightly colored and some of its distinctive yellow hues were still visible. Catherwood, barely able to see through his swollen eyelids and unable to use his left hand, faithfully copied the figures. He worked at a frantic pace, totally absorbed in the magnificence of the ornamentation of the Temple.

When they entered the vault of the Temple of Inscriptions they stopped and peered into the blackness of the interior. Again there was the familiar musky scent of decay. The jungle was silent except for the subdued hiss of the light rain on countless leaves and the screech of bats, which hung from the ceilings of the dark, fetid vault.

Augustin crossed himself and crept slowly forward, a pine torch in his hand which threw immense shadows on the dripping walls. The explorers found that the large seventy-foot-long vault was entirely empty. Then suddenly Augustin called out to them and pointed excitedly to the side wall, where two great limestone slabs covered with glyphs were barely visible through the thick slime and moss which covered them.

Augustin was told to bring up a pair of scrub brushes and was set to work trying to remove the deep verdure of centuries. Catherwood and Stephens watched with great excitement as the glyphs came through the dissolving slime. Slowly, almost magically, the carving was becoming visible—row upon row of complex signs which shouted out to them in a language which was entirely unintelligible. There was absolutely no mistaking these sculptured characters. Stephens was certain that they were the same as those found in Copan and Quirigua. He felt that these hieroglyphics told the history of Palenque and if they could be read would answer the hundreds of questions which were raised by the mysterious ruins.

In the hope that scholars and experts might be able to find these answers, Stephens asked Catherwood to copy every glyph as accurately as possible. As the artist worked in the light of the pine torches which filled the vault he paced incessantly back and forth, coming closer to the glyphs and then backing away to try to grasp the overall design of the enormous slabs upon which they were incised. His footsteps rang out resoundingly, but neither Catherwood nor Stephens could possibly have realized that immediately under their feet was one of the most startling secrets of the ancients who had built these astounding temples. That secret would not be uncovered until June 1952, when the Mexican archeologist Albert Ruz Lhullier noticed that the large slab floor of the vault of the Temple of Inscriptions was drilled with what looked like finger holes. He found these holes entirely unexplainable, until he discovered that the retaining walls of the vault did not end on the level of the floor but continued below. Raising one of the three floor slabs, Ruz found a debris-filled cobbled stairway leading downward, first in one direction and then abruptly in another. After months of labor, his workmen reached a great slab poised horizontally against what might be a doorway located sixty feet into the core of the pyramid. Just in front of this sealed doorway were the skeletons of six retainers who had been left as the guardians of the mysterious stairway.

When the slab was removed, Ruz discovered a glistening chamber draped by stalactites built up through centuries of dripping lime-saturated water. Unbelievably Ruz had discovered a tomb—which was totally unexpected, since it was the view of scholars that the Maya pyramids were definitely not used for burials.

On top of the great stone tomb was a magnificently carved slab which depicted a noble gentleman falling into the jaws of death. This was removed with great difficulty, as it weighed five tons and was located in a very cramped space in the center of the huge pyramid. Beneath it was found a skeleton bedecked with jade earrings, necklaces and other precious objects.

Far overhead, 112 years earlier, Frederick Catherwood was carefully copying the rows of glyphs which covered two impressive slabs in the Temple without the slightest awareness of what the signs meant or that a grave of some unknown royal person lay far beneath his feet. Today those who have spent a lifetime in

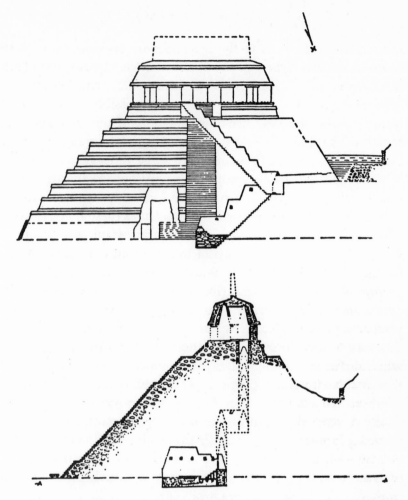

Temple of the Inscriptions, Palenque. Elevation and section to show the interior staircase leading from the rear room of the temple to the burial crypt. A light and ventilation shaft led from the stairway landing to the exterior of the pyramid.
(After A. Ruz, from J. Eric S. Thompson, *The Rise and Fall of Maya Civilization*)

the search for answers to the mysteries of the Maya know little more about the glyphs or the skeleton buried in the Temple of Inscriptions than Stephens and Catherwood did in 1840.

As the explorers stood at the summit of the pyramid they trembled with the intensity of their ignorance. "Who built these fantastic temples?" Stephens shouted almost in a rage. "Where did they come from, and where did they go and who were they?"

More than four centuries after the arrival of Columbus, almost none of the really fundamental questions concerning the indigenous people of the Americas have been successfully answered. And of unanswered riddles, those of the Maya are the most mysterious. No one has satisfactorily explained where Maya civilization began or exactly what earlier cultures influenced it. Were the Maya one of the tribes of hunters who followed huge mammals over the Bering Strait into the Americas some 30,000 years ago? And, if so, why are their achievements of such a drastically different order from those of the other Paleo-Indians who hunted Ice Age monsters? Were they members of the same race of non-Mongoloid people of Asiatic affinity who came to the Americas from northeastern Asia, and if so, why is their blood type different from that of the tribes of North America? Were these Maya people really cut off from the rest of mankind once they reached the Americas, and did they really have to invent their entire culture for themselves, or were there alien influences from the Orient and Africa even after they were apparently isolated by the melting glacial land bridges? If they arrived in America with almost no cultural baggage, if they left the worlds of Asia, Europe and Africa before the creation of any of the modern languages, before the invention of the wheel and before the evolution of the current races of mankind, why are there so many indisputable parallels between Maya culture and those of places far across the oceans?

These questions remain largely unanswered.

No one has explained the origins of the Maya world or exactly how it managed to evolve in an extremely hostile environment where conditions of weather and landscape made the construction of large complex social units almost unthinkable. There is no reliable information on the origin of the complex Maya calendar, their hieroglyphic writing and their mathematics, though all of these inventions are highly evolved and forward-looking, even to the extent that the Maya were among the first people in the world to make use of zero in making mathematical calculations. Nor is there significant data on the social organization, religious life, government or even the simplest daily life of the Maya. We do not know what they called themselves or their ceremonial centers, despite the fact that living on exactly the same land where they lived for centuries are the descendants of the ancient Maya.

It was Columbus who had the first contact with these mysterious people in 1502, near the island of Guanaja off the northern coast of Honduras. His ships came upon a canoe carrying Indian traders who reportedly came from a place called Maia or Maiam, the name from which the word "Maya" was subsequently derived. But that was not the name by which they knew themselves.

At first it was thought that the calendar and hieroglyphic writing arose independently among the Maya themselves, most likely in the lowlands, where their earliest inscriptions have been found and where they evolved their most complex ceremonial centers. But later, many scholars have come to believe that the calendar and writing originated among a shadowy people called the Olmec, who lived in Tabasco and southern Veracruz at a very ancient time and were often designated as the "mother culture" of Mesoamerica. Today this view is widely debated on the basis of archeological evidence of the Maya found in Belize which predates Olmec achievements of the same kind.

Yet it seems that whether the Olmec did or did not predate the Maya, their cultural influence was extremely important and widespread. Olmec sculpture, noted for its originality, boldness and realism, is unique in Mexico and Central America, and students consider it the first major art style of the region. It focuses upon full-figure and bas-relief depictions of fat baby-faced humans who often display a very pronounced Negroid or Oriental appearance, a strange situation when it is considered that the first blacks did not arrive in the Americas until 1700 years later, when slaves were introduced from Africa.

For years, one of the major challenges facing scholars was the effort to decipher Maya hieroglyphic writing. The first major breakthrough was the discovery that many of the glyphs have a calendrical significance which researchers managed to correlate with our own calendar. The Maya were apparently a people obsessed with time. They had an extensive theological view of time and it was the core of their ceremonial life. They incised dates on almost every monument they erected, and in fact the stelae and other sculptures appear to have been created to commemorate and celebrate certain important dates: events and the succession of rulers.

Glyphs saturated the surface of every sculpture produced by the Maya, and Stephens insisted that this mysterious writing contained the entire history of the people who produced the monuments. But this viewpoint, at least for many years, was contested. Specialists felt certain that the mysterious glyphs were concerned solely with dates. Today that viewpoint is being revised, but obviously no comprehensive information about the Maya world can really be assembled without a reliable knowledge of the contents of the thousands upon thousands of inscriptions which survived the burning and destruction of Spanish padres and soldiers, who believed that the monuments and glyphs were barbarous and pagan.

There is overwhelming irony in the fact that a people who spent most of their energies leaving careful records of their lives and times left them in inscriptions which are unintelligible to us. Deciphering the Maya glyphs has proved very difficult since the system of writing is unique to pre-Columbian America and totally unrelated to any Indo-European scripts. Those who made the inscriptions vanished long before the arrival of the European invaders, leaving few traces of the meaning of their glyphs. Today, in the age of computers, the decipherability of Maya writing remains elusive, though very recent work by anthropologists is making eventual understanding a possibility.

Equally uncertain is the origin of many elements of Maya culture and by what means these elements retained a highly similar form throughout Mesoamerica. Despite regional variation in art and architecture, the fundamental ideas of cosmology, iconography, ritualism, calendrics and hieroglyphics were essentially the same throughout the lowland region, a fact which strongly suggests a strong and pervasive orthodoxy of spiritual ideals. Yet, whatever produced this cultural similarity and by what government and social power these elements were made so pervasive in the Maya civilization are totally unknown. The striking dissimilarities between the nature orientation of most North American Indians and the highly contrasting empire orientation of most Central American Indians has not been explained. While the tribes outside Mesoamerica had few dreams of empire, or of wide military and political domination, and sought instead to remain faithfully within the domain of nature, the ancients of Central America and Mexico sought to conquer nature and possessed the kind of mentality which is concerned with human supremacy and which is similar to the ideologies of the Indo-European world. Did these concepts evolve independently in Mesoamerica, or were they somehow brought there from Japan and North Africa? No one knows.

But probably the most pressing question concerning the Maya is the disappearance of their whole civilization. For even the shattering catastrophe that led to the sudden abandonment of the greatest cities during the ninth century A.D. is still totally unknown except for highly debated and contradictory conjectures about natural disasters, insurrection, plague and famine. It is one of the most baffling archeological mysteries ever uncovered.

In our day, as in that of John Lloyd Stephens, the world of the Maya remains one of the last great frontiers of archeology, one of the last places on earth which is a source of profound mystery. We know astonishingly little more about this vast civilization than Stephens and Catherwood did as they stood at the base of the Temple of Inscriptions and gazed in silence over the broad jungle-covered landscape of Palenque. They could see the wide plazas which were once covered with brightly painted plaster. The gleaming pyramids on which processions of bejeweled priests in great feathered headdresses made flamboyant patterns on the endless gleaming stairways as they presided over rites of war and of peace, of time and of death and of fertility.

Then, suddenly, disaster. Six hundred years before Columbus, early in the ninth century, a catastrophic event crushed the people of the lowlands. Copan raised a last monument, and then by A.D. 810 it became a dying city. One after another the cities ceased construction, and in some sites building and monuments were left half finished, as if the great architects had been swept away in the midst of their work. Even the practice of erecting dated stelae came to an abrupt end, a circumstance which has provided the only accurate chronology of the dissolution of Maya civilization. Within a hundred years—from A.D. 800 to 900—all of the once populous centers were abandoned. The great monumental cities were left in silence. Incredibly, the buildings were left entirely untouched, without the least sign of any kind of invasion, insurrection or natural calamity—almost as if the people had been suddenly carried away. As if, at any moment, the inhabitants might return to their monuments and plazas.

Instead an immense decay descended upon the cities from which they never recovered. The rains came, and after them came the suns of many summers. The regal, ornate stucco and stone figures atop the pyramids stared out into the deserted plazas where countless seedlings began to sprout through the eroding plaster pavements. Succulent vines crawled without restraint over the sculptured stonework. Saplings were born in the dust of centuries which piled upon the high ledges and terraces where trees gradually sank tiny tendrils between the stones, took hold and began to grow into the massive roots which shattered the walls and threw down the stones in great silent heaps.

The silence also grew, until it was eventually broken by the roaming monkeys and parrots who came to explore the new jungle which had piled itself, layer by layer, upon these mighty works of man. Wild figs climbed the towers and intertwined among their own branches until they had made a leafy tomb for the abandoned stone people of the monuments and stelae. Then came the giant fruit bats, attracted by the putrescent ponds and the stench of rotting leaves, and the clouds of millions upon millions of mosquitoes and gnats and beetles. The copious rain sent rivulets of mineral-rich water over the walls, encasing whole buildings in delicate crystalline cocoons. Ficus raced to the tops of the temples and brought down their lofty summits like fallen birds. Time devoured Palenque and spat out its precious bones, scattering stones and bits of monumental art across the bottom of a great, deep sea of vegetation. Time ate Copan and licked its memories clean. And after the feast of time was over there were only the piled bones of a people's whole world, blotted out and lost. All they had known and said and done, all they had built, all the gods they had praised and the ideals for which they had died sank beyond reach to the bottom of the vast deep sea of human dream and memory.

On May 13, 1840, the daily storm opened with a whirlwind. At night the crash of falling trees rang through the forest, rain fell in deluges, the roar of thunder was terrific, and as Stephens and Catherwood lay looking out, the ruined Palace and the pyramids of Palenque, lighted only by the glare of lightning, were more grand than anything they had ever seen. "In fact," Stephens murmured, "they are too sublime and too terrible. There is something fatalistic here. I can feel it. For all its strangeness and for all the remoteness of the forgotten people who built it, I get the awful feeling that Palenque is not really so very different from our own world. It is truly marvelous, Cath, but at the same time I cannot shake the feeling that it is also terrifying. Do you know what I mean?"

Catherwood said nothing, and the thunder exploded into echoes which threatened to bring down the ancient walls.

"It is too sublime and too terrible," Stephens murmured again, "... like the time I climbed a cliff in Greece, totally unaware of anything except the difficulty of the climb. But when I got to the top, Cath, I was far less struck by my achievement than by the great peril of the unimaginable height I had reached."

By morning the courtyard and the ground below the Palace was entirely flooded, and the whole front of the building was so wet that the explorers were forced to desert it and move to the other side of the corridor. But even there they were little better off; for the rain and dampness was carried in gusts into every alcove. Clearly, it was time to desert Palenque. The explorers managed to remain until Catherwood finally completed his drawings. And then on the first day of June, with wounds and infections, fever and emaciated bodies, they broke camp and left the ruins.

"What we had before our eyes," Stephens wrote, "was grand, curious and remarkable enough. Here were the remains of a cultivated, polished, and peculiar people, who had passed through all the stages incident of rise and fall of nations; reached their golden age, and perished. We lived in the ruined palaces. We went to their desolated temples; and whenever we moved we saw the evidences of their taste, their skill in art. In the midst of desolation and ruin we looked back to the past, cleared away the gloomy forest, and imagined every building perfect, with its terraces and pyramids, its sculptured and painted ornaments, grand, lofty, and imposing, and overlooking an immense inhabited plain; we called back into life the strange people who gazed at us in sadness from the walls; pictured them, in fanciful costumes and adorned with plumes of feathers, ascending the terraces of the palace and the steps leading to the temples. In the romance of the world's history nothing ever impressed me more forcibly than the spectacle of this once great and lovely city, over-turned, desolate, and lost . . . overgrown with trees for miles around and without even a name to distinguish it."

Epilogue: *Aftermath*

 John Stephens and Frederick Catherwood planned to make their way across Yucatan to the Atlantic, where they would embark for New York. But prior to leaving Palenque, Stephens compulsively entered negotiations for the purchase of the ruins. There was, at least according to the prefect, no legal restriction against Stephens' purchase of the property as long as he was married to a Mexican. There were moments, Stephens was the first to admit, when helpless and without a proper dinner, alone and lonely, he had considered marrying one of the lovely local women, but as a devoted bachelor he had resisted. The ruins, however, were more of a temptation than the ladies, and so he looked over the women and found that the oldest of those who were young was only fourteen, and the prettiest of them were already married. What was left was a pair of sisters, both about forty, though rather pleasant to look at. But Stephens was inclined to find a means of staying single, and politely noted that it was impossible to choose between them. Therefore he did not marry but, at the prefect's suggestion, made the purchase through a third party—Mr. Charles Russell, the American Consul already at Carmen, who was already married to a Mexican.

Henry Pawling was left behind in Palenque as Stephens' agent, to make plaster casts of the ruins and to complete the complicated arrangements to purchase the land. But before he could accomplish those objectives the Governor of Chiapas interceded and prohibited the removal of valuable Mexican artifacts. In addition to the Governor's wise prohibition, there was a new enthusiasm for the ruins by the citizens of Palenque. Three of them asked the Governor to demand a fee for Pawling's plaster casts which he intended to ship to the United States. Pawling was asked for $4000 to $5000 for permission to export his casts. In the end Pawling was officially ordered to leave the ruins, and his casts were seized by the prefect. Despite three ambitious plans, John Lloyd Stephens never managed to buy any of the ruins.

Stephens and Catherwood meanwhile began the long descent to the sea in a thirty-foot canoe loaned to them by the *alcade* of the town of Las Playas, and poled by three Indians. Following a canal they entered the lovely Catazaja Lagoon which abounded in wild life and a great variety of tropical birds. Following the channel from the lagoon, they drifted through sleeping alligators and entered the Rio Chico, a sluggish brown waterway which reeked of stagnation. As the sun arranged its brilliant crimson light into a lavish sunset, the canoe swept through a wide passage which brought it into the Chiquinto River. The current became turbulent as the river joined the mighty Usumacinta River and rushed toward its junction with waterways that emptied into the sea. They finally reached the little town of Palizada, and from there went down to the sea with a cargo of dyewoods, bananas, mangoes and papayas.

Down to the Laguna they went on a roaring river, with rain and hail and wind whirling violently around their boat. At last they reached the Boca Chica of the Laguna. A storm on the lagoon very nearly capsized their heavily loaded bungo and for a while Stephens and the ailing Catherwood did not think they would reach the port of Carmen. The English artist was very nearly unconscious from fever, and Stephens frantically tied a balsawood life preserver around his chest as the waves broke over their little boat. They took off their boots and coats and anxiously waited to be plunged into the sea. Miraculously the ill-equipped little vessel with its inept crew did not sink, and the explorers finally reached Carmen, where they presented themselves to Charles Russell, Esq., United States Consul. Russell was asked to undertake the scheme which later failed—that of purchasing Palenque's ruins in Stephens' behalf for the sum of $1500.

It had been Stephens' hope to continue the expedition—exploring other ruined cities—but Frederick Catherwood was violently ill and seemed unable to recover from the fever and pain which caused him so much discomfort that he was unable to stay on his feet. Stephens considered the idea of going on by himself, but Catherwood was anxious not to break up the expedition and insisted that he was well enough to accompany his friend on the rest of the journey. Augustin, however, was beginning to suspect his employers of trying to kidnap him and take him to El Norte. He had never before been more than ten miles from Belize in his adult life and was completely dependent upon Stephens and Catherwood, who had promised, as part of his contract, to send him safely home at the end of the journey.

"Well, Augustin," Stephens said with a smile, "what shall it be? Will you be going with us to Uxmal?"

"Well, señor, since I do not know where I am, it really doesn't matter that I don't know where I'm going."

And so they boarded a ship in the open harbor at Carmen and traveled 120 miles northeast to the port of Sisal, the gateway to Merida, the capital city of Yucatan.

By now Catherwood was far too ill with malaria to travel. He grew paler and weaker by the day, but insisted that Stephens ride out with a guide to visit the fabled ruins of Uxmal, which lay

F. Catherwood.   H. Jordan.

Uxmal. House of the Dwarf and House of the Nuns.

about fifty miles from Merida. Catherwood remained in bed while his friend set out.

John Stephens didn't know that Uxmal, the third and last goal of the expedition, stood on a plain completely cleared of underbrush and trees, permitting for the first time a wide and open panorama of the entire city. The most engaging structure was the Pyramid of the Dwarf, with its carved stone ornamental top. Then he found the Nunnery, and the House of the Turtles—that sublimely simple architectural marvel. But what most fascinated him was the Governor's House. "It is the grandest building," he told Catherwood when he rushed back to Merida with news of his exploration. "It is absolutely the most stately structure and the most perfect in preservation of all the buildings remaining at Uxmal. Cath, you must see it!"

"My dear fellow," Catherwood said weakly from his bed, "you are romancing."

"No, I tell you it is true."

That was enough to rouse the feverish artist. Despite a disease which would have most men in the hospital, Catherwood stumbled from his sickbed, pulled on his clothes and went out to Uxmal the next day, laboriously dragging himself among the vast ruins under the ceaseless blast of the ferocious sun.

"My dear fellow," he murmured, "you did not do it justice. These buildings exceed your description!" And with this Catherwood immediately set up his easel and began to draw a panorama of the pyramid called the House of the Dwarf. He worked exhaustedly, barely able to see in the glare of the sunlight, feeling as if his skull were about to split with the violence of a headache.

At three in the afternoon Stephens found him collapsed at his easel. It was unthinkable to remain any longer. And with some urgency the expedition to Central America came to an end.

On June 24, 1840, Augustin stood on the deserted dock with Stephens' mule at his side, as a launch took his beloved masters to the awaiting Spanish brig, the *Alexandre*, bound for Havana. Catherwood was unconscious, tied to a litter and breathing with difficulty. But Stephens stood up for a moment in the launch and waved with a deep sense of loss at the diminishing figures of his dear servant and his little mule. Tears came to Augustin's eyes as he watched after *los americanos locos,* and he turned away with embarrassment and muttered, *"Merde!"*

On board, Stephens crouched over Catherwood in great apprehension for his health, taking charge of his precious drawings and notebooks and doing everything in his power to attend the sick friend. He had deeply regretted leaving Central America, but now that he was on his way, he longed to be back to New York where Catherwood could find proper medical attention. He gazed out to sea, anxious for the sight of the United States, where a new race of master builders were dreaming of monuments and empire.

But the problems of the expedition were not yet over. It seemed that Stephens and Catherwood, after surviving all the violence and rigors of their journey, might perish at sea, for the *Alexandre* ran into the equatorial doldrums and drifted helplessly for days. By July 13 the water ran out. Sharks surrounded the ship. Food was nonexistent. And the heat was unbearable. Then, just as Stephens had given up and sat over the unconscious body of his friend, whose pulse was ebbing, thinking that all their discoveries would be lost forever on a ghost ship, the wind came up and another vessel was sighted.

Almost in a trance, Stephens rushed to the railing and shouted in English to the approaching vessel. To his amazement the answer came back with a distinct American accent. It was the *Helen Maria* en route to New York harbor!

Catherwood was lifted on board and Stephens joyously scrambled aboard behind him, shaking every hand in sight. Then the wind caught the sails and the *Helen Maria* glided northwards, reaching New York City on the last day of July.

John Lloyd Stephens' account of his adventures, the two volumes of *Incidents of Travel in Central America, Chiapas, and Yucatan,* was a great hit in America, ending with an appeal to Britain and France to leave American antiquities to the Americans. However, it took American archeologists fifty years before they concurred with Stephens' excitement for the Maya. If the scholars were slow to fall under the spell of the Maya, Stephens and Catherwood were unquestionably hooked; they went back to Yucatan to finish their work almost as soon as *Incidents of Travel* had been published.

They returned to Yucatan about fifteen months from the date of their departure, in October of 1841. On this expedition they were accompanied by Samuel Cabot, a doctor of medicine and an ornithologist. Cabot, a young man of twenty-six, had another useful achievement. He had held the bare-knuckle boxing championship at Harvard for two years.

Together, the three young men began the second journey at Merida, where they sought information about the ruins of Yucatan. They were given little data but had numerous visits from cross-eyed ladies. Among the Maya, strabismus, crossed eyes, was once a mark of beauty, and the trait had been perpetuated genetically, though it was no longer desirable. Dr. Cabot had skill in a new corrective operation pioneered in France. A young boy was brought to him and after his crossed eyes were successfully uncrossed by a very simple but precise surgical technique, Dr. Cabot found himself overwhelmed by young ladies requesting the same operation. One mother was so delighted by the results of the technique when used on her pretty daughter that she sent to Cabot, on the day of the explorers' departure for the interior, a three-foot-wide cake which had to be unceremoniously stuffed into a pair of saddlebags in order not to offend the good lady. With this unorthodox packing accomplished, Stephens, Catherwood and Cabot set out for Uxmal to complete the work left unfinished when illness had forced the curtailing of the earlier expedition to Central America.

To their surprise the site was no longer clear of underbrush. In just fifteen months since their last visit the entire area was overgrown, and twenty-foot saplings waved from the top of the Pyramid of the Dwarf. They took up quarters in the Governor's House and made a detailed examination of the surrounding

Uxmal. Casa de los Palomos.

mounds, buildings and monuments. Then the evil wind from the
north which brings illness began to blow, and by the time their
work at Uxmal was completed Stephens, Catherwood, and Cabot
were all worn out by fever and had to be carried away on litters.
But they would not give in to the illness and managed to reach
Kabah and Labna. After penetrating the peninsula as far south as
Iturbide, they traveled north to the immense ruins of Chichen
Itza. Then pushing north to the Gulf of Mexico, the explorers
sailed to the eastern part of Yucatan, visiting the island ruins of
Isla Mujeres and Cozumel as well as Tulum on the rocky coast of
the mainland.

The travelers were growing weary and their illness kept after
them despite occasional days when the fever mysteriously vanished. En route back to Merida they passed through the ruins of
Aké and then went on to Izamal, where Catherwood fortunately
sketched the huge stucco face that has since unaccountably
disappeared. By the journey's end Stephens and his party had
visited forty-four sites, all of them previously unexplored, and
Catherwood had made a unique map of the entire Mesoamerican
area and provided drawings of almost every major structure

among the sites visited. Then, exhausted and homesick, the travelers finally bid farewell to ruins and boarded a vessel for Cuba. After eight months of travel in Yucatan, they were anxious for home.

On the night of June 4, 1842, they were bound for New York harbor.

John Lloyd Stephens and Frederick Catherwood remained friends at a distance. After 1845, Catherwood became a civil engineer, working with various railroad companies. Then, in the autumn of 1845, he was hired on a year's contract by the Demerara Railway to survey the route of a proposed rail line between Georgetown and the interior of British Guiana along the Demerara River. Catherwood's malaria soon returned and his querulousness was given free rein, alarming his employers by the frequency of his frantic outbursts. This unruliness was not new, for it had caused friction between Catherwood and his colleagues in the Mideast, and had very nearly brought the second expedition with Stephens and Cabot to an end when there was a completely unreasonable fight over the appropriation of Catherwood's penknife. On September 27, 1847, in a letter from British Guiana, the unhappy Catherwood said, "I have heard nothing of Stephens. I shall be very glad of any news that you will be pleased to send me. You must not be surprised to see me back some day in New York and trying to start anew in business." Then, for reasons of economy and impatience with Catherwood, the railroad terminated him in May of 1849.

Meanwhile John Lloyd Stephens was briefly involved in the steamship business, which took him to Europe. He then became one of the founders of the Panama Railroad Company. At the time there was constant discussion of a railroad and a canal between the Atlantic and Pacific. The canal which was utterly beyond the technology of the day gave way to the more realistic aim of creating a rail line. And in 1846, the government of New Granada signed with M. Mateo Klein, a representative of Saloman et Compagnie, an exclusive agreement to build a railroad across

F. Catherwood.

Gambrede.

Monjas Chichen Itza

Terminus of the Panama Railway below Panama City. This was the rallying point of the Californians, the gold miners, and the adventurers of three continents.
(Woodcut from *Harper's Monthly Magazine*, January, 1859)

the Isthmus of Panama. John Lloyd Stephens ultimately became the driving force behind the formation of the Panama Railroad Company when the Saloman enterprise went down in bankruptcy during the French Revolution of 1848, which put Louis Napoleon Bonaparte at the head of state. But the railroad, like the canal, proved that white men could not come to terms with the jungle—not with the ease of the Indians who had evolved lifestyles there for centuries. The white man hoped to conquer the wilderness, to remove it and pave it. But the challenge was not the jungle but the tiny life forms which swarmed in the air. The insects were the most ferocious adversaries of the whites. They brought yellow fever and malaria . . . typhoid, dysentery, typhus, sprue, bubonic plague, filariasis and encephalitis. These were the enemies which the American engineers could not conquer.

Stephens became Vice-President of the railway and tried to interest his friend Catherwood in coming back to Central America as his assistant on the difficult project. At the time Catherwood was at his family's residence in England and was very reluctant to leave his wife and three children behind, especially in the poor financial state he had found himself since returning to England. Stephens made him a good offer, and finally in 1850 Catherwood sailed for Panama. Almost at once his malaria returned and he was constantly ill. And if this was not enough, Stephens, after a severe fall from a horse, was sent back to New York City to recuperate, leaving Catherwood alone to face the abysmal problems of the railroad.

While in New York, Stephens was elected President of the Panama Railway Company, which had been suddenly placed in a position of momentous importance because of the discovery of gold in California and the eagerness of easterners to find a quick route to the West, rather than the normal months-long voyage around the tip of South America. So Stephens hurried back to Panama to push the rail line to its completion. His health, however, was worse than Catherwood's; tertiary malaria already had overtaken his liver and kidneys; and the severe fever which had been intermittent was now constant. There was no effective treatment for this disease, which was slowly killing Stephens. Medical experts believed that the fever was caused "by *miasma* ...making it essential to avoid the night air because of the unhealthy exhalation which hovers near the earth at that time of the day, like a smoke or a fog."

Meanwhile, Catherwood, caught up by a different fever—gold fever—had left Panama for San Francisco, arriving there at the end of August 1850. By 1851 he was a happy Californian (California had become the thirty-first state of the Union, and all inhabitants of the region automatically became citizens of the United States). He had money and comfort enough to invite Stephens to come to California and run for the U.S. Senate. But this success didn't last long. Land speculation proved the ruin of most of the high-living gold-rich Californians. Catherwood lost $7000 in a single deal. But he was desperate to succeed and reinvested $5000 more in a mining scheme with the hope of making a modest fortune or losing everything. Then he prepared, on June 11, 1851, to return to England for a visit. He made the

Stephens' Tree
(Woodcut from *Harper's Monthly Magazine,* January, 1859)

passage through Panama on the rail line he had helped to build, and there he had his last meeting with his friend John Lloyd Stephens.

From his home in London, Catherwood wrote Stephens about his good fortune in California: the mining venture was a great success and he was about to invest $1,000,000 more in the mine. Again he urged Stephens to come to California, where both the old friends might share Catherwood's unexpected success. The offer, however, was never accepted. By the time the letter reached John Stephens, he was no longer able to respond.

Deep within the jungle of the Isthmus of Panama Stephens was found unconscious under a huge ceiba tree. The Indians who discovered his body were certain that he was dead, and for years the ceiba was called "Stephens' Tree," for a legend grew that the famous explorer had died there in the jungle beneath the Maya Tree of Life. No one knew how long he had lain in a coma under the great ceiba, but somehow there was still a faint pulse in his body. He was rushed away and put on a ship for New York City. His ailment was diagnosed as terminal hepatitis. His body was jolted with pain. His energy ebbed and his mind could not focus on ideas.

New York was turning chilly with the coming of fall in 1852. At 13 Leroy Place, Stephens sat listlessly gazing at the lovely Catherwood pictures of the ruins of Central America. On September 22, 1852, a 275-foot vessel destined for the long California run was christened the S.S. *John L. Stephens*. That same morning the forty-seven-year-old John Lloyd Stephens fell into a deep coma. He died on October 13, 1852, without regaining consciousness. His body was taken to the Old Marble Cemetery in New York and placed in a temporary vault. There his remains stayed without a stone or a marker of any kind, for he was never legally buried. And John Lloyd Stephens was forgotten.

His friend Frederick Catherwood remembered him with an enduring, deep sense of loss. Still grieving for his great companion and partner in adventure, Catherwood embarked on the S.S. *Arctic*, sailing out of Liverpool for New York en route to California. It was early September of 1854, hardly ten years since his last archeological expedition to Central America. On the seventh day of the sea voyage, the *Arctic* sighted Newfoundland and proceeded along the coast toward New York harbor. Then a heavy fog overtook the vessel and suddenly the French ship the *Vesta* came up out of the mist, and the two ships rammed head on. There were few lifeboats. The unruly crew leaped into the available boats and escaped. The 385 passengers were left alone without any hope of rescue in the frigid sea, more than a hundred miles from shore.

The winter moon rose. Its pale light hovered over the decks of the foundering ship. The moans and murmurs grew silent. The water gradually reached the portholes and decks. A soft green light rippled on the ceilings of the cabins as the waves claimed them one by one. People, like figures of stucco and stone, fell into the rising tide, entirely consumed except for the pathetic souvenirs which floated in the waves. At five P.M. the *Arctic* sank and carried with it into oblivion the irrepressible Frederick Catherwood.

After the Journey:
An Acknowledgment

Writing *Journey to the Sky* started out as a complex three-year research project and ended as a very personal journey. I began simply enough with several huge stacks of books in English, French and Spanish. My non-stop reading eventually became a balancing feat when I packed tons of tomes and went off on strenuous excursions to Honduras, Guatemala and Yucatan by mule, biplane, jet, jeep and time-honored leg power. But ultimately it was the process of actually writing this book, scene by scene and month by month, which made it clear to me how completely I felt associated with John Lloyd Stephens. Like him, I finished my graduate studies in the eastern U.S.A. and then wandered all over the vast American West, where I had been born. I made long, exciting and very difficult treks across North Africa, Turkey and the Arabic world. I also followed Stephens' footsteps, un-

knowingly at the time, among the ruins of Greece, Crete and Italy. In other words, my wanderlust over a decade took in all the landmarks which John Lloyd Stephens found so attractive. Then, coincidentally, I rented an apartment in New York City—just three blocks from Prince and Houston streets, where Frederick Catherwood had lived and had built his "Panorama of Jerusalem."

When I went to Central America I was just about the same age that Stephens had been when he visited there. I traveled almost the identical route that Stephens and Catherwood had followed during the months I researched the sites they had rediscovered. My "Catherwood" was an American with a British wit, psycho-analyst Richard Thurn, who doubled as sidekick and researcher for the incidents of my travels in Central America. During our research we also visited many sites which Stephens and Catherwood did not know existed at the time of their travels, and we descended into the tombs they did not discover among the sites they did visit.

Our guide in Guatemala and Honduras—Federico Rodriguez—coincidentally turned out to be the great-grandson of the Secretary of the Interior of Guatemala who had been one of John Stephens' diplomatic contacts when he was in Central America, and Mr. Rodriguez helped us discover at the bottom of his family's closet and in the earthquake-shattered National Archives of Guatemala numerous documents related to Stephens' explorations.

All of these strange parallels between John Stephens and me greatly enlivened my excitement and involvement in writing *Journey to the Sky*. But my inspiration was not limited to the ghost of John Lloyd Stephens, for I had a good deal of more substantial and academic assistance. The writings of John Stephens himself were, of course, the major sources of my work; while the biographical research and writing of Victor von Hagen were indispensable, for it was Mr. von Hagen who, in the 1940s, rediscovered the forgotten Stephens and Catherwood just as they had rediscovered the world of the Maya in 1839. The J. L.

Stephens papers, located in the Bancroft Library of the University of California at Berkeley, were invaluable in my work, as were the assists of the Museum of the American Indian of the Heye Foundation in New York City, the History Department of the New York Public Library and the New York City Historical Society.

My research also covered a good deal of ground in Europe, where I was assisted by the staff of the Museum of Man of the British Museum, and by the director of the Museum für Völkerkunde, Berlin, and by the director of the Museum of the Americas, Madrid—all of whose holdings in Maya art and artifacts are excellent. My writing is also greatly indebted to the major scholars and writers in the field of Mesoamerican history and culture: such as the books of Michael D. Coe, John Eric Thompson, Herbert J. Spinder, Tatiana Proskouriakoff, Alfred P. Maudsley, C. Bruce Hunter, Charles Gallenkamp and the several other major authors whose works are listed in the selected bibliography.

I also had other and more practical assistance which I wish to acknowledge, since a project such as the researching and writing of *Journey to the Sky* is not possible without the help and generosity of many people, like my editor Nick Ellison, who shared my enthusiasm for the adventures of Stephens and Catherwood and helped to bring my ideas to print, and Dr. Richard Thurn, who was a good companion on the long road with its endless difficulties and near disasters. I am also deeply grateful to Jeffrey F. Kriendler of Pan American World Airlines, who put all the excellent facilities of his organization at my disposal and provided the kind of ideal itineraries and transport which every world traveler dreams about. I was also exceedingly fortunate in having the help and hospitality of the tourist agencies of Mexico (specifically Don Miguel Gonzalez Marin, Secretario de Turismo, Yucatan), of Guatemala (specifically Señora Dolores Yurrita Gignard and Señor Federico Rodriguez of the Instituto Guatemalteco de Turismo), and Señor Jaime Ferrara of Pan Am's Merida office, Señor Ramon (Monty) Castillo of Yucatan, Monsieur Claude O.

Bertin of Villahermosa, Tabasco, Mexico, and finally the gracious hospitality of Herr Karl Herrmannsdorfer, general director of the handsome Hotel Cortijo Reforma, Guatemala City.

These are the essential scenes and characters in my own exciting voyage through the world of the Maya. In some ways my adventures were, for my own day, as amazing as those of Stephens and Catherwood, experiences which brought my subjects and their voyages so close to me that while writing *Journey to the Sky*, despite my insistence upon historical accuracy, I often forgot that the tale was not my own.

JAMAKE HIGHWATER

Soho district, New York City
1978

A Selected Bibliography

Adamson, David. *The Ruins of Time: Four and a Half Centuries of Conquest and Discovery among the Maya.* New York, Praeger, 1975.

Andrews, George F. *Maya Cities: Placemaking and Urbanization.* Norman, University of Oklahoma Press, 1975.

Brunhouse, Robert L. *Sylvanus G. Morley and the World of the Ancient Mayas.* Norman, University of Oklahoma Press, 1971.

————. *In Search of the Maya.* Albuquerque, University of New Mexico Press, 1973.

Carmichael, Elizabeth. *The British and the Maya.* London, The British Museum, 1973.

Catherwood, Frederick. *Views of the Ancient Monuments in Central America, Chiapas, and Yucatan.* New York, 1844.

Charnay, Désiré. *The Ancient Cities of the New World.* New York, Harper and Brothers, 1887.

Coe, Michael D. *The Maya.* New York, Praeger, 1966.

Gallenkamp, Charles. *Maya: The Riddle and the Rediscovery of a Lost Civilization.* New York, David McKay, 1976.

Hardoy, Jorge E. *Pre-Columbian Cities.* New York, George Braziller, 1972.

Hunter, C. Bruce. *A Guide to Ancient Maya Ruins.* Norman, University of Oklahoma Press, 1974.

Kingsborough, Edward King, Lord. *Antiquities of Mexico.* 9 vols. London, 1831–1848.

Maudsley, Alfred Percival. *Biologia Centrali-Americana: Archaeology.* 5 vols. London, 1889–1902.

Norman, B. M. *Rambles in Yucatan.* New York, J. & J. H. Langly, 1843.

Pendergast, David M., ed. *Palenque: The Walker-Caddy Expedition to the Ancient Maya City, 1839–1840.* Norman, University of Oklahoma Press, 1967.

Proskouriakoff, Tatiana. *An Album of Maya Architecture.* Norman, University of Oklahoma Press, 1963.

Spinder, Herbert Joseph. *Maya Art and Civilization.* Indian Hills Colorado, Falcon's Wing Press, 1957.

Stephens, John Lloyd. *Incidents of Travel in Central America, Chiapas, and Yucatan.* New York, Harper and Brothers, 1841. Illustrated by Frederick Catherwood.

———. *Incidents of Travel in Yucatan.* 2 vols. New York, Harper and Brothers, 1843.

Thompson, John Eric. *Maya Archaeologist.* Norman, University of Oklahoma Press, 1963.

———. *The Rise and Fall of Maya Civilization.* Norman, University of Oklahoma Press, 1966.

Von Hagen, Victor. *Maya Explorer John Lloyd Stephens and the Lost Cities of Central America and Yucatan.* Norman, University of Oklahoma Press, 1947.

———. *Search for the Maya: The Story of Stephens and Catherwood.* London, Saxon House, 1973.

Wauchope, Robert, ed. *Handbook of Middle American Indians.* 12 vols. Austin, University of Texas Press, 1964.